I0721549

Broken Wings

and other dark stories

Josie Jaffrey

CONTENT WARNINGS

There is a full list of content warnings at the back of this book.

Copyright © 2025 Josie Jaffrey

Cover images © DepositPhotos

Cover design © Josie Jaffrey

Published under licence by Silver Sun Books.

All rights reserved.

The right of Josie Jaffrey to be identified as the author of this work has been asserted by her in accordance with the Copyright, Designs and Patents Act 1988.

All characters and events in this publication are fictitious and any resemblance to real persons, living or dead, is purely coincidental.

By Josie Jaffrey

Other Short Stories

Ring the Bell

The Deluge Series

The Wolf and the Water

The Silverse Stories

The Seekers Series

Killian's Dead (short story prequel, free to Josie's subscribers)
May Day
Judgement Day
Winta's Day
Valentine's Day

The Solis Invicti Series

A Bargain in Silver
The Price of Silver
Bound in Silver
The Silver Bullet

The Sovereign Trilogy

The Gilded King
The Silver Queen
The Blood Prince

Silverse Short Stories

Blood Brothers
Blood Work
Bad Blood
Ex Marks the Spot
Cara Mia (free to Josie's subscribers)
Bella Donna (free to Josie's subscribers)
Dead Road Rules
Ungilded
The Blue Empress
The Red Lady

By Josie Jaffrey

Other Short Stories

Ring the Bell

The Deluge Series

The Wolf and the Water

The Silverse Stories

The Seekers Series

Killian's Dead (short story prequel, free to Josie's
subscribers)
May Day
Judgement Day
Winta's Day
Valentine's Day

The Solis Invicti Series

A Bargain in Silver
The Price of Silver
Bound in Silver
The Silver Bullet

The Sovereign Trilogy

The Gilded King
The Silver Queen
The Blood Prince

Silverse Short Stories

Blood Brothers
Blood Work
Bad Blood
Ex Marks the Spot
Cara Mia (free to Josie's subscribers)
Bella Donna (free to Josie's subscribers)
Dead Road Rules
Ungilded
The Blue Empress
The Red Lady

For Max

Contents

Introduction

I DON'T OFTEN set out with the intention of writing dark stories. They just seem to come out that way.

A good chunk of this book started out as dreams, or fragments of dreams. Nightmares, if you like. I've tried to capture them on waking, but – as with all faint memories – the more time I spend squinting at them, the more I change them, and the more I twist them into something new.

This is how it goes: I take a glimmering promise of an idea in my hands and try to stroke it into shape. I imagine gently rising arcs and plunging depths of story that coalesce into an uplifting, joyful crescendo of redemption. But I plot my journey through the shallows inattentively, so I end up blown off course.

This has happened so many times that the darker waters now feel comfortably familiar. In fact, I can no longer remember what it was about the shallows that I found so attractive in the first place. Part of me is sure that this is dangerous and irresponsible, but I have no control over it, so I lean in.

Here I am, adrift. Perhaps you'd like to join me.

Introduction

I DON'T OFTEN set out with the intention of writing dark stories. They just seem to come out that way.

A good chunk of this book started out as dreams, or fragments of dreams. Nightmares, if you like. I've tried to capture them on waking, but – as with all faint memories – the more time I spend squinting at them, the more I change them, and the more I twist them into something new.

This is how it goes: I take a glimmering promise of an idea in my hands and try to stroke it into shape. I imagine gently rising arcs and plunging depths of story that coalesce into an uplifting, joyful crescendo of redemption. But I plot my journey through the shallows inattentively, so I end up blown off course.

This has happened so many times that the darker waters now feel comfortably familiar. In fact, I can no longer remember what it was about the shallows that I found so attractive in the first place. Part of me is sure that this is dangerous and irresponsible, but I have no control over it, so I lean in.

Here I am, adrift. Perhaps you'd like to join me.

Broken Wings

In the airless crypts beneath the sinking city of Evesend, a treasure hunt has been playing out for three centuries. Maybe longer, but that's as far back as the manuscripts track. The old records went up in the fire, or the flood, or the war, or whatever it was that happened in Evesend three hundred and twenty-one years previously. It razed the buildings to the ground, leaving behind only the bodies buried in the catacombs beneath them.

Which is a lucky thing for Adelka, because some of those bodies – crystal-encrusted, immortality-granting skeletons they call Shiners – are now worth their weight in cobalt. Unfortunately, she's not the only one looking for them.

'This is *my* seam,' she says, thudding her spade into the ground next to her as she faces off against her competitor.

'You can't claim seams,' the man says calmly, spitting a brown stream of filthy saliva onto the dirt of the tunnel floor. The splashback sprays across the blade of Adelka's shovel.

She shudders, but composes herself enough to respond. 'There are courtesies of the trade,' she says. 'They make the tombs safer for all of us. If we work with each other, rather than against each other, then we'll be sure that every inch of the—'

'Don't care,' the man says. He spits again, as though to punctuate his point, then pushes past Adelka into the tunnel she was trying to guard. She doesn't fight him; she's half a foot shorter and half his weight.

Adelka wants to cry. She wants to scream, but then the spitting bastard would hear. Instead she takes her rage, screws it up into a ball and channels it down her arm, through her hand, and into the shovel, which spears point-first into the ground. Right through the base of her little toe.

She screams, then. If the spitting bastard hears at all, he doesn't care enough to come back and look.

'What did you do?'

'It's nothing.'

'Nothing? Adelka, your shoe is bleeding.'

Adelka has struggled to mask her walk of shame. She had to lean on her shovel as she limped forlornly up from the tunnels, through the basement of the meeting hall, into the alley behind the ruined temple and along Main Street to the staircase leading to the second-storey room she shares with her sister. But this last stretch is the worst, because now she has an audience. She's trying not to hobble up the uneven risers, but she's leaving a scarlet drip with every sixth step as Thea watches from the doorway above her and judges.

'It's nothing,' Adelka insists when she finally reaches the top. 'A stupid accident, that's all. I'll be fine.'

'You're not going back down there,' Thea says. She takes the shovel from Adelka and ducks under her arm to support her sister as she limps inside. 'It's too dangerous.'

'You want to get out of Evesend, don't you?'

'Of course I do.'

'Then I need to find us a Shiner to sell to the bone merchant. It's the only way.'

'No, Adelka, it's not. I can hire myself out as a healer. You can hire yourself out as… I don't know. A nanny.'

Adelka scoffs in response. 'Because I'm so good with children.'

'Well, you can do something. My point is that we can make money. We can save.'

'Maybe in twenty years, but by then the train tickets will be more expensive, and our money won't go as far. Face it: unless we do something drastic, we're never getting out of this shithole. And that's not good enough.'

Not for Thea, anyway. Adelka's always known her sister was too soft for this hard place, too gentle for the sharp edges of Evesend society, such as it is. She can't stand the thought of Thea being stuck here forever, tending the wounds of grubby old bastards like the one she met in the tunnels tonight, all in exchange for a smear of cobalt dust and a clumsy leer. Thea would be a star in Watersedge, and Adelka means to see her shine there, rather than rot here on the marshy limits of civilisation.

Thea sits Adelka down on their only chair and gently removes her sister's work boot, then her bloody sock. Adelka tries to not wince, and fails.

'I wouldn't look,' Thea advises.

Adelka – obtuse by nature – does exactly that, then wishes she hadn't. Her little toe is hanging on by a single thread of skin and drying blood.

'Can you fix it?' Adelka asks.

'I'm a healer, not a miracle worker.'

'What about the surgeon?'

'Do you want to die of infection?'

'Then what am I supposed to do?' Panic makes Adelka's voice shrill.

'Look,' Thea says, 'you don't need all of your toes. Better to give it up as a lost cause, remove the toe entirely and let the wound heal.'

'Give up on my toe?'

'It could even be useful,' Thea says, gathering her tools. 'If you insist on going back to the catacombs, you could use it to make a canary. A toe is about the right size, with the right density of bone and flesh and everything else, for a small one at least. It could save your life down there in the crypts.'

'A canary?'

Adelka's only seen such a thing once in her life, just a brief glimpse snatched around the corner of a crypt wall when a trainload of treasure-hunting foreigners came visiting one frigid season. Adelka was wrapped in every scrap of clothing she and Thea owned, because even that far underground the earth was frozen solid, but the tourists were toasty warm in quilted jackets, layered furs and thick knits. They don't have clothes like that in Evesend anymore, nor do they have the sweetly-chirruping birds that sat on the foreigners' shoulders. Adelka had heard about those, of course. The bone miners still tell stories about them in scandalised tones, all the while secretly wishing they had one of their own. The tiny creatures can warn you about bad air, feel a cave-in coming seconds before the first stone drops, and even exchange their life for yours if you don't get out of harm's way in time. They only work underground, only in proximity to the graves of the Shiners, and only for the person from whose body they're crafted, but if you get all that right, then for one fatal event they can give you a free pass. To some people, that kind of invulnerability is worth any price, however gruesome. To others, the mere existence of the canaries is heresy, calling back to the archaic religion that burned or drowned or died in the cataclysm three hundred and twenty-one years previously.

Long story short, the Evesenders no longer have canaries, nor the knowledge to create them. At least, that's what Adelka thought up until right now.

Thea is quiet as she lays out her medical kit on the ground at Adelka's feet: cloths, warm water, alcohol, powders, and a bundle of sharp and spiky implements that Adelka is trying to ignore.

'And where exactly am I going to learn how to make a canary?' Adelka asks.

Thea whispers her reply. 'Kamara showed me.'

For a moment, neither of them breathes.

'You haven't told anyone else about that, have you?' Adelka asks.

'No.'

'Then don't. Please. You know how people feel about those things.'

'But you already have the toe going spare, and if it could keep you safe—'

'Assuming you can actually remove the bloody thing in the first place.'

Thea looks into Adelka's eyes and smiles with the reassuring bedside manner that'll make her a fortune in Watersedge. 'Don't worry,' she says. 'I know what I'm doing, and I promise you won't even feel it once I've got the numbing powder on. Trust me.'

Adelka sniffs back her pain and takes a deep breath. 'All right. I trust you.'

The canaries in Watersedge, they say, are made from ornate frames crafted by artisans in precious metals and silks. The owners contribute just a little of their blood to seal the bond, and most will only do it once; the living there is so safe and leisurely that a single canary will last a lifetime. But Adelka doesn't have the cobalt for such artistry and Thea doesn't know how to make a canary with so little of its maker inside it, so instead she has Adelka spit and piss and bleed in a bowl, then adds the severed toe with words and gestures that Adelka commits to memory. Finally, they bake the thing in the tepid oven overnight and wake in the morning to find it tweeting and bashing its little body desperately against the oven door as it tries to escape. The moment they release it, it flies to Adelka's shoulder, and there it sits, needing neither sustenance nor sleep, watching every second for the moment that its sacrifice will be required.

Adelka hates it.

Instead of the beautiful multicoloured feathers of the tourists' canaries, or even the plain blue-black of the feeble scavenger crows in Evesend's marshes, the small bird Adelka carries has feathers the sickly grey of corpse flesh and wings that seem to be jointed in the wrong place, so they get stuck every time it tries to unfurl them. Adelka smoothes them back in place, not so much because she cares for the pitiful thing, but because it turns her stomach to see its limbs twisted so far out of alignment. Soon, the bird is performing its failed flaps so frequently that Adelka begins to suspect it is doing so simply so she will stroke it again. It craves her contact, leaning into her touch while it digs its claws into her shoulder, as though it wants to be inside her skin, as though it envies her the body it once inhabited.

'Why is it so strange?' Adelka asks her sister.

'Strange? Everything about canaries is strange. You'll have to be more specific.'

'You know. Creepy. The way it moves its wings. It's not right.'

Thea shrugs and looks away. 'I did my best, but maybe your little toe wasn't big enough. Maybe there wasn't enough to make it perfect.'

'Can you fix it?'

'*Fix* it?' Thea looks heartbroken at the suggestion that she might have done it wrong.

'I don't mean fix it. I mean… never mind. It's great,

Thea. Thank you,' Adelka says quickly, but her unease remains as she takes the cursed thing down to the catacombs with her.

Whatever existed on the waterlogged coast before Evesend, it must have been pretty spectacular. Now its ashes are condensed into pavements, its tombs into foundations, and its streets into sewers, but Adelka still finds traces of its wonders as she searches the graves: a glimmer of metallic thread here, a lump of waxy colour there, and all the time the alluring and indecipherable carvings on the crypt walls. There are swirling patterns, sparkling stars, feathers and wings, bones and skulls, in configurations Adelka doesn't understand. Often there are people, too, ranged in battle or facing each other one-on-one with strange weapons in their hands. Some of the bone miners say they depict the events of the cataclysm. Some say they're just stories. Adelka thinks they must be important either way, because why else would people expend that much energy on pictures that would remain underground, unseen? But whatever meaning they once had, it has been lost along with the rest of the prior world.

It is a comfort to Adelka that the past is so distant. Although she's actively looking for a Shiner, she still collects the plain old skeletons she finds as she searches, because there are a thousand uses for old bones in Evesend. The alchemists grind them up for tinctures, the constructioners use them for plaster and, if you're really lucky, you might sell them to an artist looking for just the right shade of bone-white paint. When you're feeding that trade, the last thing you want to do is think of the bones as human beings, so Adelka avoids the temptation to wonder about these peoples' lives, or to think of them as people at all.

At least, she did. But now, as she dumps tibias and rib cages and phalanges into her sack, she can't help but notice how many of the skeletons she finds are missing a toe, or three, or entire limbs. Before the canary, she might have ascribed the loss to scavengers or water damage, but now that she's looking for them, she sees the cuts of bones that have been removed rather than lost. She and the dead are not so distant after all, even if most of them are destined to be ground up for bonemeal.

That's how the Evesenders found out about the Shiners in the first place, of course. When a bunch of cows led to the slaughterhouse simply *wouldn't* die, even the least-educated of Evesend's uneducated populace began to suspect that something might be up. It took some time to trace the source back to the skeletons in the animal fodder, longer than you'd think given that the cows and the bones shared the same shimmering glow, but when they finally made the connection, demand for the immortal skeletons soared. Now a single thigh bone can set you up like a prince in Watersedge, even once you've taken enough crystals to make sure you and yours will live forever. That's not just Adelka's dream, but the dream of every bone miner who braves the dangers of the catacombs: eternal life, countless riches and, most of all, a ticket out of Evesend.

For a chance at that, Adelka is willing to suffer the sinister feeling of the canary's claws digging into her flesh. Perhaps the birds the Watersedgers make are less unsettling, but even after a whole day to get used to it, Adelka still gets shivers down her spine each time she looks at the thing on her shoulder. She is almost glad when the roof falls in on her at the bottom of the seam for which she had such high hopes, because when she digs her way out of the rubble her canary is nothing but a lingering sparkle of dust in the air where she had been standing, right in the path of the cave-in.

Good riddance, she thinks. But as she stumbles back up to the surface, lucky to be alive, she already misses the feeling of invincibility the canary gave her.

It's not the end of the world. After all, she has more toes.

They're still alive, by the way, the magic cows. You'd think they might be revered, or at least exhibited as interesting specimens of magical zoology, but that's not really the way of things in Evesend. Instead, they're working mills, pulling ploughs, hauling timber, underfed and abused. It's not nice, but then Evesend's not very nice. If you want civilised attitudes and refined sensibilities, try the other side of the continent.

Adelka means to do just that.

'You want me to *what*?'

'It's really not that complicated, Thea. I just need another canary.'

Adelka is standing in the doorway of their room, one booted foot inside the threshold and one bare foot out on the landing at the top of the stairs as she unrolls Thea's bundle of medical instruments. It is clear what she has in mind, but Thea isn't playing along.

'Why?' Thea asks.

'To replace the other one.'

'Why?'

'So if I get stuck in another cave-in I won't die.'

'You never would have got stuck in that cave-in without the canary, because you never would have followed the seam down that far, because it's too dangerous, Adelka, and you know it.'

'Yes, but I'm never going to find us a Shiner if I don't take risks, am I? They've been cleared out of the safer tunnels. I can't keep picking over what the others leave behind. I have to dig out the dodgy caves that no one else will explore, so I need another canary. Just come outside and cut off my toe, then I can get back to work.'

'No!' Thea snatches her bundle of sharp and spiky implements out of Adelka's hands, rolls it up and stuffs it under the mattress that the two of them share in one corner of the room, then sits on top of it with her arms crossed. 'I am not cutting off your toe, and neither are you.'

'Why not? You said it yourself: I don't need my toes.'

'No. You don't need *all* of them, I said. I was trying to reassure you about losing one, not encourage you to cut them all off and throw them away.'

'I'm not throwing them away.'

'Aren't you?' Thea gives her sister a level look. 'What happens if you never find a Shiner?'

'I will. With another canary—'

'But what if you don't? Will it have been worth it?'

Adelka sighs, because there's no way for her to explain this need to Thea in a way she will understand. Her sister doesn't live in the real world. Ever since their parents— Well, ever since they've been on their own, Adelka's been the one who's had to risk it all to bring in the money they need to survive. She doesn't want Thea to know that, or to carry the guilt of it, but the truth is that if it hadn't been for Thea, Adelka never would have gone bone mining in the first place. Almost any other trade would be safer, but none of them pays as well, even when all she digs up are dull skeletons without the slightest hint of shine. The money from those bones keeps her sister housed and fed and means she has the time to train with Kamara as a healer, to have a *profession*.

But it won't get her out of Evesend. Nothing will, unless Adelka finds that Shiner, and to find a Shiner she needs another canary. It's their only hope.

Instead of trying to put this into words, Adelka says, 'You're not going to change my mind, Thea.'

'And you're not going to change mine,' Thea replies, just as stubbornly. They have that in common.

'Fine,' Adelka says, grabbing her mining bag from inside the door. 'Then I'll do it myself.'

Before Thea can stop her, Adelka has her hammer raised in one hand and the chisel in the other, poised over the two smallest toes on her undamaged foot.

She hears Thea scream before it all goes black.

When she wakes up, her foot is bandaged and there are dark circles under Thea's eyes. She's rubbing something along Adelka's lips. A sedative, she guesses. The toes are in a bowl on the floor, along with a fair portion of Adelka's blood.

'Make it with both of them this time,' she says before whatever Thea's given her takes hold. 'Just to be sure there's enough.'

Then it all goes black again.

All things considered, it really wasn't that bad.

Within a week, Adelka and her shiny new blood-red canary – functional wings and everything – find a new seam. It's a sneaky one, in a tunnel hinted at by odd turns and intrusions in the passages around it. Looking at the maps she's drawn over the years, she's long known it was there in the blank space between pathways, but she was never able to find its entrance.

Until now.

There is a life-sized statue in the recess at the back of the ruined temple, beneath the spot where the altar sits in the building above. It depicts a woman in thickly-draped robes with birds perched on her shoulders, a curled staff in one hand and a basket full of bones in the other. Behind her, a skeletal figure wraps its arms around her stomach, around her throat, tipping her chin up towards its gaping jaws. The gesture is half threatening, half sexual, and all creepy. Adelka's not sure who it represents, or what it's supposed to make her feel, but she knows she doesn't like it, and that's been enough to keep her hurrying past it for all the years she's been heading down to the catacombs.

But on this day, just as she approaches the relic, her new blood-red canary begins to sing.

It's a warning cry, signalling bad air, but Adelka isn't underground yet and the air outside is fine. At first she thinks perhaps this second canary is defective too, perhaps they still haven't used enough of her flesh and bone in its making, and she just keeps on walking. The canary stops singing. She walks back the way she came and there, right in front of the statue, the canary begins to sing again. Adelka steps away, and back, away, and back, and every time she comes close to the statue, the canary sings out for all it's worth.

For the first time, Adelka looks more closely at the grim couple, locked in their eternal embrace, and sees the cracks in the panel behind their alcove. Cracks that describe the shape of a door. Adelka slips into the recess, squeezes behind the statue and finds, in the centre of the door shape, hidden behind the figure of the skeleton, a carving of a bone.

She runs her fingers over its surface.

The carving depresses.

The stone doorway moves.

The anticipation fizzes over her skin.

This is big. This is momentous. If there are going to be Shiners buried anywhere beneath Evesend that's still accessible, it's going to be here.

The canary sings.

When the bad air washes over them both, so dense that it's toxic even under the open sky, the blood-red creature detonates in a shower of glittering rose-gold, leaving Adelka to stand in the doorway alone and contemplate her discovery. She can already see skeletons thick on each side of the tunnel, piled one on top of the other in their recessed beds of stone. Quickly, stepping just inside, she opens her sack and drops in one, two, three, four entire skeletons' worth of bones –

not a single toe missing – then bundles her treasure up, drags it out after her and seals the doorway tightly before any more bad air can catch her, and before anyone can see her and discover what she has just discovered.

Her mind is spinning.

It's an untested, unpropped tunnel. There will be dangers enough, like the bad air she just avoided, like the inevitable cave-ins and flooded paths she'll find as she maps it out.

But.

Ten seconds' work for four entire skeletons.

Even if she never finds a Shiner down there – which she will, she is now certain – there are enough easy pickings in that seam to keep her and Thea going for years. Decades. Maybe forever.

She just needs a new canary.

'If you don't do it for me, you know I'll do it myself. Badly.'

'No, you won't,' Thea says, trying to pry her tool bundle from Adelka's hands for the third time that evening. 'I didn't want to tell you like this, but… there's another way.'

'What?' Adelka's interest sharpens. 'You mean you've learned how to make canaries like the Watersedgers do?'

'No, I mean I think I might have found a job.'

Adelka stops fighting, but she doesn't let go of the bundle. 'What kind of job?' she asks.

'House healer.'

'For?'

Thea releases her grip and looks away. 'House Karillon.'

'*No.*'

Adelka throws the tool bundle onto the floor and unrolls it, fingering each of the blades as she chooses her weapon. She will not think about House Karillon. She will not remember the way Karillon Silas kicked open their door and turned her and Thea out into the night. She will not remember the blood on his hands, the blood that rubbed off onto her skin as she fought him every step of the way.

'It's in Watersedge.' Thea speaks softly, crouching down so she can reach out and still her sister's hands on her tools. 'They'll provide housing for both of us, and a monthly salary of five times what you make here in a year. We can get out of Evesend together, safely, without you losing any more toes.'

'You think living at House Karillon is safe? Have you forgotten what they did?'

'Karillon Silas is dead, Adelka. Years ago now. They executed him for the murder of our parents. No one condoned what he did. They're sorry for it.'

'They will be,' Adelka says. She selects a knife and pulls it from its pocket in the bundle. 'When we have a Shiner, we'll be rich enough to buy our own place in Watersedge. We don't need the charity of our enemies, Thea.'

'*Charity*?' Thea replies, and she is furious. 'Is that how little you think of me and what I do? You think I need *charity* to get a job as a House healer?'

'If it wasn't charity then you'd get a job for someone else. Anyone else. Tell me I'm wrong.'

For a moment, Thea says nothing, and for a moment, Adelka is sure she has the measure of the situation, just as she believes she has always had the measure of her little sister and her little endeavours.

For a moment.

Then Adelka looks up and sees the rage in her eyes.

'You are wrong,' Thea says. 'You've seen how your wounds healed. You've tasted my salves and powders. You've even had the benefit of my canaries. Can you honestly tell me that you've suffered even a second of pain under my care? No,' Thea rushes on before Adelka can grudgingly admit the same. 'Because despite what you think of me, I'm good at what I do, and they're clamouring for me, Adelka. *Clamouring*. I have invitations to attend every House on the far side of the continent at the end of my training. Did you know that?'

Adelka did not know that. She is surprised, just as Thea wants her to be. Slightly incredulous, even, which she should probably keep to herself. What she should do is congratulate her sister and acknowledge her success. She knows that's what Thea wants.

Instead, she asks, 'Then why choose them, of all the bastard houses you could choose?'

'I chose House Karillon because it's the only one that has enough space to accommodate staff *and* their family,' Thea says, then adds quietly, 'I chose it so I could take you with me. Ideally, with the rest of your digits intact.'

But Adelka doesn't want to be taken with Thea. She's supposed to be looking after her little sister, not the other way around, and especially not in House Karillon.

'No,' Adelka says.

'No?'

'No. You don't know what I found today, Thea. A completely untapped seam. Brand new, and rich like nothing I've ever seen. I was in there less than a hundred heartbeats and I came back out with four full skeletons, intact. There's a fortune in that tunnel, and I'll bet there's a Shiner besides.'

'Adelka—'

'A week,' she says desperately. 'Just until you've finished your training. Give me one week on this seam. I'll find it, Thea. I promise. And then we can go wherever we want and live like kings, forever. Just one more canary.'

'And then another, and another after that.'

'You don't understand. This is the find of a lifetime. The other bone miners would be salivating if they knew about it, but not one of them does. It's my secret. You have to give me a chance to run the seam down, Thea. Please.'

For a long time, the only sound is the tapping of Thea's fingernails on the floor.

'A week,' she says eventually.

'A week,' Adelka agrees as Thea takes the knife from her hand. 'So you'll give me a canary?'

'Two more toes,' Thea says. 'And only two more. Then we're leaving, with or without your Shiner.'

There are… *things* in the tunnel beyond the disturbing statue.

The first time they come for her, Adelka's lantern goes out, leaving her in the dark with her new canary –

it has feathers sickly pink like uncooked pig flesh – and an unknown number of unknown creatures whose toenails screech across the stone tunnel floor as they skitter towards her like nothing she has ever heard before. The twittering warning call of her canary comes to an abrupt stop, and Adelka races blindly back towards the statue with the skittering chasing her every step of the way. When she emerges into the night, she is alone, though her shoulder shines with the pale pink glitter of her canary's demise.

It has only been two days.

Faced with Adelka's threats to go back with or without protection, Thea is persuaded to cut out another canary, and another, until Adelka has only one big toe remaining and nothing to show for it but an effective trap for giant rats, a pile of pale bones and a bird in her shirt pocket with feathers the colour of a ripening bruise.

At least she still has her secret seam. Or so she thinks, until she arrives at the statue one morning to find the door to the tunnel cracked open. For a moment, she thinks she must have left it open herself when she set off for home the night before, but then she hears the rhythmic clanging thump of a pickaxe reverberating inside and knows her secret is no longer hers alone.

She rushes along the passages, bag weighing heavy on her shoulder, shovel in her hand, lantern held high above her head, until she has followed the noise to its source.

'*You*,' she says, sneering at the bastard who spat on her shovel. 'How did you find my seam?'

'Should have been more careful,' he replies, not even

bothering to look her way. 'Didn't cover your trail very well, did you?' Then he carries right on with his work. He's chipping a hole into a panel at the side of one of the grave recesses, destroying the wall and the carvings it holds.

'What are you doing?' Adelka says, horrified. 'You're ruining it.'

'Ruining it? You don't know much, do you, girlie.'

'I knew enough to find this place.'

'And too little to mine it properly. Bugger off home and let the real bone miners do what you can't.'

Adelka's about to argue with the loathsome man, but then his pickaxe breaks through the panel and something shines out from the hollow behind it.

'Is that—'

'Now don't you go getting any ideas,' the man says, turning to face her with the pickaxe in his hands.

'This is my seam!' Adelka yells. 'By rights, whatever is in there is mine.'

'Not likely.' The man squares up to her, swinging the pickaxe gently as he speaks. 'You would never have found it. You're too stupid to know where to look.'

'You can at least share it. That's fair.'

'Sorry, girlie,' the man says, swinging the pickaxe properly now. 'But I don't share.'

It's a short fight. In fact, it's not much of a fight at all.

The man swings the pickaxe back. Adelka tries to sidestep out of the way, but trips over her shovel in her haste and ends up sprawled on the tunnel floor on her back. The man brings the pickaxe down on her head. The point is aimed right at Adelka's eye. It should be a death blow, but the world twists sideways for a blink and the pickaxe embeds itself in the dirt next to Adelka's ear.

The canary tucked into her shirt pocket goes *poof.*

The man is unbalanced by the sudden change in reality. He topples over, landing half on the ground and half on top of Adelka. He's so surprised to see the cloud of purple glitter the canary has left behind that he doesn't notice what Adelka is doing with her hands.

'Hey, those things are outlawed,' he says, pushing himself up onto his elbows. 'You can't have them in the mines. Every time they pop like that, the magic destroys one of the—'

The pickaxe takes the end of his sentence along with his life. There's a lot of blood, but then Adelka is used to that by now, and in truth she hardly notices. Instead, her attention is fixed on the thing she glimpsed shining behind the panel. She hauls the pickaxe out of the man's back and applies it to the tiny hole, widening it bit by bit, strike by strike.

She knew the canaries would be worth it. She may have lost nine toes, but this is it, she knows it is. It might be dark now, but she saw the glow, and so did the man whose blood is now making her grip on the pickaxe handle slick. The Shiner is there, right behind this panel, where – Adelka has to admit – she would never have thought to look for it. Perhaps she should have stopped for a moment before she started swinging, just long enough to memorise the markings on the panel so she'd know what tipped the spitting bastard off to the Shiner's location. But she only needs one skeleton, and anyway it's too late now; the carvings have been obliterated under her frenzied blows.

Three more strikes.

Two more strikes.

One more.

The hole is as big as Adelka's head now, but there's nothing. No glow. No glimmer. Just darkness.

She takes her lantern and shoves it inside the hole, then peers in after it. There's a skeleton there, all right, but it's every bit as dull and chalky as all the others she's found in this hidden tunnel so far.

She wants to cry. There's no Shiner here.

Perhaps all she saw was a glint of light off the pickaxe head, or a flare from the lantern, or some trick of the tunnel gas. It wouldn't be the first time a bone miner came out of the ground raving about finding Shiners, only to discover that he'd lost a little of his mind instead.

Adelka steps over the spitting bastard's body on her way home. He's going to rot down here, which is no more than he deserves, but she isn't looking forward to the odour in the tunnel when she returns.

'Just one more. I still have one night left.'

'And is that really worth your last toe?'

'It's my toe. I can do what I want with it.'

The sisters have been arguing gently all the way through preparing and eating their gritty stew, but Thea's heart isn't in it and Adelka can tell. Her sister's mind is elsewhere, her belongings already packed, her mind already halfway to Watersedge.

'I want you to come with me in the morning,' Thea says.

'I will.'

'Will you? Will you really?'

'Of course,' Adelka replies, mopping up the last of her gritty gravy with a solid hunk of gritty bread. 'And I'll bring a Shiner with me.'

Thea stands from where they've been sitting together on the floor and throws her wooden bowl into the bucket they use as a sink. It's a helpless, careless gesture, and it's out of character.

'What?' Adelka asks.

'There's something toxic about the Shiners, and no amount of canaries are going to protect you from it if you keep going back for more. This obsession is eating you alive, Adelka. Can't you see that?'

'You don't understand. I found something, Thea.'

'I know, your secret tunnel.'

'No, not just that. I was looking in the wrong place. I nearly found one today. I was so close. I swear, I could almost taste it.'

'And, what? It ran away?'

Adelka shakes her head, still unable to explain what she saw in the tunnel. Between the bad air and the excitement and the… other thing that happened, it feels messy in her head. All she needs is to get back down there with a new canary, find another panel just like the one from today, and then they'll be set.

Easy.

'I can do this,' Adelka says. 'For us. For you.'

'If you were doing it for me, you'd still have nine toes.'

'You'll see, Thea. It'll change our lives. I just need one more. Please.'

There's no point in arguing, so Thea gets her kits,

administers her powders, makes her cuts and works her magic. Adelka won't wait for the wounds to heal. She won't even wait for a proper goodbye.

'If I'm not here when you get back, then you know where I've gone,' Thea says. She is sadder than Adelka has ever seen her.

'I have to do this.'

'I know. At least once this last canary is gone, there'll be an end to it all. When that happens, I'll be waiting in Watersedge for you.'

She hands Adelka a pass for the train – her ticket out of Evesend – and kisses her on the cheek as Adelka leaves, back to the statue of the skeleton's embrace, back to the catacombs behind it, back to the bones of the pale and silent dead.

Adelka needn't have worried about the smell; the spitting bastard's body has been scavenged almost to naked bone in the space of a few hours. Just along the tunnel from his final resting place – at least until he dries out enough for Adelka to sell him for bone dust – there is a carving that looks familiar. She can't be sure, but Adelka thinks it might be the same one that was on the panel they destroyed yesterday.

At the top, two figures face each other with strange weapons outstretched as though they are in the middle of a duel. One seems to be stepping forwards, surrounded by winged creatures Adelka doesn't recognise, while the other falls to the ground surrounded by swirls and stars and odd angular shapes that resemble gemstones. The falling figure has to be a Shiner, Adelka thinks. This must be his epitaph, the story of his death, so this must be his gravestone, which means that right behind this panel should be…

Adelka takes the pickaxe she has now claimed as her own and gets swinging. As she does, her new bone-white canary hops up and down her arm, tweeting anxiously. This panel is thicker than the other was, and it's sweaty work, but eventually the point of the pickaxe bursts through the stone. As Adelka drags the tool back out, hoping to bring the panel with it, she sees a radiant glimmer of wonderful brightness for the tiniest fraction of a second before the whole panel comes tumbling towards her along with the rest of the wall. She is about to be buried alive.

The canary pops in a shower of silver light, the world comes out of alignment, and the next thing she knows Adelka is standing on a pile of rubble. Despite searching through it for the rest of the night and much of the next day, she finds nothing but boring white bones and silver glitter. Again, she is frustrated.

But no matter. There are more carvings to search, more panels to check, and it won't be long now, she's certain.

Thea can wait one more day.

Adelka might be out of toes, but she doesn't need all her fingers, either.

Invidious Bitches

The air makes my teeth ache as I smile at the cameras. It can't be the temperature, because the red carpet is baking in the kind of heat that makes London sweat, releasing all the noxious smells that the cold and rain usually hide. The problem must be the peroxide I left on overnight. There are only so many times you can whiten them, the dentist told me, before the chemicals dig their way through the enamel to the nerve.

I guess I've reached my limit.

'Lisa! Lisa!'

The reporter is young, her hair shining like a waterfall as she holds out the mic towards me. Those golden strands look naturally healthy rather than cosmetically enhanced, like mine are. I wonder if she's one of *them*. I can't see a single wrinkle on her face and her teeth are dazzling, whiter than mine will ever get without veneers.

'Lisa, what's next for you now that the last season of Hard Collateral has wrapped?' she asks, pretending innocence, the bitch.

She knows.

'Oh, plenty on the horizon,' I say, stretching my smile until my canines clang with pain. 'I can't let you have any details yet—'

'Of course not,' she says sweetly.

The bitch. The bitch *knows* that the only thing on the horizon for me is a slow decline into retirement. She just wants to watch me squirm.

'But I can tell you,' I continue, leaning in close to whisper, 'that one upcoming project involves a certain superhero with shape-shifting powers, if you know who I mean.' I'm lying my arse off, of course, but my delivery sells it: I hold a finger to my lips as I twinkle with mischief. It's an expression I have practised in the mirror to perfection, just like all my others.

The bitch is suitably impressed, and surprised enough that it's frankly insulting.

'You don't mean Lok—'

'I'd love to tell you more,' I say, holding up my hands to ward off her questions, 'but you'll have to wait for the press release. I'm sworn to secrecy. Watch this space!'

I step back to take a few more questions from other reporters, then smile and wave as I walk the rest of the carpet, smile and wave to the cameras, smile and wave to the bitch of a reporter who's going to be printing bullshit about my prospects that will, with any luck, seriously piss off her editor and the studio involved.

Not that anyone seems to care about lies in this

business. Sometimes I wonder if they're all we have.

'Lisa!'

I'm expecting another reporter, but instead it's Madeleine Carpenter, my former co-star from Space Rangers. She throws her arms wide before air-kissing me on both sides, grasping my shoulders in a hug that is designed to keep me at a distance. She's the same age as me, but she looks ten years younger than she did the last time I saw her. Even up close, I can't see the lines beneath her make up, not even around her eyes. She must have an incredible surgeon.

'Madeleine!' I say brightly, playing for the cameras. 'You look fabulous!'

'Thanks, darling.' She doesn't return the compliment. 'It's been an absolute *age*. I must tell you all about my new show!'

'Oh, yes,' I can feel my smile slipping into a grimace. 'Something about heartburn, wasn't it?'

'Heartachers and Heartbreakers.'

'Of course. My mistake.'

I know the title perfectly well. I've been following Madeleine's ascent with jealous attention, watching her rise out of the ashes of our last project into a prime-time TV role that eclipsed Hard Collateral in the ratings. I should be where she is now, but her show didn't have a sex scandal. Her show didn't have a director who was too drunk to direct. Her show didn't get cancelled mid-season. No wonder she looks so good. I bet she can afford the best of everything.

'Not to worry,' she says, laughing off my faux pas. 'The memory starts to go at your age, I'm sure.'

The bloody cheek.

I'm still suppressing my indignation, trying to come up with a subtle sucker-punch retort, when Madeleine takes my arm and starts leading me inside.

'You should see my beautician,' she whispers. 'She'll do wonders for those eye-bags of yours.'

I laugh at her audacity. Does she really expect me to believe that she turned the clock back a decade without surgery?

'Seriously,' she says, and indeed she is serious now. She pulls a business card out of her clutch bag and tucks it into my own. 'See her, darling. All the top crowd do. Trust me: it'll be the best call you ever make.'

I smile back, but I have no intention of contacting anyone recommended to me by Madeleine bitchface Carpenter. Either she's hoping for a referral discount or, more likely, it's some kind of prank. I'll play along for the sake of appearances at this event, but I'll be tearing up that card the moment I get home.

The ceremony itself is utter bollocks. I knew it was going to be. I'm only here because my co-star in Hard Collateral, Joey Farelli, made the shortlist for Best Actor, but he's far from that and predictably misses out on the prize. With any luck, the tabloids might run a few photos tomorrow of the two of us together, Joey crying on my shoulder while I offer sympathetic support. He's a petulant little snot of a man who used to make his assistant dump his girlfriends for him and the last thing I want to do is console him, but my calendar is wide open and I need all the publicity I can get.

That's why I agree to talk to the cameras at the end of

the night. Unlike my so-called peers, I am stone-cold sober and, thanks to frequent touch-ups, just as polished as I was on the red carpet.

'How's Joey doing?' the interviewer asks.

'Proud to have been nominated,' I say, lying through my aching teeth. 'He was honoured to be to be up for the award with so many incredible actors and I have no doubt that even greater things are on the way for him.' Like a cracking hangover and, I hope, a recurring case of genital herpes from the soap star I saw following him into the toilets half an hour ago.

The interviewer asks about the other categories and awards, and I smile blithely as I give my sanitised opinions. I'm about to excuse myself when he throws in the grenade, the question everyone else is too refined to ask.

'What did you think about Iris Kemp's nomination?'

He's talking about the lead actress in Howling Man, the latest film about Werewolves to grace our screens. There's been a glut of them ever since the Werepeople revealed their existence a decade ago, and it shows no sign of letting up any time soon. The world has gone crazy for the slow-aging, fast-healing, bright-eyed creatures, particularly the film and television industry. They see them as an opportunity. A studio can invest in an upcoming actor and lock them into a long-term, low-pay contract for multiple films, comfortable in the knowledge that the actor will stay looking exactly the same way for a century, beautiful and timeless, perfect for long-running franchises. If we're not careful, human actors are going to be relegated to the transience of the stage. Organisations like the BAFTAs are standing with us humans, thanks to persuasive lobbying from people like Madeleine Carpenter.

Unlike most of the actors in Howling Man, Iris is a genuine Wereperson. She was up for Best Actress, but we all knew she never stood a chance of walking away with the trophy, not with her pedigree.

'I think it's great,' I say, summoning up more generosity than I feel.

'So you think she should have won?'

I laugh. 'The competition was pretty stiff.'

'But you think a Wereperson *could* win a BAFTA?' he insists.

I'm tired and it's late and this guy is really getting on my nerves, so I do the one thing that people in my position never do: I tell the truth.

'Are we going to have a Werewolf winning a BAFTA anytime soon?' I say. 'Probably not. They've got the looks, sure, but you have to remember that they are, after all, a different species, so they're never going to be able to portray humans with the same nuance we can. But I fully support the board's proposal that we create a separate awards ceremony, the BAWFTA, so the Werepeople can have their own space. That makes a lot of sense to me.'

'You don't think, as the Weres argue, that keeping them out of the BAFTAs is discriminatory? Particularly given that Howling Man is a film about Werewolves?'

'Didn't I just say I thought it was great that Iris was shortlisted?' I reply. 'But the point is that she didn't win, and she won't ever have a chance at winning against humans. That's not really fair on her, is it? But a BAWFTA, that she could win. Give the Weres their own award ceremony and you give everyone a chance to shine. Leave the BAFTAs to the humans.'

He opens his mouth to ask another question, but I wave and walk away before he can. Not one question about me. Not one question about my career, or my gown, or my plans. All anyone wants to hear about these days is the Werepeople.

The selfish fucks.

I hear my comments debated on the breakfast show while I do my morning cardio. The Werepeople think I'm just jealous of their looks and longevity, but the Actors' Guild are leading the charge to defend me.

'It's hard to keep up with the immortal crowd – no one's denying that – but there's more to our profession than how you look. What the Actors' Guild cares about, what audiences care about, is the craft of acting, not youth and beauty. That's where Lisa got it absolutely right: we need human actors to play human characters.'

'And Wereperson characters as well, apparently. It's pure discrimination—'

'What's discriminatory about awarding merit?'

'How can you judge merit when you won't even let us play in the same league? We already get a tiny percentage of your rates, and now you want to limit our involvement in the industry altogether?'

'We're not the ones setting quotas here, Bob.'

And so it goes on, until it's no longer about me at all. What's happening in creative spheres is a pale shadow of what's playing out in the wider world, where politicians call for detention camps and microchipping, as though Werepeople were no more than dogs. In comparison, my opinions and those of the Actors' Guild seem mild indeed, but the global debate rages so hot that I have to withdraw from social media. I don't mind. In the end, I get what I want: my name is on everyone's lips. Suddenly, I'm more in demand than I have been for years. My agent calls three times that first day with new roles and that's just the start.

When the big one comes in, I'm waiting for it. It's Heartachers and Heartbreakers, and they've promised that my role will be bigger than bitchface Madeleine's.

'No audition?' I ask my agent.

'No audition. They want you. You'd start shooting next month. Shall I tell them yes?'

'Yes!'

It's only later that the doubts start to set in. Sure, I'm on the rise right now, but the fad will fade and in the meantime I'm not getting any younger. Yet, somehow, Madeleine is.

At first, I dismiss the idea. I think I've put it out of my mind entirely, but when I see the designer clutch discarded on my dressing table some impulse makes me reach inside for the card.

Be the envy of your friends, it says. *Let our all-natural techniques wash away the years. Call Rejuven∞te today.*

All-natural techniques, my arse. The only way Madeleine could have lost all those wrinkles and broken veins is surgery. A few essential oils and a bit of yoghurt can't possibly have turned the clock back so far. Whatever she did, it wasn't this. I toss the card onto my dressing table and forget all about it.

* * *

There are cameras waiting outside the studio when I arrive for the first day of filming. It's five in the morning, so they must really want to speak to me. Granted, I've been hard to find for the past few weeks – I've been stuck in an endless cycle of beauty therapies and exercise since I got the role – but this kind of persistence smacks of desperation.

'Lisa!' one of them yells as I get out of the cab. 'What do you think of the testing proposals?'

Ah. So that's why they're here.

It's something the Actors' Guild has come up with: blood tests for all its members. It won't be accepting Werepeople as full members anymore; they'll only be associate members, making them ineligible for certain awards and opportunities. I'm reluctant to comment, but being outspoken is what got me this role and, like they say, there's no such thing as bad press.

'I appreciate the hard work of the Actors' Guild in championing acting excellence,' I say, turning to face my audience. 'It should be about who can deliver the best performance, not about who can look young and beautiful for the longest time.'

'So you stand by your comments that Werepeople can't act as well as humans?' another asks.

'No Wereperson has ever won any acting award, ever, even before they revealed themselves. Doesn't that speak for itself?'

'Some might argue they were trying to fly under the radar, and that up until now they haven't had an opportunity to shine.'

'People might argue that, as a last resort, when presented with undeniable facts.'

'Isn't excluding them from the industry like this tantamount to oppression?'

'You're kidding, right? They're the ones who chose to keep their existence secret. We didn't do that to them. We're not the ones barrelling into an industry established on acting excellence and flooding out the people who actually have talent because of a superficial trend. If anyone's being oppressed here, it's us. We're just trying to protect what we've built here before they overrun us.'

'And you're not at all uncomfortable about the proposals to prefer human actors over Werepeople, even when the role is a Were character? Isn't that just appropriation, pure and simple?'

I smile. 'Look, there's a very good reason that normal people can portray Weres but Weres can't portray normal people. They simply don't bring the depth of performance that humans do. When normal people play Werepeople, they bring that depth with them to create characters the audience finds more sympathetic. Test screenings have shown that. You're not helping the Weres or us by ignoring the truth. Give them their space and let us keep ours.'

'And the testing?'

'I stand with the Actors' Guild, as they've stood with me. Now if you'll excuse me, I have a show to perform.'

I'm buzzing from the debate when I hit the studio, but that buzz quickly diminishes when I realise that I've been called in early so I can have extra time in hair and make-up. Madeleine breezes through with only a few quick corrections, but they pull out all the industrial tools to beat my face.

It gets worse when the interview from this morning hits the internet. There are photos of me everywhere, looking tired and old. The bags under my eyes – bags I'd never noticed until bitchface Madeleine pointed them out to me – are so dark that they look like yesterday's mascara. I break down when I get home from the set, and by nine o'clock I'm still crying into my dressing table, wet cheeks pillowed on my arms.

Then my fingertip brushes against card. *The* card.

It's stupid and it'll probably come to nothing, but I'm desperate enough to try anything.

The Rejuven∞te clinic is hidden down a winding alley in Soho. It looks like exactly the kind of invitation-only place that I've been angling to get into my entire career. That the invitation should finally have come from Madeleine, of all people, is galling beyond words.

The reception area is crafted in reclaimed wood and natural colours, with so many potted yuccas and monsteras that it feels like walking into a jungle. It smells of rosemary, lavender and neroli oil. The woman who greets me is beautiful in a soft, non-threatening way. Her smile is wrinkle-free.

'Welcome,' she says, without asking for my name. 'Emmanuelle is waiting for you in treatment room five, just here on the left. Can I offer you a herbal tea, or perhaps a kombucha?'

I decline.

The treatment room is much the same as the reception area, though the aromatic smell is stronger here. Emmanuelle looks about seventeen, but she moves with a confidence that speaks of more years and there's age in her eyes. Maybe Madeleine was right: maybe this is the best call I ever made.

'Has Ms Carpenter told you much about what we do here?' Emmanuelle asks.

'Not much.'

'It's as simple as this: we turn back time.'

'That doesn't sound very simple.'

'You'd be surprised.' She smiles. 'Our age is held in our self-image. When we look tired, it's because we feel tired. When we look old, it's because we feel old. The power of our treatment lies in reminding our bodies of our inner youth and, with the help of our rejuvenation serum, encouraging them to make us look on the outside the way we see ourselves on the inside. But for the treatment to work, you have to do your part too, and in some ways that's the hardest bit: you have to be able to visualise your true self, the perfect version of yourself that you would like to be. Do you think you can do that?'

It all sounds like mystic mumbo-jumbo to me, but I'm impatient to get on with it, so I assure her that I can. While Emmanuelle leaves the room, I strip and hop up onto a treatment table covered with soft towels. Apparently this is a full-body treatment. When she returns to the room, she gets me to lie on my back with my eyes closed, then rests her fingers at my temples.

'I want you to remember the last time you were truly happy with the way you looked,' she says. 'I want you to visualise a particular moment, or a particular day, and hold it in your mind.'

I scramble for a moment, testing the memories in my

mind and finding each one faulty. Finally, I have it: my last day at RADA, when the prettiest girl on my course looked at me with envy in her eyes. I have never felt so beautiful.

'Have you got it?' she asks.

'Yes.'

'Good. Now I want you to breathe deeply with me, in and out, as you sink into the memory until it's not a memory at all. The woman you see isn't the woman you were, it's the woman you are. Feel the energy flowing through your limbs, feel the electricity and buoyancy in your skin. You are her. She is you. Focus on that thought as I apply the serum.'

She strokes the cream over every inch of me – and I mean *every* inch of me – as she coaxes memories of each part of my body to the forefront of my mind. I remember how strong my legs were when I played netball at university. I remember the way my teeth sparkled white on the TV in my first speaking role. I remember the time my first boyfriend kissed the back of my hand, and I can almost feel his lips on my skin.

The time seems to pass in a blink, but soon Emmanuelle is rubbing the last of the serum into my skin and saying, 'All right. You're done.'

'I'm done?'

I blink my eyes open. The wall clock says I've been in this room for two hours. *Two hours.*

'Do you want to see?' she asks.

'Sure.' But I'm hesitant.

Emmanuelle walks over to the corner of the room and pulls a towel off the full-length mirror that is standing there. I have a moment of fear. I feel so good, so energised, that the thought of looking in that mirror and seeing the same, sagging face that has been looking back at me lately… It hurts my chest.

She helps me from the couch, promising that I'll like what I see, but I keep my gaze fixed on my feet as I shuffle across the room. Only they don't look like my feet. The ever-growing bunions, the protruding veins and tendons, they're gone. My feet look soft. They look young.

I raise my eyes to the mirror.

And freeze.

I can't believe it. I haven't seen the woman looking back at me for at least twenty years. I smile at my reflection and, for the first time in weeks, my teeth don't hurt.

I'm on every talk show, in every magazine, every blog, every YouTube beauty video, every TikTok, every Instagram post for months. The world loves the new me and hates that they can't achieve the same results for themselves with clean eating and exercise. But they know it wasn't surgery, it can't be surgery, because doesn't it look so natural? That's because it *is* natural, I laugh, then advise them to try a juice cleanse. They keep watching, and they keep wanting, and they keep wishing they were me.

I eat their envy in wrinkle-free handfuls.

At the same time, I've become the darling of the protesting movement. *She's just as gorgeous as any of the Werepeople*, the Actors' Guild says, *but she also has the talent. Why settle for just one when we can have both?*

Soon enough, the Werepeople buckle and create their

own guild. With that defeat, it becomes easy for the industry to push ahead with a prohibition against Werepeople depicting humans on stage or screen. It snowballs within the year.

They did it to themselves, really. They gave up the fight and let us win.

In the circumstances, I shouldn't be surprised that the first movie role I am offered is related to the controversy. The storm has died down, but the battle still looms in the public consciousness. They want to see it played out in fiction, to dissect what happened and reassure themselves that the morally correct end was reached. The studio knows its audience and the script delivers sanctimony in spades.

I play Kirsty Allman, a university student whose life is ruined when a Werewolf seduces her boyfriend then murders him, framing Kirsty for the crime. The Werewolf gets her comeuppance when she fails to perform well enough in court to convince a jury of her innocence. She goes wild with rage in the Old Bailey and Kirsty beats her to death with the judge's gavel, even though that's physically impossible and judges in English courts don't even have gavels. It's a crowd-pleasing thriller of a movie.

Bitchface Madeleine is brought in to play the Werewolf opposite me, partly because the studio likes our dynamic from Heartachers and Heartbreakers and partly because she tells me I owe her for the referral to Rejuven∞te. I call in a favour and get her cast. At least this means I'll get to kill her, which has been a life goal ever since Hard Collateral tanked, even if I have to do it on screen instead of in real life.

I'm determined to make this shot count, so I spend months immersed in the script. Maybe that's why I'm a little out of touch when I arrive on set for the first day of filming.

'Hand,' the security guard says to me.

'Excuse me?'

'I need your hand.'

'What for?'

'The blood tests.' He points to a sign by the gate. *Blood testing required before entry*, it says, then it sets out a load of new regulations from the film industry about Werepeople. 'Please, your hand.'

He administers a prick test, stares at the plastic strip for a while, then waves me through. Unfortunately, Madeleine has arrived during the time it's taken for the test to run. She rushes up to join me in a flutter of excitement. If possible, she's looking even younger today than she did the last time I saw her. If she gets any more treatments she's going to have to start working as a child actor.

'Darling!' she greets me, holding out her hand to the guard. Apparently she knows the drill. 'Such an exciting day!'

'Very exciting,' I reply through gritted teeth. A full year working with in close quarters has make me loathe her more, not less. I've seen it all: the temper tantrums when she fumbles her lines, her refusal to eat anything not okayed by her personal nutritionist, the pointless riders she adds to her contract. Odious woman.

I'm tempted to up my treatments at Rejuven∞te just to piss her off, even if it does mean I'll look like a twelve-year-old.

But then the security guard speaks a single word into his collar mic.

'Wereperson.'

'What?' Madeleine gapes at him. 'There must be some mistake.'

'No mistake.'

A second guard arrives at the door within seconds.

'Do the test again,' Madeleine says.

'I can't—'

'Again!' The word is a growl. The second guard fingers the taser at his belt, but the first is sympathetic enough to rerun the test. It comes back with the same result.

'No wonder you look so young,' the second guard scoffs. 'How old are you, exactly, Ms Carpenter?'

'How dare you—'

'Get out of here before we throw you out.'

There's a tense moment of stand off, then Madeleine rushes them, trying to push through the door to appeal to some higher authority, but – despite being a bonafide Wereperson – she's not strong enough. The guards wrangle her down to the pavement.

'But I'm human,' she screams. 'I'm human!'

I watch as they carry her away from the building. By this time, the director has been called. She meets me at the door, her face a mask of shock.

'Did you know?' she asks.

'No,' I breathe. 'I had no idea.'

And from what I saw, neither did Madeleine.

We shoot my scenes while Madeleine's role is recast, but the production is shaken. The press are waiting in their hordes at the end of the day. I express my shock, my horror, my betrayal for the cameras, and suppress my glee. The bitch is dead.

But something is bothering me. In the frenzy that follows her downfall, I can't put my finger on what it is.

The phone rings at midnight. I fumble for it on my bedside table.

'It's the serum,' she sobs quietly down the phone to me. 'The Rejuven∞te serum.'

'Madeleine?'

'It's the serum.'

'What's the serum?'

'I'm not a Wereperson, Lisa. I've never been a Wereperson.'

Then the meaning of her words hits home. The Rejuven∞te serum.

'You're saying Rejuven∞te turned you into a Wereperson?' I ask, sitting up now, on high alert.

'Yes. No. Maybe. I'd just been to the clinic for a last-minute treatment and maybe the test picked up the serum instead of my blood, or maybe I fixated on it too much and started visualising myself as one of them instead of... But I'm human. It's just that it's made from them. The serum. From Werepeople. That's all.'

'That's *all*?' I'm angry now, because if this gets out then she's going to take me down with her. 'You knew that and you still told me to go there?'

'It's just an extract,' she insists. 'Stem cells. They de-age your skin. It's totally natural.'

I think back to those words on Rejuven∞te's business card and they take on a sinister new meaning: *all-*

natural techniques.

'Lisa, you have to help me,' she protests. 'If you don't, then I'll never work again. They've banned me from the set, thrown me out of the Actors' Guild.'

'Then join the Wereactors' guild,' I say blithely.

'But I'm not one of them!'

I don't listen to the rest of her prattling, because I'm too busy worrying about my own prospects. Am I going to turn into one of those monsters too? And is Madeleine going to keep her mouth shut, or will I have to shut it for her?

'Lisa, are you even listening? You have to help me!'

'You're the one who got us both into this mess, Madeleine. For all I care, you can rot in hell.'

I break a nail hanging up.

It looks like Madeleine really is a bitch, after all. Now I have to make sure that I don't turn into one too.

I worry about it all night, a night plagued with dreams of transformations that terrify me. What makes it worse is that I know from Emmanuelle's warnings that believing I look a certain way could manifest that appearance into reality. I can't think about the Were cells on my skin. I can't think about them seeping into my flesh. I can't think about them changing me, turning me into exactly the kind of creature I've lobbied against, and the doublethink is crushing me.

The next morning, I decide before I've even got out of bed that I'll go down to Rejuvenɔte to get some answers, but when I call for an appointment the line goes through to a recorded message.

'Hello, former Rejuvenɔte client. Your treatment is

complete. Welcome to your worst nightmare.'

When I pull the phone away from my ear, I can feel the fur growing on my cheeks.

The Biting Cold

We think of spring as the place where everything starts: grass shoots, tree buds, flower heads, sepals and petals unfurling into life as the sap rises behind the bark. It is the beginning of the sun's return, the warming of the land and the creatures that walk on it, and the awakening of the seeds they carry within them.

But nothing comes from nothing, and some things only wake in the dark.

You have always been alone. Your mother died giving birth to you, her first child, and your father followed thirteen years later from what the vicar called pneumonia but you know was really a surfeit of gin. The parish took the house and would have taken you, too, if you'd let them, but your knees were too strong to bend. You would not spend your life atoning for your father's sins. The only thing left of your childhood is your mother's charm bracelet, a chain of wooden animals strung along leather thong. It is too precious to wear, so you keep it in a pouch at your waist as you stalk through the forest.

This is your sixth season in the wild. You have lost your puppy fat along with your illusions about the romance of living in the trees; the tips of two toes and the littlest finger on your left hand are black with frostbite. You already know that winter is a thing with teeth.

Still you stay, not just because you have nowhere else to go, but because of this.

Look.

The forest should be three colours – the black of the bare trees, the dark hue of the evergreens, the white of the frost – but in the dusk the sky paints the snow in a rainbow from violet to red and back again. The shadows are purple and blue, like dark water pooling around the tree roots.

Step.

It crunches. The day's sunshine had melted the very top layer of the snow, but the chill of the approaching evening has since refrozen it, so it splinters beneath your boots and gives way to the soft powder beneath. It anchors your feet to the ground.

Breathe.

The air is sharp with the clean scent of ice. It burns in your lungs, in your sinuses, at the back of your throat. You smell the animal skins wrapped around your chin, too, roughly tanned and now soaked with condensed drops of your exhalation. They smell of the knife-edge freedom in which you exult: on one side, the dangers of the forest and, on the other, the constant clamour of your body's need for comfort. There's something magical about the balance, not that you believe in magic. If you were starry-eyed enough to gamble your life on a magic bean, you'd be dead by now.

You were raised on the stories, though. Between your father's bottles, when the money was too scarce even to afford the bathtub concoctions of the widow next door, he would occasionally be lucid enough to tell a tale. You know all about cannibalistic witches, faeries snatching away children, and mutilated feet shoved into glass slippers for the sake of a prince's hand, blood pooling at the toes. You understand these stories because they are true: out here on the edge of civilisation, you do what you can to survive. The forest has no morals and neither must you.

But there's a difference between truth and reality; something can be *true* without it being *real*. You know they're only stories. You've seen the faerie hills and mushroom circles, but you've never believed that fantastical creatures lurked within them. The dying light of the winter sun is magic enough for you. The dying light and the prey it awakens.

You slip into the ragged pile of branches that forms your hunting hide and let yourself fade in your stillness, waiting for movement. At first, it is nothing more than a single twig poking up through the patchy blanket of snow. It twitches and you imagine that a woodlouse is moving beneath the leaf litter, maybe a centipede, or perhaps a worm has dislodged the foliage with its burrowing. You spend your life beneath these trees and if you've learned anything about the forest it's that —

even in the depths of winter – the world is alive beneath your feet. You are about to look away, but a second movement has you reaching back to your quiver instead.

Whatever is pushing its way up out of the snow, it's definitely bigger than an insect. The forest floor shifts up and down like a rug over a trap door, the snow and the leaves beneath moving in a single carpet. The something must be burrowing its way up from deep in the earth, which makes you think it must be a rabbit or, perhaps, a badger. There would be eating enough on that to last you days, weeks even. You slip an arrow free from its holder and nock it to your bow.

Breathe in.

You steady the tip and sight on your target.

Breathe out.

You wait for it to breach the surface. You might have a second, two if you're lucky, to fix your aim before the creature spots you and ducks out of sight. It'll be coming out head first, which is good news if it emerges facing away from you, but bad news otherwise. It'll be alert, looking for predators, and you are nothing if not that.

You are so focussed on the spot that you almost miss the rush of deer through the conifers. They have been hiding in the arbours created by the weight of snow on the lowest branches, bending them down into natural shelters that are so secret you have walked straight past them. The deer should be hiding there still, curling up in each others' heat to weather the night, and yet they are running past your hide in a frantic herd.

Something has spooked them, but you don't stop to

question your good fortune. You turn and follow them with the point of your arrow, aim and shoot, run and chase. Your head is filled with the thought of hot meat sizzling over your fire and the knowledge that with the weather this cold, you can store as many deer as you can bring down. You run.

By the time you return to the hide with your prizes, there's a hole in the earth where you saw the twig move. You were expecting the entrance to a badger sett, but instead there's a chasm ten feet wide that spills dark soil up onto the snow like a wound. You shift the two deer carcasses on your shoulders as you turn, squinting between the trees. Discomfort tickles up your spine with an intensity you have not felt since you first ran out into the forest six seasons ago. This is your home and your sanctuary.

And yet.

You shrug the deer up higher until they rub their cooling fur against your cheeks, then retreat carefully to your hut, leaving the gash in the earth behind you.

Beneath the snow, where you can't see it, a circle of death caps rings the void.

Your fire is lively, even when it starts to snow outside. The fireplace pulls well. You turn the hunk of venison on its spit as sizzling drops of fat splash onto the coals and fill the hut with a scent that calls to your appetite. Outside in your meat larder, the balance of your hunt hangs cooling in its lean-to beside the woodpile that feeds your fire and insulates your walls. There's a water butt, too, collecting rain from your roof, though its contents are frozen now. Under the snow, your garden waits for spring. This year's crop and forage is hibernating in your root cellar or pickling there in jars.

You think of each of these things in turn, the resources you have marshalled, and you sigh happily. You are proud, because this comfort is entirely of your own making.

It wasn't always like this.

The hut you built in your first season fell into ruin before three months had passed, leaving you shivering in wet skins and waking with digits that ached and burned, then blistered and turned cold as the snow. This year you were more careful. As soon as the ground was soft enough, you dug into a sheltered bank and sank struts to prop its roof. That's your bedroom now, lined with clay and cocooned in the warm earth. You built out from its open side with wood and dirt, lined with animal skins and topped with flattened cans to make it waterproof and sturdy. Discarded metal is easy to come by at the edges of your domain, littering rivers and ditches. There is always enough to tip your arrows, tin your food and bend for your gutters.

So that's your hut, complete with crude pipe chimney and stone fireplace. Nothing in here is pretty, nothing smells fresh, and some of it itches, but it works, and you have earned every unyielding inch of it with blood and sweat and flesh. You take your mother's charm bracelet from your pouch and stroke the smooth contours of the carvings with the tips of your unblackened fingers. You think that she would be proud too.

The venison pops on its spit and you take that as your cue to serve your dinner for one. You need not share nor concern yourself with politeness, so you bite into the meat as greedily as a dog might chew a bone. Perhaps you should yearn for more company than your mother's ghost, but in moments like this you think you might be happy alone forever.

Outside in the blizzard, a hundred yards from the door of your hut, a creature made of leaves and twigs tips back its head and swallows the snow in hungry mouthfuls.

Time moves quickly at the edge of the forest. Civilisation encroaches further and further each season, and before many years have passed there are fewer deer to be had, fewer birds, fewer rodents, fewer grubs. The jars and tins you have scavenged from the river by the village are filled with the last few mushrooms you have managed to pickle and wild berries you have boiled into something almost like jam, but they won't be enough to see you through the winter. You are taller and more muscular now so your belly demands more, but your root cellar is almost empty and the meat larder full of nothing but skins and one last, precious haunch of venison. By the time the first snow comes, early and cold and more bitter than ever, you are already hungry and lean.

You return to your old haunts. You lurk in the branch-built hide and remember that glorious winter evening when the deer pelted past like a living wave, and you wish that it might happen again. You don't pray, because if you learned anything as a child in that alcohol-fumed house it was that God doesn't listen to your prayers, but you hope and yearn and imagine that if you bring the memory to the forefront of your mind and hold it there, the forest might hear and be merciful.

But the trees sing their own mournful song as the wind cuts through their naked branches like a whip. The pines keep their own counsel; the wind is their friend. It's the hazel, rowan and crab apple trees that shriek: bereft of birds and squirrels and bees, their blossom dropped to the dirt this autumn without being pollinated. They need all their mercy for themselves.

You crouch within your skins and try to be still, but weeks of poor nourishment in freezing temperatures have undone you. When finally, after hours of waiting, you spot something moving in the undergrowth, the tip of your arrow shakes with your shivering.

A rabbit. Somehow, hopping its way through three inches of snow, is the fattest, whitest rabbit you have ever seen. Whatever cache of food it has stashed away, it's clearly better than yours.

You have to take three deep, steadying breaths before you can stop your arrow from weaving. When it finally points true, you are so anxious to make the shot that you fumble your release and it goes long, but the rabbit must have heard the twang of your bowstring because in that moment it turns and jumps right into the arrow's course. The point skewers the rabbit through the neck and pins it to the ground, turning the white snow crimson.

Maybe the forest heard your prayer after all.

You say a quick thank you to the air with a voice that rasps with disuse, then turn and take your prize back home. You've been driven this far by the relentless growl of your stomach, but now you've secured another day's meal you can let yourself rest. Eat and sleep. Preserve your energy. Live to hunt again tomorrow.

After making a meal of half the rabbit – you wish you could have saved more, but you're so *hungry* – you step outside to stash the remaining half in your meat larder with the venison, but the meat has gone. The makeshift door of the larder is standing open, shattered and mangled, and the skins and haunch that you have carefully preserved and denied yourself over the past months are simply gone.

Gone.

It hasn't snowed since the last time you checked your larder, but there are no tracks here except your own. It is as though the contents simply flew out, taking some of the door with them in their flight.

Gone.

Knowing that it won't last long enough, you store the remaining rabbit in your root cellar and curl up in your bed, wondering at the possibility of a thief without feet.

You sleep long and late the next day, feeling the weight of your misery, so it's not until evening that you make your way back to the hide. Maybe the forest will be merciful again, you think. Maybe yesterday's rabbit has friends.

When you arrive, you try to pinpoint the spot where you felled yesterday's dinner. It should be easy to see – the snow was stained red – but there's nothing here now except a freshly-dug drift of soil scarring the snow. It is unpleasant in its familiarity. You try to reason away the coincidence, but your instincts know what your mind tries to deny: the gash in the earth is the same size, and in the same spot, as the one you tried to forget in the year of the deer. You'd returned to it after that night and found nothing but the flat forest floor, so you'd almost convinced yourself that it was a dream. A dream of earthbound leviathans moving beneath your feet.

Perhaps you're dreaming now. Perhaps the haunch of deer is still safe in your meat larder and the newly-tanned skins are waiting beside it to line your bed when it's too cold to leave the hut. Or maybe you've been so long in the cold that you're seeing things that aren't there.

Giving up on the rabbits, you abandon the hide and walk to the edge of the chasm, insisting to yourself that it won't seem so ominous once you know the whole of it. It's only the night, and the mystery, and the fact that the venison thief has made you worry.

You peer over the lip and have to catch your weight on your bow, digging one end into the snow. The devastation is worse than you thought.

The hole is wide only because it is deep, so the spoil has spread out around it. It funnels from a broad mouth into a deep vertical tunnel, so deep that you can't see the bottom of it; it fades into a darkness so complete that beyond twenty feet or so you can't distinguish the walls of frozen earth from the emptiness between them. Around the sloping edges, drifts of snow are spattered with blood and white fur. It looks as though whatever dug this hole has also found the rest of your rabbits.

You hear the crunching noise before you notice the shadow lumbering towards you. It's as tall as a tree, moving with the unsteady gait of a newborn fawn as it lurches into the clearing. Its bones are branches, its flesh a moving morass of dead bugs and worms, its skin the pulpy paleness of rotting petals. In the joint of an elbow, you recognise the wooden planks that are missing from the door of your meat larder and the half-tanned fox pelt you left there to dry. When it reaches the hole, it doesn't so much kneel as collapse to the ground in a pile of limbs that move independently of its control, bending into impossible shapes before reforming into something new.

You wondered where the creatures of the forest had gone and here is your answer: they've been disassembled and rearticulated into this. When it scrapes the snow from the ground and shovels the rotting earth beneath into its mouth, it does so with fingers made of squirrel bones and tipped with rooks' beaks for claws. Its teeth are shards of rock and flint lancing out of muddy gums, its face a patchwork of leaves, feathers and insect carapaces that glint like tar in the moonlight. There are snail shells in place of its ears and spiderwebs trail across its face like a veil. It eats the leaf litter in gulps as big as your torso, stomach never swelling, jaws never stopping, and you know that its hunger will never be sated. You don't know what it is, but you know that you have to stop it before it destroys everything that keeps you alive.

You draw an arrow and let it fly. It lands in the creature's cheek with the thunk of metal into tree bark, peeling apart the leaves that cover the wooden skeleton. You expect retaliation or at least acknowledgement, but the creature doesn't look at you. Instead, it looks at the arrow, pulling it free to examine the metal tip. Then, deliberately and slowly, it puts the arrow into its mouth point-first and chews. You let loose another arrow, and another, again and again until your quiver is empty, and each ends up crushed between its flint teeth and swallowed into its bottomless belly.

It is relentless. It is unstoppable.

It will eat the forest whole.

You run without looking back.

After that, you don't go out after dark. When you return in the daylight to the spot where you saw the creature, there is nothing but level earth and the snow that covers it. It is beyond your comprehension, so you choose to ignore it.

Until spring comes, and the forest begins to change. The plants that rise from the earth are deformed in places, plated with foil and speckled with shot that twinkles in the sunshine. Your garden spits out spinach that hardens to metal at its tips. The flesh of an errant spring lamb is threaded through with wire-like veins, making it inedible. The radishes you grow are lush and fresh at their roots, but the stalks and leaves are covered with tiny splinters of iron that drive themselves into your fingertips when you harvest them and take hours of careful work to coax from your skin. Your home is seeded with these foreign bodies, lurking unseen in places that were previously free from hazard. You can no longer trust the earth and you grow thin on its meagre fruits.

But outside the forest, life seems harder still. The roads are lined with graves, so many that most remain unmarked weeks after they have been filled. You are not the only one struggling to stay alive, nor are you the only one looking to the forest for sustenance. Trees are cut from its edges as the towns creep ever further towards its heart and your hearth. At the same time, you're finding shining sheets of wrapping material in the forest and bottles in the rivers, both made from something new, resilient and brightly-coloured, sometimes pliable, sometimes stiff. The townsfolk call it plastic. You collect the bottles and fill them with water from the clear spring by your hut, the only source from which you'll drink; the surface of the river now glints with multi-coloured oil that tastes like burned vegetables and makes you vomit.

You strip and save what plants you can over the next few seasons, thankful that at least the autumn blackberries and nuts are free from corruption, and settle in for the hardest winter you've ever known. You've dug a new, secure meat larder and you fill it with what you can, hunting only the animals that belong in the woods; the livestock you poach from the surrounding farms is so laced with metal that you abandon it for the crows. You don't think too hard about why this should be. You're busy trying to stay alive.

The first snow comes hard and fast, freezing alpine strawberries on their stalks and potatoes in the ground before you have a chance to dig them all up. You tear open the black flesh of your frostbitten finger on the flattened tins you use to excavate the crop – you can't feel the pain in the dead flesh – but it's all for nothing because the potatoes defrost into a rotten mush that fizzes with a fermented smell that reminds you of your father. It makes you so sick that, despite your hunger, you carry the remains away from your hut and scatter them in a clearing for the birds. You're angry enough and sickened enough that you pay no attention to the dusk, nor do you hear the creature approaching. When you do, you freeze as still as the icicles that drape the trees around the glade.

The creature walks past you, as though you are invisible.

It's quieter this year, smaller, barely twice as tall as you, but it still walks in the same shambling half-stumble, lurching as though it is only one gust of wind away from collapse. It drops to its almost-knees in a heap of dizzying disassembly and scoops the mess of fermented potato into its mouth along with the snow, the leaves, the twigs, and the shining wrappers that now litter the forest floor. It, too, is hungry, for even the leaf litter is thin. There has not been a mast year for as long as you have lived.

As you watch it shovelling, wondering whether you should run or stay and fight for the remains of the forest that it is devouring, your eye catches on a spray of small wooden shapes amongst the ruined potatoes. Your hand slaps against the pouch at your waist, the pouch that – now you feel the ragged edges with your fingertips – you realise has broken, spilling your mother's precious animal charms across the ground and into the fermented mess that reeks of your father's sour breath. You watch in horror as the creature scoops the delicate carvings into its metal-tipped claws and swallows them whole.

You feel a snap in your chest as something breaks loose, then you're running towards the creature without thinking, thumping at its side with balled fists, catching your knuckles on metal mesh, broken plastic and the occasional bone. When you finally collapse exhausted beside the impassive creature, it turns its glass eyes towards your bloodied hands and blinks once with eyelids made of blue eggshell. Its pinecone nose shifts up and down. Then slowly, its frame writhing with leaves and dirt and teeth and crushed cans and bottle caps as it rearranges its form, it brings its face down to your hands. You are too tired to fight it now, so tired that you almost welcome its attentions, but the bite and swallow you are expecting never comes. Instead, the creature reaches out with a tongue made of fabric and fur and licks the blood from your fingers, one by one.

This task completed, it turns away to gobble up the last of the ruined potato, then gets awkwardly to its feet and ambles away, leaving you alone in the snow.

It has left no footprints in its wake.

In the spring, the trees put forth branches ornamented with shining sweet wrappers and tiny wooden animals that nestle like flowers among the leaves, and you begin to understand that the creature is not the enemy you believed it to be. You harvest a handful of the charms and make a necklace from them, stringing deer and rabbits and hedgehogs and badgers in miniature around your throat.

It's been years since you last approached the creature. The forest is little more than a copse now and there are cities where the towns once stood. People press in from all sides, rambling along deer trails that are now empty of their original denizens, crushing strange hybrid mushrooms beneath their feet. It's been months since you last saw the slightest trace of a rabbit, and the birds have all but deserted the forest, yet the people keep on multiplying. So far you have kept them away from your little hut with judicious planting of holly and other discouraging shrubs, all of which bristle with sharp metal thorns and plastic spikes, but you know it won't be long before the interlopers chase you from your warren. Maybe you should go, you think. If there are so many of them, there must be more food out there than there is in here.

Or so you imagine, but then you see exactly what they eat and what it has done to them. A couple of them cross your path not two hundred yards from your hut. They're clad in dangerous colours – red and pink and orange – but their skin is snow white and so translucent that you can see the veins snaking across their cheeks. One has a metal plate where his eyebrow should be and the eye beneath it looks wrong. The other's hair glints with coloured lights that run along the shell of her ear like water flowing uphill. It is grotesquely beautiful, but the skin around it is rotten and waxy. Their faces gleam with oily sweat. They're loud, shouting and squinting at each other as they stomp through the undergrowth with their guns, boxier and less elegant than the one your father had before he sold it for gin. This is no way to hunt, but that hardly matters because there are no animals left here to kill. There are precious few trees to form their habitats, and every one is corrupted in bark, root and branch. In these straitened days, you must scrape morsels of plant matter from plastic and metal and glass to make your meals.

But what you watch the city people eat is worse. They unwrap it from shining leaves of plastic and bite into bricks of paste that smacks distastefully around their mouths as though it is sucking the moisture from their gums. When they leave, you take their abandoned wrappers from the ground and lick the reflective insides. They taste of nothing at all.

When the cold comes, the people leave. It's just you out here now, you and the creature that the first snow brings. You see it in the distance sometimes, moving between the trees outside your hut, but you don't leave your sputtering fire long enough to risk meeting it. There is little for either of you to eat, but you try to abstain, understanding that it is more vital that the creature eats than that you do, knowing that its hunger today means no food at all for you come the spring. You live on the mouldering remains of your root cellar and are frugal with every scrap that the forest still offers.

Your abstinence takes its toll. Without wood to burn, without leaves to fill the cracks in your walls and without the warmth of new animal hides around you, the cold is insurmountable. You lose five more fingers to frostbite, leaving you with only the thumb and index finger on one hand, index and middle finger on the other. You can still use your bow, just, but this is small consolation; there's nothing to shoot at except metal-plated trees. Your dead fingers hang from your hands like rotten carrots and burn with an ache that screams through your bones. It feels like you are dying with them.

When the frostbite blisters swell and pop, nothing soothes the pain except icing your fingers with snow.

The cold numbs them, giving you some blessed relief. You have a vague memory of being told not to do this as a child, but if you were ever told the reason then you have forgotten it. You don't realise that rubbing your frostbitten digits with handfuls of ice is just killing them quicker, hurrying the cell death into your bone marrow. They look entirely black now, but they feel better, so you are surprised when you wake one morning under mouldering skins to find that they are missing. A brief search locates them in your bed. During the long, cold night, your fingers have amputated themselves at your knuckles, leaving nothing but glistening raw flesh behind.

It takes you all day to clean the stumps of your hands in the water of the forest spring – the one resource that remains clear and uncontaminated – and bind them in old rabbit skins that you have scraped clean into thin leather. It is dark by the time you go out to bury your dead fingers, and the creature is waiting for you. It is hunched and distorted, netted with mesh and packed with artificial detritus that will not bend into the shapes its contorting body requires. Its ears are glass bottle-bottoms, its fingers are plastic pipes and its shoulders are crowned with painted tin-can epaulettes, but these aren't ornaments; they're awkward pieces of a body that is no longer functional. Metal limbs spark as their parts scrape against each other in desperate attempts at rearrangement. Rubber screeches against glass, raising the last few birds from the synthetic tree tops in pathetic mimicry of their former flocks. Here and there you see a glimmer of nature in the creature: its teeth are real this year, perhaps bovine or perhaps human, and they are anchored by flesh. It has clearly found something living to eat, but not here. There is nothing on the forest floor except bundles of wire and glass encased in plastic shells. You don't know what the devices are, but you know they've been multiplying over the past few years along with the people. Now they litter the forest floor in heaps: objects of all shapes and sizes that shine and beep and flash with lights.

The creature is not deterred. Mindlessly, it picks up a handful of them in clumsy fingers and brings it to its soft lips. The metal shatters its enamel teeth, but still it crams the pieces into its mouth, smashing the devices into shards of plastic and wire that stick in its gums. It bleeds, but if it feels the pain at all then it doesn't show it.

You wait until it has swallowed its empty meal, then feed it your frostbitten fingers, one by one.

Winter ends, but it may as well not have bothered. Nothing natural grows in the forest. In truth, it is not much of a forest anymore, but a valley instead. The trees are few and stunted. Unable to sustain the weight of their metal branches on a patchwork construction of plastic and tin, they crumple at their bases and topple to the ground, smashing apart the glassy grasses at their feet. The few birds that hatch from the cellophane eggshells in their boughs grow foil feathers on flesh that is black and dead. You see no rodents or deer at all, but you find a blistered rabbit's foot that appears to have amputated itself from its owner. You do not consider this talisman to be lucky.

Over the coming years, there is almost nothing for

you to eat. You have given up on growing your own fruit and vegetables – they are filled with plastic seeds and wire filaments. Instead, you survive on nuts and the apples stored in your root cellar, holding your nose as you eat them sparingly in an attempt to ignore the fermented hum of their flesh. Supplementing this with rare carrion, you waste away through what should be the fattest months of the year. By the time the first snow arrives, you are too starved to do anything but lie in bed and slurp at the last dregs of your nut porridge.

The creature comes to you like a lover on his knees, though it is no taller than you now. It crouches at the side of your bed as its artificial body barks out a series of squeaks and wails.

It is hungry, you know, because you are hungry too.

Its eyes are plaintive; they reflect your own in their metallic depths. You see your hurt there, your desperation, and know that it is nothing compared to the ravenous agony the creature feels. There is nothing of the forest left in it, just oil and shine and veneer. It may still be able to stand under its own power, but it is dying as surely as you are.

You feed it the last of your porridge, ladling the cold mixture between its blade-like teeth and then, at the end, letting it chew up the wooden spoon and bowl as well. You feed it the animal hides from your bed, which it rips into shreds then swallows in greedy, slurping strings. It eats the walls of your hut, gulping down stone and wood and fibre, then returns to your bedside. You laugh as it paws with glass fingertips at the leather that covers the stumps of your hands, then you unwrap the brittle stuff and feed it that too, and the clothes from your back, and the charms from around your neck, one by one.

When it turns towards your metal chimney, you call it back. It shouldn't eat that, so you must give it something else. You've been keeping the knife beneath your pillow for weeks, waiting for the moment when you had strength enough for this final act. It is time.

You will not see another spring. But with luck, and with one proper meal, the forest might.

In the spring, the valley is a carpet of poppies, blood red and lush in their profusion. Beneath the ground, metal acorns crack open to send up sprouts that are unmarred by human interference. They will grow tall and strong in time. Around them, burrows are filled with breeding creatures of every shape and size, each made only of flesh and blood, with one small exception: each has a small wooden simulacrum of itself that hangs from an ear, or a tail, or at its neck.

You have been prolific. When Winter comes again, there will be plenty of you to satisfy his appetite.

Good and Beautiful

In the middle of the Aegean Sea, there's an island. It's not a big island, nor is it popular: the salt wind whips too harshly against its coast, flat and unprotected as it is, and scours the land to bare rock. Those who take the Grand Tour in search of adventure might spend weeks hopping around the Greek islands, but they don't come here. The only figures on the beach are the bone-white statues that litter the shore, bleached and smashed and weed-slicked.

They're not beautiful. You might call their faces handsome and their bodies well-formed – those parts of them you can find, at least – but you might also note the slight widening of their eyes and the mania of their smiles. If you were superstitious, you might wonder if it wasn't the landscape so much as its occupants that keeps the tourists away.

Once upon a time, the island was different.

Once upon a time, it was filled with fishermen and smallholders and their families, plus skilled craftsmen and the merchants they attracted. It bustled, not in the way that cities bustle, but with the slumbering labour of orchards in late summer and the fierce desperation of boats borne by winter storms.

Once upon a time, it was home to a girl named Dew.

Her house was so close to the beach that it was permanently filled with sand, and so small that there was only just enough space for the three of them inside. When her father brought his friends home after a long day's fishing, they had to sit outside to eat. None of them much minded, because the food was worth it: Dew's mother was the best cook on the island. She was so good that nearby smallholders gave her a share of their produce in return for finished meals.

Just as well, because when Dew's father made his final trip to the sea, never to return, that trade was all that kept Dew and her mother alive.

Tides ebb and flow, taking the months with them. Dew grows up. She helps with the cooking and waits the tables that are their livelihood – permanent fixtures on the sand, now – and all the time she grows. Soon she'll grow out of being a child.

When her mother raises the subject for the first time, it's late in the year, late enough that the harvests are in and the frost on the wind makes Dew's nose run. Late enough that she can't deny how the cracks in the walls have begun to gape, letting the cold creep into their ramshackle home to rime the flagstones with ice.

'Dew,' her mother says, softly entreating. 'We should

think about finding you a husband.'

Dew knew it was coming, knows it's inevitable, knows all the reasons that make it wise counsel, but still it jolts her.

'No,' she counters, 'we should find *you* a husband. I'm still a child.'

Her mother holds her gaze, but it costs her. There's shame in her eyes. They both know why her mother can't remarry. It's not just that she has Dew, it's… everything else. There were lean times when there was no food to be had, when her mother sent Dew away on errands more often – away to the beach for seaweed, away to the hills for herbs, away to anywhere as long as it was far from the house – while a single man dined alone on the beach and lingered. Different men, but always with the same intent darkening their eyes when they looked at her mother.

Now Dew feels like she is the one trapped by their gaze.

'No,' she says again.

Her mother is defeated.

'All right. Not yet.'

But soon. Before it's too late.

The changes start with the spring, slowly enough that Dew doesn't notice at first, but soon – too soon – it's inescapable. By the end of May, Dew's a girl who looks fully-grown. She doesn't want to be. All she wants is to be left alone.

But there's no hiding from the rest of the island. The boys her age and older start chuckling behind their hands as she serves their food, exchanging significant glances with each other over wine-flushed cheeks. She hears their laughter as she walks away and wonders what she's done to upset them. It's only later, when the first one corners her beside the woodpile, that she realises her mistake.

He's good-looking. The light brown of his hair startles her. Most of the island's inhabitants share Dew's colouring: ink-black hair, tan skin, dark eyes. His are grey. He looks like one of the heroes from the stories her mother recites by the fire. The problem is that stories lie. The old stories are the worst, filled with untruths that grow as they percolate through the years. The lie about pretty boys is the biggest of them all.

'What do you want?'

'Shhh,' he soothes, like she's a baby. 'I only want to say hello.'

Dew doesn't know that *only* is a threshold word.

He steps towards her and then he's stroking her face as he whispers soft words that are meant to reassure, but instead they make her heart race with something that scares her. When he touches her hair, she rears back and pushes away, running into the house and her mother's arms.

Dew cries, just for a moment. It's shock more than anything else.

Her mother doesn't ask why; she doesn't need to. She just says, 'The Angelos boy?'

Dew nods against her shoulder.

'He works the smallholding with his father,' she says, her tone thoughtful as she strokes her daughter's hair. 'He's a good boy. Handsome.'

The words sting Dew – the injustice, the betrayal – because she doesn't understand how the island works, how precarious their place in it is. Her mother explains: no one will believe her. The boys get away with everything because they are beautiful and charming, but it doesn't matter how beautiful a girl is. She will never be any good. Her best chance is to charm one of them into marriage. Then at least she will be safe from the others.

The next time the Angelos boy corners her by the woodpile, she lets him stroke her hair. She lets the others too.

They only want to talk.

They only want to kiss.

They only want to touch.

She only wants to be left alone, but she is overruled. After all, how is it fair that the needs of one should outweigh the wants of so many others? Her *only* weighs less than theirs.

There's a man called Andros. He comes around a lot these days, first and last at the dining tables. Dew's mother sits with him sometimes while the islanders raise their eyebrows. Some of the older women tut at her mother, making Dew blush, but not with embarrassment. Inside, she is raging. They have their comfortable smallholdings and their labouring husbands, safe from the sea. They don't understand that Dew and her mother have to take kindness wherever they can get it, and they get plenty from Andros. He brings game and fish and fine wooden objects he's carved himself, all of which he gives without asking for recompense.

Not from Dew, anyway, but her mother actually likes

him. This is more than trade.

Andros is handsome, too. Dew thinks that's a good thing for her mother. Handsome men don't need to buy women with gifts, don't need to lie, because they always get what they want. They only have to ask, so why bother with deception? In its way, that is comforting. Andros must be genuine, or he wouldn't bring them anything at all.

He travels a lot, he says, skipping from island to island to trade the things he picks up along the way, so he's never around for more than a few days at a time, but he spends them at the beach. The boys learn to avoid Dew on those days, but they come running back the moment he's left.

It's a game to them, this dance of dominance. Dew never wins. She isn't even a player, just a piece.

Until she flips the board.

While Andros is away, the Angelos boy traps her by the woodpile again. He usually leaves off after some kisses and a fumbling grope – they all do – but this time he tangles his fingers in her hair and won't let go. He knows Andros will be back any day now and he means to snatch his chance while he still can.

She could scream. She thinks about it, but she knows how he'll twist the truth. He'll smile and laugh and say she was asking for it, then come back with his fists the next day to strike where it won't show. She's seen enough marks on her mother over the years that she knows what to expect from boys that snatch. There are no heroes to come to her rescue; none that will believe her, anyway. She's heard the stories and she knows what they teach.

Beautiful boys are virtuous, but every girl is poison.

If only that were true, she prays, eyes and lips pressed shut against his kiss and the ripping pain in her scalp. *If I could bite and sting and paralyse, I could protect myself. If I were made of venom, they'd taste me and die.*

It's a bitter prayer to a god Dew didn't think was listening, but it works. She is granted one *if only* to counter all their *onlys*.

There's a quickening at the roots of her hair. It's long and thick, bound back with a rag and the boy's hands, but now it breaks free in coils of silky smoothness that glide across Dew's cheeks and embrace her shoulders, not with the threat of a lover, but bringing comfort like her mother's arms. The boy doesn't notice at first, intent as he is on his object. For a second, a split-second, there is satisfaction in his eyes. He thinks she's relenting, mistaking the touch at his neck, his shoulder, his waist for Dew's questing fingers. His blood is too high to admit the discrepancy: three touches, two hands.

Three touches, three bites.

The Angelos boy keeps his distance after that night. He says nothing about what happened, because who would believe it? He isn't sure what happened himself. His skin is scarred with the marks of sunk teeth, but Dew's lips were trapped by his, her hands crushed between them, so it couldn't have been her. He thought he saw her hair… but it's ridiculous. Her hair looks just like anyone else's now. It must have been insects, he thinks, though he's never seen bites like these. They fester and stink of rotting flesh, as though he is dissolving from the inside out. He is in too much pain to think of romance.

Dew has no time to celebrate over the coming weeks, or to ponder the divine intervention; her mother is sick. She looks tired, drawn, and she can't cook without vomiting. Their neighbours' scant goodwill is just enough to keep the trade flowing, but their generosity wanes with time. Dew's food lacks the culinary magic of her mother's: her pies are too flaky, her bread not as light and fluffy as she wishes. She's learned a lot in her short years, but she can't yet replace her mother at the stove.

When Andros returns, he finds Dew desperate and scared. She greets him with relief and leaves him alone with her mother, hoping they will come up with a cure. Despite her better instincts, she thinks he is there to help.

The yelling drifts down to the beach in fragments: *already have three... what did you expect me to... wife... can't support another...*

Then the violence: the kick, the clatter, the muffled scream.

The end.

When Dew reaches the door, Andros pushes past her and out. Dew's mother is lying on the doorstep, blood surrounding her, legs coated with gore. Gone: the pulse at her throat, the breath from her lungs, and the life she carried, along with her own.

Andros backs away. His last words are 'I only...'

Dew meets his eyes as the echoes of memory swim around her head, dredging up all the *onlys* that have been imposed upon her.

I only want to touch.

I only do it because you want it.

It'll only hurt for a second.

And in a flash of certainty, Dew feels the weight of all the *onlys* her mother has suffered through her short life, until this final one: *I only wanted you at my convenience.*

It doesn't matter that he doesn't speak the words. It's what they all want, at the end of their *onlys*.

Dew becomes conscious of the writhing of her hair. She had half-convinced herself that she'd dreamed it the first time, and for a second she chooses to believe that it's the wind tugging her braid loose, hoping the feeling will pass. It doesn't. The locks circle her shoulders and hold her as she falls to the sand at Andros's frozen feet, stroking her back and blanketing their warmth around her.

The wind blows sand across the beach and waves against the shore, but Andros is still. His skin is unnaturally white and hard as marble. His feet are planted like roots, his hands held out to placate, his eyes frozen wide with panic. He looks scared, as though he knew in his last seconds that if the men had found out what he'd done, they would have come for him.

Maybe they would have.

When they see her mother's body and the unnatural sculpture that Andros has become, they'll definitely come for Dew. They'll call her a witch and throw rocks at her until she's buried alive. They'll be lining up to condemn her, all the boys who've stolen kisses and squeezes and stroked her hair.

Dew's hair strokes her now, wiping away her tears,

offering solutions.

Andros doesn't move.

Dew's mother doesn't move.

Her hair…

In the middle of the Aegean Sea, there is still an island. It was bare to start with, but now it's stripped clean, the fragments of every statue collected and reassembled in its proper place. The figures have been measured and studied until the truth has been mined from their bones, and this is the verdict: they are role models and heroes, the template for manhood. The stories call them *kalokagathia*, good and beautiful, and with that word they lock the qualities into one inseparable equation.

Beautiful = good.

They're in museums now. You can go to see them, if you want. You can look into their handsome faces, their blank eyes, and decide for yourself what fate they have earned; whether they'll spend eternity smiling, or grimacing with fear.

Peyton's End

As the car turned into the village, the cottage came into view. It was perched on the cliff edge at the top of the hill. From this distance, it looked as though it were balanced there, as though a sharp gust of wind might blow it straight into the sea below.

'Oh,' Mrs Larson sighed. 'Look at it, Gem. Isn't it gorgeous?'

In the backseat, twelve-year-old Gemma lifted her attention from her handheld game for the briefest moment before returning to it, unimpressed.

'Gem?' Mrs Larson prompted.

'Yeah. Looks great, Mum.'

'And I'm sure you'll find some friends on the beach,' she said as she followed the road through the dunes. 'Loads of kids your age.'

The Devon village of Leestow was so tiny that they had driven through it in a blink. Now the car was climbing up to the promontory where the cottage sat exposed. The Larsons had a clear view of the beach in the bay beneath. It was a small stretch of sand, bright with sparse towels and umbrellas.

'I was expecting it to be more crowded on a bank holiday weekend, but it looks like we've got lucky,' Mr Larson said, rolling down the passenger-side window to let the breeze into the car. 'God, that's good. I love the smell of the sea.'

Gemma put aside her game. She didn't think it was lucky that there were so few people here. She didn't want yet another summer holiday spent amusing herself while her parents raved about local cheeses or spent hours sitting in the sun reading books in silence. She wanted someone to talk to who wasn't too grown up to have fun. Sadly, the youngest people she could see on the sand were all old enough for bikinis and beer.

But Gemma wasn't the only person in Leestow looking for a friend, and her arrival did not go unnoticed.

'Are you ready, darling?' Mrs Larson shouted up the stairs.

Gemma had slipped up to her room to unpack her bag quietly while her mother exclaimed over every aspect of the cottage. Apparently, the window seat in the sitting room was 'quaint', the kitchen was 'rustic' and the garden was 'bucolic'. Sometimes Gemma thought her mum only opened her mouth because she liked the way words sounded.

'I'm coming,' she shouted back down.

They'd arrived late, so her parents had decided to go

to the pub in Leestow for dinner. Gemma hated pubs. The old ones smelled of stale beer and smoke, and the new ones had chirpy waitresses who offered her colour-in children's menus, as though she were a child and not very nearly a teenager, actually.

In a place as small as Leestow she wasn't expecting much, but she still put on some smart trousers and her best sandals. It would make her mother happy and the happier her mother was, the more likely it was that they'd get to order pudding.

'You look nice,' Mr Larson said as Gemma came down the narrow stairs into the kitchen.

'Thanks,' she mumbled back.

Then the strap on one of her sandals snapped in half. She pitched off the final step as it broke, and fell straight into Mr Larson's arms.

'Oof. Are you all right, Gem-Gem? What was that?'

Gemma took off the shoe and looked it over sadly. The heel strap was broken clean through, weakened by the clasp of the buckle. There was no way it could be fixed.

'They were my favourite pair,' she said softly.

'Gem?' said Mrs Larson, walking in from the sitting room. 'What's wrong?'

Gemma held up the sandal. She had to blink away tears and hoped her parents didn't notice. It was stupid to cry over a shoe. It was the kind of thing a kid would do.

'Oh well,' said Mrs Larson. 'Just as well I got you a present, then. I was going to save it until tomorrow, but I suppose you'd better have it now.'

Mrs Larson fetched the parcel from a bag hanging by

the front door. It was wrapped up in birthday paper, even though Gemma's birthday wasn't until November.

'Open it,' Mrs Larson said, putting it on the kitchen table.

Gemma removed her other sandal and opened the present carefully, saving the paper. Inside was a beach towel, a pair of rainbow flip-flops and a bottle of sun cream. Only her mum would wrap suncream. It was a pointed gift: with her red hair and pale skin, Gemma couldn't go outside without the stuff.

'See?' said Mrs Larson, holding up the flip-flops with a smile. 'Perfect timing.'

Gemma smiled back and thanked her parents as she put on the flip-flops.

They'd do.

But they weren't her sandals.

Gemma was overdressed. The pub was the dingy, old sort that her mum called 'traditional' and 'charming', but Gemma thought was more like a wet hole in the ground. Despite the summer heat outside, inside it was cold enough to make Gemma wish for a thicker jumper.

There were a couple of middle-aged men drinking dark pints at the bar and a small family in the room beyond.

'Hello,' Mr Larson said to the barman. 'Are you still serving food?'

The two men at the bar exchanged a look. Gemma could understand why: there was a chalkboard sign right next to where her father stood that read 'Food served till 9pm'.

And that was the least embarrassing thing her father

did that evening.

For starters, he decided they should stay at the bar and chat until their food was ready. He introduced himself to the two men, who were just trying to have a quiet beer together and clearly wanted nothing to do with Mr Larson or his family. Then he discovered that the men were a couple and made a big fuss of how wonderful it was that 'even out here, it's all right to be gay'.

At that, Gemma left her parents behind and went to find a table in the dining area. They could join her when her dad had stopped being awful.

It was nicer back here. There was a big window, currently flung wide to let the warmth in. An open door led out to a beer garden where she could see more drinkers congregated, mostly young, smoking and laughing and enjoying the sunshine. Gemma envied them. She didn't get to sit in the sun without slathering on sun cream first. She hated the smell of it and the way it made her skin sticky, so instead of going outside she sat at an empty table in the damp-smelling shade.

The walls were covered with framed watercolour paintings. A couple of them had price stickers on the corners, so Gemma guessed they were by local artists. The views certainly looked familiar: the beach, the cliffs, the sea. There was something lonely about them, though. There was little sunshine, but lots of clouds, and there were no people in them, just landscapes and the occasional bird. They felt empty.

'Good, aren't they?' Mr Larson said as he joined her at the table, as though he had been the first to see them. 'One of the chaps at the bar knew the artist. She used to live in our cottage, apparently. But she moved away.'

'Ah,' said Mrs Larson, interrupting. 'Here comes your scampi, Gem. Doesn't that look lovely?'

After some wheedling, Gemma persuaded her parents that she could walk back to the cottage on her own. They wanted to stay for another drink, which Gemma knew meant badgering the barman, and she didn't want to hang around for that.

It wasn't a long walk, no more than a mile or two, but the views were dramatic enough to make it stretch. The pathway skirted the cliff edge with wilful intention at some points, before diving back into the gorse to weave through sandy brush and the occasional patch of wild orchids. It was as though nature was holding the reins here, so different from Gemma's home in Reading, so different even from the village down the road.

The salt wind in her face made sense of the paintings back at the pub. The isolation here matched the sense of isolation in the watercolours; the remoteness of the holiday cottage was peaceful, but there was no help for miles around. It was that tension that shivered down her spine as she turned the last corner up the path to the cottage and let herself inside.

The place was too quiet without her parents there.

But it was perfect for a bit of exploring.

There was no cellar to the cottage, at least none that Gemma had found, but there was a hatch in the ceiling on the landing at the top of the stairs. Her mum and dad wouldn't want her poking about, but it would be at least another hour until they were back from the pub. She found a stick with a hook on its end in the wardrobe in her parents' bedroom and used it to pull at the ring on the hatch. A ladder came down with it, triggering an automatic light.

For such an old cottage, the mechanism was smart. The ladder was sturdy. She didn't think twice before climbing up into the attic room.

It wasn't as cramped as Gemma had expected. The room was long and thin, set between the gables, but she could stand up straight in the centre. There was an easel set up by a circular window at one end, the watercolours long-congealed in the palette. And paintings. So many paintings. They were propped up against the walls in rows five deep, canvas after canvas, sheet after sheet. It wasn't just watercolours, either, but oils and charcoals and pencil drawings, every medium possible tested and perfected.

The older pictures, the ones at the back of the rows, were portraits. There seemed to be no pattern to the subjects – men, women and children of every shape and form – as though the artist had wanted as many models as possible, with no interest in portraying particular individuals. Then something obviously shifted, because the more recent paintings were only landscapes: fields of flowers and the sea.

Gemma ran her fingers along the tops of the frames as she flicked through the canvases. There was no dust. Someone looked after these paintings, probably hoping to make money off them by selling them at the pub. But if the artist who once lived here had moved away, why had she left the paintings behind?

It was only when Gemma got back down to her room, shutting up the attic behind her, that she saw that one of the same artist's paintings hung over her bed, a huge canvas. She wasn't sure how she hadn't noticed it before.

That night, she dreamed she was standing at the spot it portrayed, the edge of the cliff beyond the garden. The wind was strong and sharp, the darkness harsh with the dawn, but it felt warm.

Welcoming.

Safe.

The next day, Gemma wolfed down her lunch and escaped to the cliffs before her dad could suggest touring the model village, or going to the train museum, or something equally painful. The morning had been spent driving around the area in the car, which seemed to Gemma to be a stupid way to spend your holidays when you could be outside.

'Take your phone!' her mum yelled as she ran out of the door.

'I've got it.'

'And keep it on.'

'I will!'

That was enough to buy her an afternoon of freedom.

The path along the cliff followed close to the coast, so there were never more than two minutes in a row that Gemma couldn't see the sea. It looked calm from up here, but it was windy enough that she could imagine waves smashing into the beaches below. She liked the drama of it.

She headed away from the cottage and up, climbing past windswept trees and rocky outcroppings to even higher reaches of the promontory. From the village, the cottage seemed like the highest point for miles, but the trees behind it concealed the curving rise of the coast. Up here, there was more than nature. It was clearly a well-trodden path, because the National Trust had put signs here and there talking about the fortifications in the nearby harbour. There were wartime relics hidden in the trees, too, where the mud path occasionally turned into slabs of concrete peppered with broken iron fixings.

Modern ruins. So much less interesting than ancient ruins, to Gemma's mind. She walked past without slowing.

A few more minutes of walking took her down again, and then out to a grassy spur from which she could see the whole horizon. There was someone sitting on a fallen tree by the edge.

'Hi,' the girl said. She was about Gemma's age, with blonde hair and freckles, wearing blue shorts with a white blouse.

'I'm Toni,' the girl said.

'Um, hi. I'm Gemma.'

They looked at each other for a moment, taking each other's measure, then Gemma sat down next to Toni on the fallen tree.

'Where are you staying?' Toni asked.

'A cottage near here.'

'Me too. But I live here all the time.'

'What's that like?'

'Boring.'

Toni kicked at the grass tufts with her heels. She was wearing navy leather sandals that Gemma envied instantly. They were even lovelier than the pair that she'd broken. Next to them, her flip-flops looked cheap and plasticky. She pulled her feet back self-consciously.

'I love your shoes,' Gemma said.

'I love *your* shoes.'

The girls looked at each other for a long moment.

'Size five?' Toni asked.

Then both of them said 'Swap?' at the same time and laughed.

When the navy sandals were on Gemma's feet, she stretched her legs out long in front of her to admire them.

'You don't like them?' she asked Toni.

Toni shrugged. 'They're old. It's nice to have something new, and these are so colourful.'

She wiggled her feet so the shoes made their flip-flop sound in the air.

'Well, if you like them,' Gemma said, 'they're yours.'

'Ditto.'

They sat in the sunshine for a while, weaving plaits from the dry grasses gathered around the fallen tree. Later, Toni took her to a sloping meadow filled with daisies. They made garlands of them, and played hide and seek amongst the trees, and had rolling races down the hills.

Toni was such good company that Gemma didn't once stop to worry that it was childish.

'Gemma,' Mrs Larson said when she came back from the cliffs that day. 'What happened to your new flip-flops?'

'Lost in the sea,' she lied, because she didn't want to admit she'd given them away willingly. 'A girl I met gave me these instead.' She showed off the sandals on her feet.

That diverted Mrs Larson enough that she forgot her irritation.

'You made a friend? That's great, Gem. Who is she?'

'She lives around here.'

'What's her surname? Have you met her parents? What do they do?'

'I don't know.'

'Well, you should ask her next time you see her.'

'Why?'

Gemma's mother was always asking the most stupid questions. As if Gemma was going to ask Toni what her parents did. As if it mattered. Her mum hadn't even asked for Toni's first name, so why did she care about her surname?

'We might know them,' her mother replied. 'Or know people who know them. The Fairleys live down here, and the Dawsons.'

'The Dawsons?' Mr Larson said. 'Really? They had that double-spread in the homes section of the paper last month.'

'Exactly,' Mrs Larson said quietly, before turning back to Gemma. 'Maybe your new friend would like to introduce us to her family. Wouldn't it be nice if we could all get together for dinner?'

'I don't know if I'll see her again,' Gemma said.

'Well, you should. In fact, we should all go down to the beach together tomorrow and see if your friend is there. Doesn't that sound nice? I'll pack some sandwiches and we can sit together as a family and make sandcastles. Yes?'

'I'm twelve, Mum.'

'Come on, Gem,' said Mr Larson. 'You're never too old for sandcastles, are you? It'll be fun. I'll help. We'll make a sand palace. Maybe walk to the village for ice cream, take in the local colour.'

Gemma nodded, because there wasn't much point in arguing. And if he was horribly condescending to everyone tomorrow, at least she'd get an ice cream to cool her blushes. It was the best she could hope for.

When Gemma went to bed that night, she took Toni's sandals with her. Normally, she would have left them lined up next to her parents' by the front door, but she didn't trust her dad not to put his own shoes on top of them. She didn't want him to crush the straps.

Instead, she carefully stowed them in the bottom of the wardrobe in her room, closing the buckle to keep them properly shaped. The leather was so soft, the stitches so fine, that they deserved to be looked after. Her old, broken pair were stiff and inelegant by comparison. She couldn't believe that she'd had the good fortune to meet someone so generous, so kind, who was willing to give such wonderful shoes away to someone she'd only just met.

Gemma hoped she'd see her again. Ideally alone.

The bedroom was hot and stuffy, so Gemma opened her window before turning in for the night. It was on the wall opposite the bed, opposite the painting of the cliff, and it gave the same view. She'd spent some time examining that watercolour earlier in the day, kneeling on her bed with her face close to the canvas. There was no glass covering it, but it wasn't dusty either. Like the paintings in the attic, someone took care to make sure it remained in good condition.

Which begged the question: why put it opposite a window? Gemma had been on enough school trips to museums and art galleries that she knew keeping paintings in direct sunlight was a bad idea. They got bleached. It had happened to the rug in the front room at home; when they moved the coffee table, you could see the dark rectangle it left behind like a shadow.

But the watercolour didn't seem bleached. In fact, its colours were startlingly bright. It was so real that Gemma had almost believed that she could reach out and stretch her fingers into the painting, just as she could stretch her hand out of the window opposite into the same landscape. They were almost mirrors of each other – the same in size, shape and content – although not quite; whichever you were looking at, the bay was down to the left.

That mirroring might have explained why, when Gemma went to bed that night, she didn't pay attention to the direction of the breeze that rustled over her sheets. As she drowsed into sleep, she knew only that it was refreshing and assumed it came from the window. But the air outside was unnaturally still for the coast.

The breeze was coming from the painting.

The next day was Saturday, so the beach was busier than it had been up until now. Still not *busy*, as such, but full enough that the Larsons couldn't find a space that was entirely out of earshot of the other groups of towels and bodies that had collected on the sand. This was bad news for Gemma, who really didn't want to be seen building sandcastles with her dad, but good news for Mrs Larson, who was keen to meet the Devon well-to-dos.

'Most of them probably have their own gardens, of course,' she said as she set up her deckchair. 'They might not come to the beach, but if Gemma can make friends with–' She turned to Gemma. 'What did you say your little friend's name was, Gem?'

'She's not *little*,' Gemma grumbled, 'and her name's Toni.'

'Toni,' Mrs Larson murmured. 'Toni.'

'Don't the Dawsons have a daughter called Antonia?' Mr Larson asked. He was already elbow-deep in the sand, playing with a plastic bucket and spade they'd bought at the nearby café.

'No,' said Mrs Larson. 'No, you're thinking of the Fitzroys. But I think Angelica Hargreaves has a daughter called Antoinette, doesn't she?'

Mr Larson clapped his hands together, showering Gemma with sand.

'That's it! Antoinette Hargreaves. Our little Gem-Gem, friends with Antoinette Hargreaves. Well, well.'

'I'm not *little*,' Gemma protested.

'Of course you're not, darling,' said Mrs Larson. 'Now why don't you point out your friend to us?'

But Toni wasn't on the beach. That wasn't much of a surprise to Gemma, because they hadn't met on the beach in the first place. If Toni was waiting for her anywhere, then it would be on the cliffs above the cottage, but her parents didn't know that. All in all, Gemma thought that was for the best.

The morning passed in an unpleasant heat haze of

warm fizzy drinks and sand stuck to sun-creamed legs. Mrs Larson had made sandwiches too, but they had been forgotten in the bustle to get to the beach this morning. They were still in the fridge back at the cottage – salami and tomato, Gemma's favourite – taunting her with their absence. By midday, she was ready to go back to the cottage to shower off the sand, eat her sandwich, then spend the afternoon inside with her Nintendo Switch, but her mother was having none of it.

'We want to know who you're spending your time with,' she insisted.

So they stayed on the beach until their stomachs were grumbling and even factor 50 couldn't stop Gemma's skin from pinking. It was Mr Larson who finally called the outing to a halt.

'We can come back later,' he said. 'Maybe tomorrow. We're here for a while, after all. There's plenty of days left for us to meet Toni.'

If Gemma had anything to do with it, that particular day would never come.

Mrs Larson hadn't put on enough sun cream and was too burned to venture out again that afternoon. Gemma tried not to be happy about that, but it was difficult not to feel a bit smug when her mum was always going on at Gemma about how important sun cream was. Gemma's own pinkness had vanished the moment they'd got into the shade.

'How about that ice cream, then?' her dad asked after lunch. 'We could go to the village shop while Mum rests up.'

'I don't know…' Gemma said, her gaze trailing out to the cliff beyond the window.

'Oh, let her be, David,' said Mrs Larson as she cleared away the plates. 'She doesn't want to hang around with us all holiday. I'm sure she'd much rather go and find her friend.' She smiled at Gemma conspiratorially. 'Wouldn't you, darling?'

That was exactly what Gemma wanted to do, but the fact that her mother was pushing her into it made her want to change her plans.

'Maybe later,' she said. 'I think I'll just hang out for a bit.'

She fetched her Nintendo and played until her mum fell asleep on the sofa and her dad had wandered out to the village. Only then did she pull on her special sandals and walk out through the garden. She thought she'd have to climb up past the broken concrete fortifications to find Toni, but as it happened she was right there next to the coastal footpath at the end of the garden, sitting in the grass with her feet dangling off the cliff.

'Hi,' Gemma said.

Toni looked over her shoulder.

'Hi.'

'Is it safe?' Gemma slowed as she approached the edge, eyeing the drop with hesitation.

'Are you afraid of heights?'

'A little.'

'It's fine,' said Toni. 'Look.'

She pulled up her feet then rolled onto her front in the grass, so only her head and hands were hanging off the edge.

'Do it like this,' she said. 'It's not dangerous. Come on, you'll see.'

Gemma was cautious. First she went to her knees, a good ten feet away from the edge, then to her stomach, snaking forwards until she could peek over the cliff. Then she laughed.

'See?' Toni said, turning to Gemma with a smile.

'Okay,' Gemma replied. 'I get it.' Then she swung her legs around, sitting up so that her legs were dangling over the side.

Because this wasn't *really* the edge of the cliff. It looked like it if you weren't right on top of it, but just a little beneath where Gemma's feet were now dangling there were rough steps cut into the rock that clung to the cliff face all the way down.

'Where do they lead?' Gemma asked.

Toni swung her own legs around, then pushed off to drop down onto the first step.

'Do you want to see?'

Mischief sparkled in her grey eyes.

'Um, are you sure it's safe?' Gemma asked. Even though the steps were wide enough not to feel precarious, they were really more of a rocky scramble than actual steps. They were formed from huge chunks of stone so tall that Gemma would have to sit on her bum to drop down from one to the next. She wasn't sure how she'd get back up.

'I go up and down here all the time,' Toni assured her, grabbing her beach bag before dropping down to the next rock. 'It's a smugglers' staircase. You know, back in the day when they used to bring in rum and tobacco and, I don't know, gold or whatever.'

'Like pirates?' Gemma asked, following cautiously.

'I guess. You can make up your own mind when you've seen it for yourself. Come on.'

It took a long time to get down the steps. Part of that was due to the difficulty of scrambling over them, but mostly it went slowly because Gemma was terrified. From her cliffside perch, there was nothing to see except the ocean. It stretched out from the horizon and enveloped the promontory. Even if she looked directly down, Gemma could see nothing except blue, but she tried not to do that because the more she did, the more she wobbled.

But eventually, the steps curved around the side of the cliff and into a tiny bay that Gemma had never noticed before. There was the smallest of beaches, and next to it…

'A cave?' Gemma asked as she hopped down onto the sand.

'You can only get into it at low tide. This beach is usually underwater.'

'Very cool.'

'You find all the best shells here,' said Toni, leading the way across the beach. 'Look.'

She picked up a full-sized cowrie shell from the tideline and tossed it into the air. Gemma caught it.

'Oh my god,' she said. 'It's huge! I didn't know you could find these in the U.K.'

'You can find just about anything on this beach,' said Toni. 'It all washes up here eventually. You want to see inside the cave?'

As if she had to ask. Despite the allure of beachcombing, Gemma was already walking across to the dark entrance.

'It's safe?' Gemma asked.

'Sure, as long as we're out before the tide rises. If we're not, we'll get stuck inside.'

Gemma's eyes widened in concern.

'It doesn't fill up completely,' Toni reassured her. 'I've been trapped in there before and it's really not bad. You just have to wait. It's not dangerous or anything. So, are you coming?'

Toni led the way.

The entrance was only six feet tall. Ten steps inside, a rocky floor rose abruptly out of the sand and narrowed the cave to a tunnel that Gemma had to crouch to get through. It went on for about twenty feet before finally opening out into a cavernous lagoon of clear water, surrounded by a rocky shelf that dropped to its own secret beach at the far side. The pool looked deep and the cavern ceiling loomed high above the girls' heads.

'The best stuff is always in here,' Toni said, edging along the rock path around the water. 'Things get forced in by the current, then they're stuck.'

'Stuff like what?' Gemma asked.

'Like the boat,' Toni said, pointing to a battered old rowboat that bobbed by the beach. 'I can't think why else it would be in here.'

Gemma looked back at the passage they'd just come through.

'But… how would it even fit?'

Toni shrugged. 'This place is magic. That's the best explanation I've found.'

And it did seem to be. When they reached the little

beach, rolling out their towels on the sand, Gemma couldn't help but think that it was the perfect beach holiday for the pale-skinned. She wouldn't need any sun cream here in the shade. It was a kind of paradise. There were hundreds of colourful fish playing in the water, so striking and varied that they might have been tropical. There was coral here too, which she thought only lived in warm water, but then the cave *was* warm. The pool was as well.

With Toni to entertain her, Gemma could have stayed there forever.

Gemma's phone buzzed in the pocket of her shorts, waking her from her doze. They'd been chatting, lying on their towels, but Gemma must have dropped off for a few minutes.

She pulled the phone out and groaned when she saw the message on the screen. Her dad had sent her a photo of himself next to the village shop with an irritated-looking woman. It was captioned 'making friends with the locals'. It looked like making friends was the last thing he was doing.

'He's so annoying,' Gemma said sleepily.

'Your dad?' Toni asked with a yawn.

'Yes. Ugh. He's so embarrassing. And my mum. They want to meet you, by the way.'

Toni screwed up her face at that.

'Why?'

'They want to meet your family. They do that. They always have to meet everyone. I don't know why.'

'Parents, right?'

Gemma sighed. 'Tell me about it.'

'We'd better get going anyway,' Toni said, gathering her things. 'Tide's coming in. We'll have to wade out as it is.'

Gemma looked over at the passage. The water was coming in. It was just a trickle so far, running down into the lagoon, but it wouldn't stay that way for long.

Gemma wrapped her sandals in her towel with her phone and tied the bundle around her shoulders. She wasn't going to get her new favourite shoes wet.

She followed Toni out. Negotiating the passage wasn't a problem, but in the mouth of the cave Gemma was walking on a floor she couldn't see. She ended up stubbing her toe on a rock and went flying. Conscious of the precious cargo in her bag, she threw her hands out to stop her fall into the water. It saved her shoes, but her T-shirt wasn't so lucky. Something caught it under the water and before she knew what was happening, the thing had ripped nearly the whole way up the middle.

'Oh no,' Gemma said, looking down at herself.

'I bet it was a nail,' Toni said, doubling back to help her. 'They hammered loops into the rocks here so they could moor their boats. At least, that's what I would have done if I were a pirate. I don't know why else there'd be nails here.'

Gemma tried to gather the ripped pieces of her T-shirt back together, but it was hopeless. She hadn't hit puberty yet, so it had been the only thing between the world and her naked chest.

'I'm wearing a vest underneath this,' said Toni, unbuttoning her shirt. 'Here.' She handed the short-sleeved blouse to Gemma.

'Will your mum not mind?' she asked.

Toni shrugged. 'I've got loads more. Don't worry about it.'

So Gemma didn't. When she finally left Toni to go home for dinner, the steps back up the cliff didn't seem so steep after all, nor the drop so far. They said goodbye on the clifftop and promised to meet again the next day.

Gemma expected her mother to be angry about the ripped T-shirt, but instead Mrs Larson exclaimed over the quality of the blouse's cotton, the prettiness of the buttons, and the fine embroidery. That grated. Where Gemma saw a thoughtful gift from a friend, her mother saw the money that had bought it.

She resolved then to ensure that Toni and her mother never, ever met.

Gemma laid the table on the patio while her mum brought out dinner: quiche and salad.

Her father had been down at the pub, bothering the locals again. He might have called it 'making friends', but Gemma knew that what he actually did was badger people into telling him what he wanted to know. It was embarrassing, the way he couldn't see how much they wanted to escape him. He treated people who lived in the country as though they were a separate species to be studied, instead of just people who lived in the country.

Sometimes, Gemma wished she could disown him.

'They told me some fascinating things about this place,' he said. 'Did you know that the promontory here is called Peyton's End, after the family who used to live in this house?'

'The same family as the artist?' asked Mrs Larson.

'That's right. Family of geniuses by all accounts, but

dreadfully poor. It all went wrong – the wife had mental health issues, apparently – and they left.'

'That's sad.'

'I suppose so, but if it hadn't happened, then we wouldn't be here now enjoying this lovely view. So there's a silver lining to every cloud, isn't there?'

Gemma was just glad that none of the locals were around to hear him talking like that. God only knew what he'd been talking about in the pub.

'Oh, and I picked something up for you, Gem-Gem,' he said, popping back inside to grab a plastic bag. Inside was a new pair of flip-flops. 'Mum said you wouldn't want to mess up your nice sandals on the beach.'

'And now you can give them back to your friend Toni, along with her shirt,' said Mrs Larson.

Gemma felt a stab of angry irritation. She didn't want to give them back. They were from Toni, so they were special.

'The sandals were a present,' she said. 'And so was the shirt.'

'Well, that's very generous of your friend,' said Mrs Larson, 'but we don't need charity. You've got plenty of clothes.'

'That's not the point. You don't return presents.'

Mrs Larson looked puzzled by Gemma's vehemence. It wasn't like her to be any less than compliant. Usually, she just nodded and did what her parents asked.

'Well,' said Mrs Larson, searching for a solution that would suit her daughter while still maintaining her own authority, 'maybe you could give her a present in return, then. How about that? We could pick something up in the village.'

Gemma didn't think Toni would want any tourist tat, but she nodded anyway then cleared away the plates. Her parents stayed out on the patio getting increasingly tipsy while she stayed inside to play her Nintendo until bedtime.

She tried to block out their words and remember the lagoon instead.

In the middle of the night, the cottage was eerily quiet. Gemma expected a place this old to creak like a pirate ship or buzz with night insects, but there was nothing to hear this close to the sea except the waves. The sound drifted in through her bedroom window in the darkness, along with the smell of fresh salt on the air.

It was unsettling, that silence. In some way that Gemma couldn't define, it seemed to be carried on the breeze. It crept into her bones and stilled her into sleep in a way that felt oppressive and unnatural, but not altogether unpleasant. It was comforting.

Almost familiar.

And yet she awoke the next morning feeling more tired than she had been before she went to bed. She didn't wake up until her mum called up the stairs for her, telling her to come and lay the table for breakfast.

'What does the day hold, then, Gem-Gem?' her father asked as he joined them in the kitchen.

'Beach, I guess.'

'Don't forget your sun cream,' said her mother.

'I talked to the boys at the pub last night,' said Mr Larson. 'They hadn't heard anything about a smugglers' staircase, Gem-Gem. Looks like you might have found yourself a local secret there. They all thought the cliff just dropped right into the sea.'

'You can't see it until you get up close,' Gemma said, shovelling baked beans into her mouth. Mrs Larson would never normally have made a cooked breakfast in the summer, but for some reason all of them felt the need for some inner warmth that morning.

'Well, maybe you can show me and your mum before we go,' said Mr Larson.

'Maybe.'

Mr and Mrs Larson exchanged a look over their daughter's head, then Mrs Larson mouthed 'Let her be'. Mr Larson shrugged back.

'I'll pick up some postcards at the shop, shall I?' Mr Larson offered. 'We'd better get them in the post before we leave, or everyone will think we've forgotten them.'

'I'm not sure you need to send postcards when you're only away for a long weekend, darling,' said Mrs Larson.

'Nonsense. I'll pick some up for you too, shall I, Gem-Gem? A few to send to your friends?'

What friends, Gemma wanted to ask. Since her parents had moved her to secondary school, she'd struggled to find any at all. It wasn't like primary school, where she'd automatically been friends with the children of her parents' friends, however awful they were. People had to like her as a person to be her friend now, and apparently they didn't.

Toni was the first one she'd had in months.

Her parents didn't understand when she tried to talk about it. They just told her she'd make friends eventually, that she needed to make an effort, or that she was exaggerating and it couldn't be that bad. There was no point talking about it, so Gemma simply declined her father's offer.

'We don't do postcards,' she said. 'I'm twelve.'

'Of course you are, Gem-Gem. Silly of me to forget.'

Gemma rolled her eyes.

'I have to go,' she said, clearing the table. 'Toni will be waiting.'

'Don't forget to invite her to dinner, okay?' said Mrs Larson.

'Uh-huh.'

'Gemma?'

'I said yes, Mum. I'll remember.'

Gemma definitely would remember. She just wouldn't necessarily ask. Not properly, anyway. She wasn't letting her only friend anywhere near her embarrassing family.

Toni wasn't waiting on the cliff, but Gemma knew where she'd be. It only took a few minutes to climb down the steps this time, then she was racing across the beach and into the cave.

If anything, it was even more perfect than Gemma had remembered. The water looked bluer, the fish more colourful, and there were glints of gold sticking out of the sand at the bottom of the lagoon.

Toni was on the little stretch of beach at the far end.

'Morning!' she called. 'I hoped you'd find your way here on your own.'

'Didn't want to come and meet me?' Gemma said as she edged around the rock shelf to join her.

'Didn't want to meet your parents,' Toni said quietly.

'Sorry.'

Gemma shrugged. 'I don't blame you. Mum invited you over for dinner again. She's obsessed.'

'Grown-ups, right?'

'Right.'

Gemma spread her towel out on the sand then went up to the very edge of the lagoon, peering into the water.

'Are those coins at the bottom? They look like coins.'

'Doubloons, I reckon,' said Toni. 'I told you this place was used for smuggling.'

'I didn't expect coins to stay that shiny in the water. If they're old, I mean.'

'That's gold for you.'

'Gold?' Gemma's heartbeat picked up a notch.

Treasure.

'I thought you might want to be pirates,' Toni said, holding up a plastic bag. It was stuffed so full that clothes were spilling out of the top. 'I brought everything piratey that I could find. Scarves and hats and lots of red stuff.' Toni put the bag down on the sand and started hauling things out. 'Pirates liked red.'

'Why?' Gemma asked.

Toni looked up at her with a gleeful smile. 'Colour of blood, isn't it?'

Gemma laughed and joined in with the dressing up. After some searching, she found a red skirt and a straw hat with a striped ribbon that she thought would fit the bill.

'I'm a lady pirate,' she said, taking off her baseball cap and putting the boater on instead. 'When I'm not being the scourge of the high seas, I go punting on the river with strawberries and champagne.'

'And I'm a swashbuckling scoundrel called One-eyed Anthony,' Toni said, tying a scarf across her left eye. 'I steal from the rich to feed the poor, and I won't rest until I find the scurvy dog who took my eye.'

'To the boat, then, One-eyed Anthony?'

'After you... Er...'

'Um.' Gemma thought for a moment. 'How about Vicious Veronica?'

Toni laughed. 'Suits you.'

They pushed the old rowboat off the beach and punted out into the middle of the water, using the oar to prod coins loose from the bottom of the lagoon. They collected them all in a plastic bag with the idea of taking it back to Toni's dad, who was a historian, but in the excitement of the day the bag was abandoned in a corner of the boat and forgotten about. The fish were more interesting in their multicoloured glory, and the pirate game was soon put aside in favour of watching the water.

Even lunch was eaten in the boat – Toni had brought sandwiches and pomegranate seeds, because she thought they were exotic and the colour would appeal to pirates – and the day passed quickly in the timeless cave.

It was Toni who noticed the tide rising and rowed them to shore so they could get changed. As Gemma was packing away her things, she noticed Toni's attention on her baseball cap and remembered what her mother had said about giving Toni a gift in return for the blouse and shoes.

'Did you want it?' she offered, holding it out. 'It's

just an old hat, but–'

'Seriously? I'd love it. Thank you. My mum doesn't buy me things like this.' Toni took it and turned it in her hands. She was examining the cap with a kind of awe that made Gemma feel embarrassed.

'You're welcome. Do you think…'

Toni looked up at her friend's hesitation.

'Do you think I could wear this home?' Gemma said, swaying from side to side to make the red skirt swing around her calves. 'Just to borrow. I'll bring it back tomorrow.'

'Of course. But we'd better hurry, unless you want to get stuck in here overnight. With the ghosts of dead pirates…'

Toni crept closer to Gemma, waving her fingers as she said, 'WoooooooOooooo.'

Gemma batted away her hands and laughed. This time, she was the one who led the way back to the beach.

Mr and Mrs Larson were in the garden drinking Aperol Spritzes when Gemma returned from the cliff.

'You missed lunch,' said Mrs Larson.

'Toni had sandwiches for us.'

'And where is your new friend? Are you going to introduce us?'

Gemma turned and looked over her shoulder, back towards the cliff.

'She's gone home now, but she was literally just there,' Gemma said, pointing. 'Didn't you see her? She came up the cliff with me.'

Her parents exchanged a look.

'How many of those have you had?' Gemma asked, looking at the empty Aperol bottle.

'Don't be rude, Gem-Gem,' said Mr Larson. 'Why don't you come and tell us what you did with your day. You can have a drink with us. Lemonade, I mean.'

He went to fetch a can from the fridge for her.

'You weren't wearing that skirt this morning,' Mrs Larson said to her.

'Toni lent it to me,' Gemma said defensively, not ready to listen to her mum go on and on about fabric quality again. 'I'm giving it back in the morning. And the hat.'

'And where's your own hat?'

'I gave it to Toni. A present. Like you said.'

Mrs Larson looked horrified.

'Your old blue baseball cap? God, they're going to think we don't have two pennies to rub together.'

'Mum—'

Mr Larson returned, handed Gemma the can and sat down next to her on the patio furniture.

'Well, then?' he said, slurping from his glass. 'Let's hear it. I'm all ears.'

So Gemma told him, if a bit reluctantly. She told him about the rocky steps and the cave and the lagoon, filling out the bare bones she'd described briefly the night before. She told him about the fish and the doubloons and the coral in every colour and shape.

'Really?' said Mr Larson. 'I didn't think there was coral in this country.'

'Well, there is.'

He pulled out his phone and Googled it.

'Only in Scotland,' he said after a few seconds, his

attention fixed on his phone. 'Cold water coral, it says.'

'Well, the water in the cave isn't cold,' Gemma replied irritably.

He looked at her sceptically. 'This is England, Gem-Gem. Not the Caribbean.'

Gemma took the excuse to go and set the table for supper. She didn't want to talk to him about it if he wasn't going to take her seriously. Why couldn't he just believe her for once? She wasn't stupid.

But he wouldn't take her at her word.

That night, after Gemma had gone to sleep, Mr and Mrs Larson walked to the end of the garden and looked over the edge of the cliff. There was nothing but the sea.

'She said you had to get really close,' Mr Larson said, lowering himself to his stomach.

'Be careful, David.'

He shimmied forwards until his head and shoulders were hanging off the cliff, until he looked so precarious that Mrs Larson grabbed hold of his ankles.

'Well?' she asked as he pulled himself back to safety.

He just shook his head.

There were no steps, no rocks, no path. There was nothing but a straight drop into the waves.

Gemma hadn't slept well. The weather had turned colder overnight, so she'd closed the window, but still there was a draught she couldn't seem to plug, even when she balled up her clothes and stuffed them into the crack under the door. It was strong enough to whistle through whatever gap it had found. Between the noise and the cold, anyone would have been hard-pressed to get their eight hours.

And it had been very cold last night, so cold that Gemma had almost believed that, if it hadn't been dark, she might have been able to see her breath pluming in the air in front of her face. Strange, for mid-summer.

But it was warm again the next morning when she joined her parents for breakfast.

'What have you done to yourself, Gem-Gem?' her dad asked, reaching over the table to touch her cheek.

'What?' Gemma hadn't brushed her teeth yet, so she'd not looked in the mirror.

'Paint,' said Mr Larson, looking at his fingers. 'Blue paint. Where did that come from?'

Gemma rubbed at her skin. 'I must have picked it up outside yesterday.'

'Well, make sure you're careful not to get it on those lovely clothes Toni lent you,' said Mrs Larson through a mouthful of toast. 'I wouldn't want her to think you were careless with her things.'

'Mum…' Gemma groaned.

'And did you talk to her about coming over for dinner? We'd love to host her and her family here, wouldn't we, David?'

'Sure,' he said absentmindedly, reading the newspaper on his iPad.

Mrs Larson looked at her daughter expectantly.

'I'll talk to her,' Gemma said.

'Good. Now, are you going to be home for lunch, or shall I pack some sandwiches for the two of you?'

Once Gemma had left with her picnic, Mr Larson looked up from his reading.

'Do you think we should have asked her about it?' he said.

'Hmm?' said Mrs Larson.

'The staircase. Do you think we should have asked her about it?'

Mrs Larson put down her coffee cup. 'What exactly would you have said?'

'She's lying to us, Trudy.'

'It's *make believe*, David. The last thing she or her friend wants is some fusty old adult sticking their nose into the game. If she wants to pretend there's a smugglers' staircase that only she can see with a cave and special beach beyond it, then where's the harm in that?'

'She's not being honest about where she is.'

'Oh, nonsense. She's got her phone, hasn't she? You can just check the tracker.'

'I shouldn't *have* to check the tracker. That's the point. She should tell us where she's going.'

'Oh for–' Mrs Larson reached over the table and took David's phone to pull up the tracking app. 'See?' she said, turning the screen to show her husband. 'She's on the cliffs just above the house. Everything's fine. Will you stop worrying?'

'All right,' he said, holding up his hands. 'All right.'

'Let the girl enjoy a bit of independence. She's perfectly safe here.'

By late afternoon, Mrs Larson was becoming irritated by her husband's inability to relax. He seemed on-edge, which was unlike him, and he kept complaining that he was cold despite the fact that it was the hottest day on record.

Accordingly, he'd been sent to the pub.

He'd been nursing a beer for half an hour and was starting to feel much better. It was good to get out of the house. Trudy was right.

It had been a good holiday all round, he thought, and they'd all enjoyed themselves. Even Gem-Gem had made a new friend, which was more than he'd hoped for. A bit of a relief, actually, given all the trouble at school. Though after the thing with the smugglers' stairs, he wasn't entirely certain that the child was real. He could well believe that Gemma would have made her up to keep them happy.

But then he could understand an almost-teenager not wanting to introduce her friends to her parents. That's what Trudy said, anyway. The truth was he worried too much.

'Well, Bill,' he said to the bartender. 'It's been an absolute pleasure. We've had a lovely time here in this beautiful part of the country. And it's such a treat to meet the locals, like yourself. Lovely to hear the local Devonshire accent, eh?'

Bill cleared his throat uncomfortably, but he took the hand Mr Larson offered and shook it.

'Will you be coming back next year then, Dave?' Bill asked, in a tone of voice that prayed for a 'No'.

'Not sure,' Mr Larson said. 'Maybe. But it's a strange place, that house, isn't it?'

Bill tipped his head to the side, equivocating.

'You could say that,' he conceded. 'Not many people stay there twice, that's true enough. In fact, I don't think anyone's ever come back to that cottage in all the time I've been here.'

'Gosh. And you're, what, mid-forties now?' asked Mr Larson, thoughtlessly rude, as was his custom. 'So no repeat business, in forty-odd years?'

'Not quite,' Bill corrected him. 'I've been here for five years. Moved down from London in 2015. Brixton, born and raised.'

'Ah,' Mr Larson said, momentarily wrong-footed.

'My predecessor, though, he was here when the Derbyshires went missing.'

'The who?'

'The Derbyshires. You know, the family who used to live in the cottage. The artist and her husband. Just upped sticks in the middle of the night, and no one saw them again.'

'The Derbyshires? I thought they were called the Peytons?'

Bill went quite still.

'Who told you that story, Mr Larson?' he asked.

'One of the gents who was in here last time. Geoff, his name was. He said the cliff behind the cottage was named for them. Peyton's End.'

'Peyton's End,' Bill said as he blew out a breath, shaking his head. 'It was that, all right. Peyton was their daughter. Peyton Derbyshire. She'd lived in that cottage all her life, playing along the cliffs, then one day she slipped and fell into the sea. She died. After that, her mother couldn't stop painting the spot where it happened. Proper morbid.'

'So all of the paintings…' said Mr Larson, nodding towards the dining room.

'Yup. They're all hers. All memories of the place

where Toni fell.'

Mr Larson stilled. 'Toni?'

'Peyton. That's what they called her, for short.'

'Toni. You're sure?'

'Pretty sure. There's a monument up on the cliff that says the same. You haven't seen it?'

Mr Larson abandoned his pint and speed-walked all the way home, telling himself with every step that he was being an overprotective, overreacting fool.

'Where's Gemma?' asked Mr Larson as he burst into the kitchen.

'I don't know,' said Mrs Larson. 'I didn't hear her come in, but she's probably in her room playing her game again.' She looked up from the salad she was preparing for dinner and noticed her husband's agitation. 'What's wrong?'

'Nothing,' he said, already moving to the stairs. 'I'm just being silly, I'm sure.'

'David.' Mrs Larson followed him. 'What is wrong?'

'Just a story I heard from Bill at the pub.' He was at the top of the stairs now, striding down the corridor towards Gemma's bedroom. 'I'm sure it's nothing.'

'*What* story, David?'

He opened the door to Gemma's room. She wasn't there.

'About the people who used to live in his house. Their daughter was called Toni. She died. I thought…'

'You thought what? That Gemma was friends with a ghost?'

'I said it was nothing, didn't I?' said Mr Larson, pushing past her to go back into the corridor. 'So, where is she?'

He took his phone out of his pocket and opened the tracking app so he could search for Gemma's location. There was a muffled 'plink' from inside the bedroom.

'Did you hear that?' he asked, pushing back past his wife to search through the clothes Gemma had strewn across her floor. 'It's here somewhere.'

'David,' said Mrs Larson from behind him.

'She must have left it behind by mistake. But she always has it with her. She knows we worry if she doesn't. She knows better than that.'

'David,' Mrs Larson said again. 'Look.'

He followed her pointing finger.

In the watercolour above the bed, a red-haired girl stood at the very tip of Peyton's End. She was wearing navy sandals, an embroidered shirt and a red skirt. A striped ribbon trailed from the straw hat in her hand. It had been caught by the wind and pulled loose, so it seemed that at any moment it might be carried away over the cliff and into the water below.

'No,' said Mr Larson. 'That's madness.'

The bedroom door swung closed. The window on the opposite wall slammed shut. The walls shook.

'Shit,' said Mr Larson, tugging at the door handle. 'It won't open.'

'Try the window.'

Mr Larson ran to it, fitting his fingers under the sash, but the moment he applied some force the window came off the wall.

'What the…'

He held the window frame in his hands, an insignificant weight of canvas, and trailed his fingers down its surface. It was a painting.

'That's not possible,' said Mr Larson.

The couple looked at each other, then looked at the painting hanging over their daughter's bed. Only it wasn't a painting anymore. Where previously the unglazed watercolour had been framed in static permanence, now there was a riot of movement within it. Grasses blew in the breeze and there, at Peyton's End, Gemma stood wearing Peyton's clothes and beckoning them forward. The other girl was at her side.

'Toni finally made a friend,' said a voice behind them. 'Isn't that nice? This was her room, you know.'

Mrs Larson turned slowly, horror tickling up the back of her neck, to see a couple standing where the window had once been. The man was wearing a brown three-piece suit and the woman was wearing a summer dress that was cut so beautifully it looked like couture.

'She was on her own for so long,' the woman went on. 'I could paint her a world as real as yours, but I couldn't paint people to life in it. They have to bring their own life with them, like we did, like a key that you leave behind you in the door. She's been lonely here with no one her own age. Until your Gemma came.'

The man smiled.

'She said you were dying to meet us.'

Lead Me Not Into Temptation

Arthur was the first to arrive at the college suite. It was just as he had always imagined it: wood-panelled, wood-floored, ragged-armchaired and saturated with the cigarette smoke of countless students who had come before him. The two bedrooms were of similar proportions, each with a narrow bed, desk and sink, so similar that there was little to choose between them, yet still he did not claim one. It seemed impolite to do so before he had met the fellow with whom he would be sharing the space. Instead, he pulled out his Latin primer and started brushing up on his grammar in preparation for the first week of term.

George was late. George was always late, although Arthur didn't know this yet. When the suite's door crashed open a couple of hours later, it was clear that he was also more than a little drunk.

'Hello there, chap,' George slurred. His collar was

askew and it looked as though he had been wearing his clothing since the previous night. It was both too formal and too dishevelled for this time of the morning. 'You'd be the fellow I'm bunking with, would you?'

Arthur had already risen to his feet and now stretched out his hand towards his inebriated fellow student. 'Arthur Morris,' he said. 'Studying Greats.'

'George Cholmondley, mostly studying rugger and rowing, I hope.' George clasped Arthur's hand tightly in his own large, sticky one, shook it once, then dropped without ceremony into one of the armchairs and fell instantly asleep.

It was an inauspicious beginning, indeed, but what can you tell from the beginning of anything?

George and Arthur went everywhere together or, more accurately, George was good-natured enough to invite Arthur everywhere he went and Arthur was grateful to be included. In that way, slowly, they became a common sight together around the quad, Arthur dragging George to tutorials and George dragging Arthur to the pub. George had become the college's top rower by the end of his first term, thanks mostly to Arthur's diligence in rousing him from bed early enough to get on the water for practice each morning, and Arthur had become something of a social butterfly by following George's example. All in all, the two could not have been better paired.

Until Lily.

Daughter of the college chaplain, Lily had been granted early admission to the university on the proviso that she continue to live with her parents in their college lodgings. This was not only convenient for her classes, but also put her in the unusual position of being one of the very few eligible young women with whom the hundreds of male students had regular contact. It was inevitable that flirtations and infatuations would occur. For some young ladies, that prospect might have intimidated. As it happened, Lily was more than fit for the challenge.

Unsurprisingly, the first encounter between the three was incited by George. It was a Saturday rugby match, the last of the term. George was on the pitch, Arthur was on the bench with his belongings and Lily was in the front row of the stands, cheering along with the crowd.

Perhaps, since her allure has thus far been described only so far as it pertains to her value as a novelty in the male-dominated world of academia, you might imagine Lily to be quite plain. You would be quite wrong. She was not beautiful, not exactly, but she was magnetic. She was bright-eyed and full-lipped, but it was the brashness of her laughter and the way she surrendered to it fully, her head tipped back with abandon, that drew Arthur's attention. Even after months under George's tutelage, he still couldn't imagine feeling settled enough in his skin that he could yield so entirely to emotion.

Arthur couldn't stop watching her. He tried to concentrate on the game, but he soon lost track of play. Eventually, he turned away from the pitch and gave himself over to the study of her face, which meant he was watching when she saw George. The ball had rolled to a stop on the grass just in front of her seat. George was the one sent to collect it and bring it back to the field, but he only accomplished the first of those tasks. Even from a distance, Arthur could see Lily's pupils dilate. When he followed her gaze, it was with resignation that he recognised his friend as the source of her bedazzlement.

She stooped to pick up the ball for him, passing it from her hands to his with an intensity forged in fluttered lashes and parted lips. Their fingers touched in the exchange, George's movements leisurely and deliberate as a smile spread across his face. And what a smile.

Arthur couldn't blame Lily for her reaction; he had to admit that George was worth staring at. In his rugby kit, mud-smeared and bare-thighed, he drew the eye. You would never have known that he'd woken up that morning in the bath, reeking of stale cognac and still wearing his suit from the night before, as usual. With his dark hair and pink cheeks, he was almost as vivid as Lily herself. Seeing them together, they looked as though they belonged to each other.

From that point on, the college considered their fates sealed. George, ever the gentleman, introduced Lily to Arthur that same day and took pains to include him in every outing the undeclared couple enjoyed together. This was uncomfortable for everyone except, apparently, for George himself.

And so it was with relief that George's two satellites saw him reclaimed by his raucous family for the Christmas break. They would both stay at college, Lily with her family in the chaplain's lodgings and Arthur in the echoing loneliness of the rooms he shared with George, with no expectation that he should meet the girl again until his return.

It was grey and rainy the day everything changed: Boxing Day, the disappointing chaser to what had been a far from white Christmas. Lily was finishing her lunch alone in the refectory, seeking a brief respite from her family under the guise of visiting the library. She didn't expect to see anyone she knew.

'Merry Christmas.' Arthur took the seat across from hers.

'Oh.' She arranged her cutlery on her empty plate and neatly dabbed at the corners of her mouth. 'I thought you would be going home for Christmas.'

Arthur smiled ruefully. He looked tired, as though the break from his studies were doing him more harm than good. Perhaps, if he had nowhere to go, that was precisely the case.

'You don't have family to visit?' she asked.

'I'm an orphan. There's no one eager for my company at this time of year.'

'That's awful.'

Arthur's face fell.

'I'm sorry,' Lily continued. 'I didn't mean to be insensitive. I only meant…' She wasn't sure what she had meant, but she knew she couldn't leave things as they were, with her cheeks heating and the young man opposite her looking increasingly wretched.

'Please,' he said, forcing a smile. 'There's no need to feel uncomfortable. I'm perfectly happy with my lot in life. I've been very fortunate, truly, to be admitted here on scholarship. This is my home now.'

His hopeful words broke Lily's heart. Here she was,

trying to escape her family, when Arthur had no family left from whom to escape. George was all he had, and she had even tried to deny him that. She had behaved shabbily, and it was time she made amends.

'Come for dinner with my family,' she said.

'Oh, no.' Arthur looked down at his hands. 'Please, there's no need to extend your pity to me. I have no desire to impose.'

'You won't be imposing. And I'd like you to come. Please. It would make me happy.'

To her surprise, Lily found that the words she'd spoken were true. Arthur must have heard that in her voice, because he agreed to the invitation and thus embarked on an evening so wonderful, so revelatory, that he wondered how he and Lily had ever been less than friends. They laughed as they ate, as they played party games with her family, as they relaxed by the fire late into the evening, long after the rest of the family had retired to their beds.

Lily was entranced. How could it be that she had never truly seen this boy before, with his gentle face, his soft voice, and the way he snatched glances at her, as though he were rationing them against future need? Subtly, smile by smile, glance by glance, she found herself overcome by his quiet charm.

The only sour note that evening was the behaviour of her father. Usually a genial and welcoming man, Lily was surprised to find that he had taken against Arthur.

The truth was that, since the moment he had invited the young man inside his home, the chaplain had felt increasingly uneasy. There was a chill rushing up and down his neck, yet the doors and windows were firmly closed and no one else complained of a draught. His fingertips felt as though they were frozen, no matter how close he held them to the fire, and the trembling in his hands was so pronounced as he tried to cut the ham for dinner that he had to cede the carving duties to Arthur. And all the time, throughout the evening, he felt as though there were eyes fixed on him, eyes with evil intent, even when there was no one looking in his direction at all. It made the chaplain unsure and defensive, which manifested in ill humour towards their guest – whose proximity, strangely enough, seemed only to exacerbate the chaplain's condition.

The moment Arthur left, the man's body was at peace.

But from that night on, his heart and soul could find no rest.

By the time George returned to college, laden with gifts and cheer, any awkwardness between Lily and Arthur had disappeared entirely. George, the merry naif, thought that the newfound accord between his friend and potential lover could only be a good thing. He saw nothing in it but the increase of their group's happiness for the future. Little did he know how short that future would be.

Over the course of the following term, the three became as close as it was proper for two men and an unmarried woman to be. Closer, perhaps.

Lily was not unaccustomed to male attention. She didn't court it, not openly, because the game lay in drawing the men to her. Besides, it was necessary to make some pretence of modesty and decorum, if only for the sake of her father's reputation. He had been behaving so oddly since Christmas, insisting she stay away from the male students, that it seemed wise to humour him. Her restraint lasted only so long, though. The moment she was away from prying eyes, she could conduct herself however she wished.

And she fully intended so to do.

With George and Arthur, the game had been long. She teased and baited, all the while appearing nothing less than chaste as she laughed her raucous laugh, and yet neither of them bit. The problem was, she believed, that they were each too loyal to the other to break the trust between them. If just one of them could have her, thus depriving the other, then neither of them would.

To Lily, this was a matter of no small frustration. But she was willing to work to find a solution, and it so happened that the perfect occasion for mischief was soon upon them.

There was much spoken of the college's masquerade ball. It was an annual tradition that, at the end of Lent, the students and faculty would mask their faces and mingle amongst each other in liquor-drenched freedom. Designed to create a freer atmosphere for the exchange of scholarly ideas, in fact the event was best known as something of a debauch, allowing lines to be crossed in anonymity that might otherwise have remained unbreached. So it proved for Arthur and Lily, for – much to her own surprise – it was Arthur on whom she had primarily fixed her sights.

He was not a handsome man, not athletic or strong of jaw like George, but he could be beautiful. Lily had seen that, finally, over the Christmas break, and now she could see nothing else. He had grace and poise, deftness and delicacy of speech and movement, and something else besides, something Lily couldn't put into words, but that felt almost ethereal. However unable she was to describe how Arthur's proximity made her feel, she knew that she wanted it again. She'd live in it if she could, if she could but dare it, if she could avoid George, and if she could only convince Arthur to accept it.

By mutual agreement, all three friends arrived at the masquerade alone, in costumes they had not revealed to each other beforehand. It was part of the fun, Lily had told George, but secretly she had hoped she might identify Arthur before he did and spirit him away. It was uncharitable to desert George, perhaps, but with Lily due to spend the Easter break away with her family, it was the only opportunity she would have to be alone with Arthur before the summer.

It was now or never.

Arthur wasn't sure about his costume. George had told him this was an opportunity to break free from themselves, to surprise their peers with masks that were the exact opposite of who they really were. If that was the intent, then George had missed the mark with the costume he had selected for Arthur: a black Venetian mask with devil horns and a suit with tails to match. If George thought him the opposite of a devil, Arthur feared he was much mistaken. With the thoughts that were crowding his head this evening, he felt far from angelic.

He knew Lily the moment she walked into the quad.

Whatever she'd worn, he would have known the defiant tip of her head, the determined set of her jaw, and the elegant shape of her long neck. Even without the lily she had tucked behind her ear for his benefit, he would have recognised her just as quickly.

They slipped away alone before Lily had even greeted George. It was a betrayal, Arthur knew, but it was also the culmination of everything George had taught him over the past six months. He couldn't turn Lily down, not now he knew what it meant when her eyes softened as she looked at him. This was something he simply had to do.

They passed through a wooded courtyard arboured with roses, blooming out of season, and it was there that Lily entwined her fingers with Arthur's and led him beneath the trees. There he let her put his back against the bark and press her lips to his neck, to his cheek, to his lips. It was cold enough that their breath was visible between their faces, and yet still they delayed in the permissive dark and claimed each other's mouths, hers demanding and his shy.

As their kisses became more urgent, Lily became aware of the limitations of their trysting spot. It was not enough to kiss him, to touch his cheek, to feel his body pressed against hers. She needed more, and this was not the appropriate venue.

There was only one place to go.

Taking his hand in hers, she led him across the college. He had to smuggle her up the staircase to the rooms he shared with George, ducking around corners as he listened carefully for the footsteps of their fellow students. Once they were safely in the suite, shut away in his room with two doors between them and the outside world, such caution was quickly abandoned. Things moved so fast from that point that it spun Lily's head, and later she couldn't imagine what had come over her to inspire such desperate hunger for the man in her arms. She might almost have believed she'd imagined it, if there had not been a witness. The worst possible witness. George.

He was standing in the doorway to Arthur's room, left unlocked in their haste, his mouth open, face white. Perhaps he had seen them slip away from the quad. Perhaps he had come back to the suite for some forgotten item. Perhaps he had simply had enough of the ball without the two of them present. Either way, he had chosen the worst possible moment to appear.

Arthur was propped up on his hands with Lily's legs wrapped around his waist. Both were naked. There was no disguising their predicament.

Arthur's face fell as his eyes met his friend's.

'George.' He looked as though he wanted to say more, but the words didn't come. For several long seconds they were stuck in that painful tableau, nothing but silence and despair between the three of them, until George turned abruptly and left the room.

The night ended quickly after that. Lily's exit from the suite was swift and silent and, she vowed, never to be repeated. She hadn't realised that George truly cared for her, not as anything more than a friend, but the look on his face…

That *look*.

It was as though his heart were breaking in two.

As she was to discover, his was not the only one.

* * *

Arthur's costume was found folded neatly on the bridge the next morning, the devil's mask balanced on top and his shoes placed underneath the pile, a sock stuffed inside each one, as though he had been hoping to keep his outfit clean and dry for his return. But there would be no return for Arthur. Later that morning, the police found a smear of blood and hair on one of the bridge abutments beneath where his clothes had been piled. The water was high that day. If there had been any other trace of his descent, it was washed away with the rain.

Arthur left nothing else behind except the belongings in his room and the child that would soon begin to grow in Lily's womb.

The memorial service was more packed than anyone had expected it would be, so packed that there were rows of mourners standing at the back of the college chapel as Lily's father led the service. At first, Lily assumed they were all friends of George's, and George assumed they had come only for the scandal, but as they conversed with one after another in the quad afterwards, it became clear that Arthur had been far better known and better liked than either of them had appreciated. He had no family, but there were countless men who seemed to consider him a brother and enough women claimed him as a 'dear friend' to make a Lothario blush. It was strange how learning of Arthur's proximity to others, so out of character for the man they'd known, made him feel that much more out of reach to them. Who was this man, who had been their friend? They were no longer sure, but far from tarnishing him in their eyes, the unsolvable mystery of the man they'd both loved just made them yearn for him more.

Drawn together in their grief and guilt, George and Lily were swiftly married. Never much of a mathematician, George was unsure whether the baby growing within his new wife was his or Arthur's, but it was of no consequence: the couple were happy to raise the child together either way.

The chaplain was not happy, however. So unhappy was he, in fact, that he refused to perform the marriage ceremony for his daughter. Although he had no objection to George – the boy seemed fit enough, if a little addled by his knocks on the rugby pitch – he was disturbed by the changes that had started manifesting in his daughter after young Mr Morris's death; by suicide, the chaplain assumed. He'd been loath to give a memorial service for someone whose demise had taken such a sinful form, but after all there was no definitive proof, and Lily had insisted. It was the last thing upon which he had allowed her to insist.

There had been a dreadful row. It was clear that there was something wrong with his Lily, something working upon her, turning her from a dutiful, devoted daughter and student into a wild creature who would not be contained indoors, would not talk to her family, would not even attend church. Some of this might have been explained by her pregnancy, but Lily kept that information to herself. It was only after the marriage – performed in secret in Scotland – that the truth came to light. Yet even after she had obtained her husband, the chaplain saw no improvement in his daughter's mental state. In fact, it became steadily worse.

By the time he received news of the birth of his grandson, the chaplain had not spoken to his daughter for six months. He would never have a chance to do so again, for within a day of the birth announcement came news of Lily's death.

George was not made for solitude. Isolated from his family, left in a shabby townhouse with an infant son, his wet-nurse and nothing but the ghosts of his former confidantes for company, he felt that any day he might follow in Lily's footsteps and lose his own mind.

He hadn't told her family the truth of it, because it was enough that he had to bear it himself, but her death had not been a peaceful one. It had started towards the end of her pregnancy, as she felt the little life quickening inside her. The more he kicked, the more agitated she became, until finally she declared her intention to rid her body of the parasite it harboured. The doctor had strapped her down then, but Lily only writhed and kicked in her restraints, yelling all sorts of crazy things: that she was carrying the child of the devil, that it was evil, that she'd been impregnated by an incubus, that the child would be a demon too, that it had to die or it would ruin them all...

When George could no longer stand her screams, the doctor kept her sedated until the birth. He had hoped it would be the turning point, but if anything her psychosis only intensified. She screamed when she finally saw the baby's face, shouting obscenities, denouncing him as the child of Satan. Fearing she might intend harm towards him, George sent for a wet-nurse and took the baby away.

Whatever evil Lily had seen, George could not discern it. He was enchanted by the tiny creature. There was no malice in its little pink face. He looked into its new eyes and saw only the innocence of every child, untarnished and desiring nothing but the care of a loving parent, which he swore he would provide just as dutifully as any mother. He began as he meant to continue, cradling the little boy for every waking second that he was not being fed, lavishing his attention on him to the exclusion of all others. Given Lily's incapacitation, he felt that he owed nothing less to his son, but the new father's devotion to his baby was his mother's demise.

Lily had been sedated following the birth, but her restraints had not been reattached. While the household was distracted by the baby, she found her peace on the cobblestoned pavement five storeys beneath her bedroom window.

These were the truths George kept locked in his mind until it threatened to break beneath their weight. He tried to face it all with denial, naming his new son Arthur after the boy's potential father and his own erstwhile friend, but he was still haunted by the too-recent losses, hollowed out so deeply that even the sight of his son's smile could not fill him up again. He clung to it nonetheless, to every cry and snuffle and gurgle, but found the spectre of his old friend's face was too present on his son's own for him to forget what he had lost.

It was in this state, with the anniversary of Arthur Morris's death approaching, that he received an invitation to the college's masquerade ball. Whether by way of penance or tribute, he sent his acceptance by return of post.

The quad looked exactly the same, and yet entirely different. Candles that a year ago had streamed merrily in their lanterns now felt blindingly garish, the drinks were unpalatable and the masks, so exciting at his first masquerade, were now less mysterious than they were alienating. George, wearing the same jester's outfit he had donned a year ago, felt locked into a lifetime as the proverbial sad clown. He had chosen this costume both literally and by every small misstep that had brought him through the past twelve months. He felt each one like a pin in his heart.

Arthur and Lily, together.

Arthur, gone.

Then Lily.

Arthur.

The figure caught George's eye at the edge of the quad as it headed under an archway and through into the small garden beyond. At this time of year, there shouldn't be any roses blooming, and yet the arbours beyond the arch were heavy with blooms and their scent. The man stopped there beneath the trees, graceful and delicate, a man wearing a suit with tails and a black devil's mask.

It couldn't be.

Arthur was dead. Arthur died a year ago.

George's head knew this well enough, but his feet weren't listening. They guided him across the quad, pushing through groups of students and tutors gathered around the braziers, his eyes blind to everything except his destination. He knew from the moment he saw the mask, but until there was grass under his shoes and Arthur's eyes were reflected in his own, he did not truly believe.

'It's you,' he whispered into the darkness.

The darkness whispered back. 'It's me, George. I was hoping you would come.'

As Arthur stepped out from beneath the trees, George could doubt it no longer. It was truly him, back from the dead, waiting for him at the masquerade as George had hoped he would be twelve months ago. If he allowed himself to fall into the moment, perhaps he might forget, for tonight at least, that the last year had happened at all. Tonight, perhaps this could be the truth instead.

'Are you really here?'

'Yes,' Arthur said. 'And no. But I am as good as here.'

The words made no sense to George, but he couldn't find it in himself to care. All he cared about was that Arthur was here, in front of him, and that he could finally say all the things he had left unsaid for so long.

'I should have told you,' George said, closing the distance between them. 'I should have told you so many things.'

'You didn't need to.' Arthur reached out and pulled the mask from George's face, letting it fall to the ground, and cupped George's cheek in his lithe fingers. 'I knew. And I'm sorry. I would have done things differently if the choice had been mine.'

'And now?'

Arthur didn't answer, but George saw the eyes behind

the mask flicker down to his mouth, and that was invitation enough. He leaned forward and kissed the lips he had loved so long, entwined his clumsy fingers in the hair at the back of Arthur's head, pressed his heart against the heart he had pined for and felt its steady beat.

Thud-thud.

It was a long time before George could compose himself enough to pull away. When he finally did, he saw sadness in Arthur's eyes.

'I have to go.'

George could only nod numbly in reply, his hands falling from his lover's face, from his hair, as he tried fruitlessly to untwine his heart as well.

'The baby?' Arthur asked.

'A boy. I named him after you.'

Something was happening, a blurring of Arthur's body, as though he were being caught up in a black sandstorm that had no substance, brought no breeze, but nonetheless began to erase the edges of his form. George snatched at him, trying to hold his love in place, but his fingers closed around thin air. Arthur's last words were distorted by the dark nothingness that was rising between them, but George heard them clearly enough.

'If you love me, keep our boy safe.'

'I will,' George whispered. 'I do and I will. I promise.'

It was a promise he never broke.

Eighteen years later, Arthur Junior took up his place at the college.

There were a lot of Arthurs that year, all following in their father's footsteps. The original Arthur was long gone, far away on the other side of the continent, sowing the seed of devilry in pastures new. It wouldn't be long before each one of his sons would do the same, however reluctantly.

The Mermaid House

It was at the beginning of my career as a lawyer that I happened upon the town of Outsmouth, a large but unassuming congregation of fishing cottages clustered nervously along the south coast.

I was just a trainee in those days, but my supervising partner was the sole executor for a client who had died recently at his home on the nearby island of Holmout, and I had been sent to take an account of the property on her behalf. It's never an enviable task to be deputised in such a way, and certainly not when a client with numerous children and indecent wealth has chosen to leave their entire fortune to the local museum. I knew that the family would be waiting at the former client's home with questions I had neither the wit nor the authority to answer – why was the executor herself not present, what right did I have to turf the family out of their ancestral home, and did I know who they were, actually? – so I was not in a rush to catch the ferry that would take me there. In any case, it turned out that the service was offered only twice a day, and I would have to wait several hours to be conveyed across the choppy waters that lay between Holmout and the mainland.

The day presented its distractions for my choosing: the cold beach, the blustery coastal path, or my book in the car. There was no contest.

I have always been an avid walker, particularly when the sea is close. I still keep my trainers in the boot in case I find myself at a loose end in some place that begs to be explored, and the coast was begging for it that day. So I parked up by the deserted ice cream stand – many months out of season by then – exchanged my heels for my walking shoes, pulled a jacket over my fancy trouser suit and set off along the empty path up into the dunes, blinking against the sandy wind.

That's how I got my first glimpse of Outsmouth: squinting through a gale as I held my jacket closed about me and wondered why on Earth the ferry crossing was located in such a bleak, out-of-the-way spot, when such a large town lurked just around the bay. The channel looked navigable enough, though it seemed to me that some large portion of the town's footprint stood on land that had been reclaimed from the sea, because instead of following the natural concave shape I expected from the shoreline, the buildings clustered on a large, oval promontory that reached out into the water. It was curious and seemed to warrant closer investigation, so I would have found my way into the town even if I had not then seen the sign at the bottom of the dunes.

Come visit the Mermaid House, it demanded. *The South Coast's most eerie and wondrous attraction. Genuine fish people! Marvel at their majesty and thrill at their sharp teeth! Plumb the mysteries of the deep!*

Those kinds of relics weren't uncommon back then. Seaside towns like Outsmouth thrived on tourism, and they all fabricated some oddity to display. I might have ignored it entirely, but the rain had quite suddenly begun to lash at my jacket, and my eyes fixed on those magic words: *Tea room!*

Praying it would be open, I hurried to the road, past the sign proclaiming that I was now entering Outsmouth, and made my way to the largest building in town. It was in a strange location, on the most inland edge of the town, and of a strange construction, four storeys of stone-built grandeur. Sitting as it did beside a spill of single-storey homes, it made the town look almost as though it had overflowed from the great stone edifice into an oil slick of habitation that spread into the sea.

But there was smoke coming from the chimney, light glowing from the windows, and the front door was standing slightly open, so I ran through the rain and straight inside.

'Welcome!'

The dark-haired teenager was cheerful. She was standing behind a polished wooden reception desk in a polished wood-panelled reception room that was far grander than I'd expected for a little backwater like Outsmouth. There was thick coir matting beneath my feet, a polished wooden hatstand and umbrella rack next to the door, and a cheerful fire roaring in the grate beneath a polished wooden mantlepiece adorned with colourful ceramic pieces like nothing I had ever seen before. Everything about the room was warm and inviting, and the teenager was going out of her way to be the same.

'Can I take your coat?'

She could only have been a couple of years my junior, but she treated me with more than proper deference as she hung my jacket and helped me to shed my soaking trainers and deposit them on the mat by the door.

'Tea room?' I asked plaintively.

'Oh.' Her face fell as she glanced out of the window at the pouring rain. 'No. Not in January. But I could make you a cup in the kitchen upstairs while you take a look around the museum, if you like?'

'Museum?'

'Yes indeed! This is the Outsmouth town hall and the Royal Museum of Holmout. If you want to know how the King of Holmout won his crown, then you've come to the right place. We've got all the history right here in this building, chronicling every swashbuckling step of his glorious triumph over the waves.'

'There's a king of Holmout?'

'Absolutely. Well, not anymore. He just died. Very sad, actually, but he left everything he owned to the museum so we can preserve his story for posterity. Isn't that neat?'

A few puzzling pieces of the Holmout client's file were starting to click into place.

'He's a *king*? Alongside the current queen? How on earth does that work?'

'You can learn everything about it just through those doors,' the teenager said, gesturing tantalisingly to the double doors behind her, access to which was barred by a fat red rope strung across from the reception desk. 'So, do you want to look around? Forty pence entry.'

I fished two coins out of my pocket and handed them over. After all, what else was I going to do on a rainy afternoon on the coast? So in I went.

Almost immediately, I began to suspect that my enthusiastic friend had oversold the swashbuckling aspect of the so-called king's 'triumph over the waves'. In fact, it seemed that my supervising partner's erstwhile client had merely reclaimed a little coastline from the sea, as I had surmised when first viewing Outsmouth from a distance. Old black and white photos and narrative display boards hung at regular intervals along the wood-panelled corridor, charting the process from start to finish as the sea was dredged and the land built up. When this proved successful, an island was constructed out in the bay and a castle was planted there to watch over Outsmouth, allowing the new 'king' to survey his fabricated kingdom. The castle was where I was heading that very afternoon.

Which was all useful context for my impending work, but hardly the *eerie and wondrous attraction* boasted by the sign for the Mermaid House.

Until I turned the corner and saw the tanks. In a long room, just as aggressively wood-panelled as the rest of the building, there were recesses in the walls that held large aquaria of dark water. From a distance, they were nothing but ink and slime, but as I approached I saw creatures I don't know how to name. There was one in each tank and they were each perhaps the size of my hand, coloured the translucent black of slug flesh, and they moved in the water like motes of dust move in the light. They trailed filaments from their bodies like jellyfish stings, or thin tentacles, which moved independently from the rest of their bodies as though they had minds of their own. And – just for a second – there was a flash of something sharp.

The Mermaids of Outsmouth, the sign read, *vanquished here fifty years ago by the King himself, and finally contained.*

In that moment, I recalled how goldfish will grow to the size of their bowls so that, if let loose into a lake, they become specimens of gargantuan proportions. A shiver ran down my spine.

I stepped away from the tanks. They weren't the only thing in the room. Here again were more of the colourful ceramic pieces I'd seen in the entrance hall, arrayed on shelves above the tanks. But there were bigger pieces too, set in recesses of their own, huge figures sculpted larger than life-size and glazed in pinks and purples and blues. They looked almost human, but their limbs were oddly cast and their heads were adorned with feathery appendages striped in all colours of the rainbow. They were the most vibrant, excessive, audacious pieces of art I had ever seen.

Since I was the only person there, since the place was silent, and since my curiosity could not be contained, I reached forward to feel the nearly-hand of one such sculpture, but where I expected to find cool porcelain beneath my fingers, there was a surprising warmth. Then I saw the signs.

Don't touch the shells.
Shells.
Shells.
The shiver was back.
'You should come and see the voting rooms,' a girl's voice said.

I jumped and, in my shock, knocked a small coloured piece from the shelf beside me to the floor. If it were china, it should have broken.

It rolled.

'Oh, I—'

'Don't worry about that,' the girl said, picking the thing up and returning it to its place. She must have been about seven, and very similar in her appearance to the teenager at the front desk. 'Jamie's always shouting at me for playing with them, but it's not as if they ever break. I can't see the harm. She's my big sister, you know,' she continued, in that flippant didactic manner that is peculiar to small girls. 'I know just as much about this place as she does, though. Do you want me to show you the voting rooms? I know all about them.'

'The voting rooms?'

'The ones where everyone voted whether to let the mermaids stay in the bay. You know, ages ago, when Grandma was little. Look, they're over here.'

Without waiting for a reply, the girl led me quickly around three corners to where two rooms – wood-panelled, of course – stood facing each other across a short corridor. One held the gift shop, and the other was marked *toilets*, but above the doors to each were other signs, older signs burned into short wooden planks.

One said *Ins* and the other said *Outs*.

'All the people in town came in here, Grandma says, and if they wanted the mermaids in the bay then they went in the *Ins* room,' she continued, pointing at the signs, 'and if they wanted them out then they went in the *Outs* room, and then they counted them all up. It's why we're called Outsmouth, you know. The Outs won, and so they started killing all the mermaids, but they fought back and the war took forever and everyone nearly died, so the town said they'd give the whole bay to the king if he'd save them, so he set up all these nets and smooshed the mermaid's homes on the seabed and used them to build his island. That's why he's the king. Was the king. He's dead now, you know.'

'I know,' I replied numbly, grasping at the one piece of information that felt real.

'I didn't like him anyway. He was awful to the mermaids. He really hated them, you know. Wanted them all dead and gone, even the little ones in the tanks. And now he's dead, so there. And he had hairy ear holes.'

The girl had several other objections to our erstwhile client, but my mind was already overfull of her stories, and in any case my attention had been caught by a third room. It was just at the end of the short corridor over which the *Ins* and the *Outs* had faced off, barred by another of the thick red ropes, but through the half-open door I could see an old woman sitting in a rocking chair. Beside her, a dog guarded a staircase that led down into darkness. I could hear the lapping of waves emanating from it and wondered how that was possible this far inland.

Without meaning to, I found that I had stepped closer

to the rope.

I could see the light, now. It was barely there, just a faint luminescence in pink and eerie green that glowed on the back wall of the staircase. Even just a step closer, I could hear the waves more loudly now, as though they were beckoning me through the rope, through the door, across the room and down the stairs to whatever watery end awaited me there. I felt that I had almost crossed that threshold already, could see the salty darkness in from of me, could feel it lapping at my bare toes as I stood on the bottom step of the wooden staircase and let it taste my skin.

'Can't go through there,' the girl said, snapping me out of whatever fantasy had taken me. 'That's what the rope means, you know.'

I looked back across the room to the staircase and saw the old woman again. There was something strange about her hair, half-hidden under a headscarf. She was looking me dead in the eye. She didn't seem angry, not exactly, but I had to blink before I could look away.

'That's Grandma,' the girl said. 'She doesn't like people much.'

'Oh,' I said.

Then, to escape the woman's stare, I walked quickly into the gift shop, though it hardly merited the name. There were a few pencils and pads with whimsical mermaid designs, enamelled spoons and thimbles decorated with mermaid-themed scenes, but not the thing for which I was really looking.

'Are there no guide books for the museum?' I asked the girl. 'No pamphlets that I might read?'

For, despite my shivering at the creatures in the

tanks, and the odd demeanour of the girl's grandmother, the story she had related had me fully in its grasp. I wanted to go back through these corridors more slowly and learn more of what had happened here, to find out what in the world these creatures were and whence they came, whether they were real or a fiction created to lure in tourists, but I wanted to do so with a guide more reliable than this small girl.

'Well, there's the orig'nal ac-a-dem-ic paper,' she said, sounding the word out as though she had been taught it by rote. She darted over to a stack of leaflets by the counter, grabbed one and handed it to me. It wasn't much, perhaps six pages in small font, but it looked official enough that something jumped in my stomach at the sight of it.

It was *real*. I held the proof in my hand.

But why then did no one talk of the Outsmouth mermaids? Why had I – who walked the whole British coast and explored all its rock pools and caves – not known anything of the creatures that lived in the tanks within the museum's walls? Why was I only now hearing of the king of Holmout and his campaign to rid the bay of their kind?

As my mind was filling with these questions, I heard a distant horn blaring out across the sea.

'Oh no,' I said. 'The ferry.' I didn't think I'd wandered the halls that long, but my watch told me hours had passed. 'I've got to go.'

Shouting a quick thank you to the girl, I raced back along the corridors in my stockinged feet, clutching the paper tightly in my hand.

'Your tea's cold,' her sister said to me when I

returned to the reception desk.

'I'm sorry, but I must go. The ferry.'

'Oh,' she said, springing into action. 'You'll have to hurry! Quickly now!'

I struggled back into my jacket and trainers with her help, then rushed out of the door.

'Hope you enjoyed the Mermaid House!' she called after me. 'Come again soon!'

'Thank you!' I called back.

It was only once I was on the ferry, rain-soaked and covered in sand from my scramble back up the dunes to the ferry landing, that I had a chance to look closely at the paper the girl had given me. It was fascinating. I read it three times through on the journey across the strait, so I had it just about memorised by the time I arrived at the island of Holmout and noticed what was in the top right-hand corner of the cover.

£1.50.

I'd been in such a rush to leave that I hadn't paid. The guilt squirmed in my stomach.

I'd pay on the way back, I told myself. My visit to the former client's family wouldn't take long, and I was sure I could make it back to the museum before closing time to settle my account.

But when I returned that evening, the vista that greeted me as I scaled the dune was very different from the one I had seen earlier that day. Instead of the large town reclaimed from the sea, there was nothing but the black water of the bay and a single building planted at the edge of the darkness. It looked as though it had sunk halfway into the surf.

I approached with caution. The fire in the entrance

hall no longer roared, the wood no longer gleamed, and the corridors were no longer lined with exhibits and display boards. Instead, the fireplace had rusted and the wood was rotting and, at the back of the building, the rooms where the *Ins* and *Outs* had voted tipped at a sharp angle.

I could see the staircase, now unguarded. I could see the glowing luminescence. I could see the water lapping at the stairs, higher now than it must have been before.

But I could hear something, too: whalesong, the soft thud of sand under footsteps, and a clicking crunch that spoke to me of teeth and beaks and terrible jaws.

I turned, dropping the academic paper in my haste, and I ran.

The sign I passed on my way back to the dunes read, *You are now leaving Insmouth*.

When I returned to the office and spoke to my supervising solicitor the next day, she knew nothing of the museum in Outsmouth, nor of the king of Holmout, nor of Holmout itself, and I had nothing to prove the truth of any of it. She had been under the impression, she said, that I was taking a trip to the coast for my health. Perhaps I should take another, she suggested.

After that day, my health was never quite the same again.

Now that I'm retired, the children are grown, and my wife is gone, there's little else to occupy my days except walking and reminiscing. I have thought often of Insmouth over the past fifty years, but I think of it more frequently every day, to the point that the thoughts have become intrusive and impossible to ignore. Now I'm finally here, at what was once the ferry crossing to an island that no longer exists. When I pull on my trainers and coat and clamber over the blustery dunes and finally spy the Mermaid House sitting on the edge of the bay, it is just as strange and grand as it was the first time I saw it, though now it sits dark and alone.

It takes minutes that feel like hours to scramble to the front door. Inside, the wood-panelled rooms are damper now. Everything smells of salt and seaweed and there are limpets scattered thickly on the walls that lead to the back room, half cellar and half rock pool. The stairs still disappear down into the dark water at the back of the building, and still that faint luminescence is leaking out from the world beneath the waves into this strange portal that straddles the threshold.

I shed my coat, my jumper, my shirt, my trainers, my trousers, my socks, and leave them in a pile by the door. I approach the staircase barefoot and swimsuit-clad. All the while, the greenish-pink glow beckons me onward.

It is begging to be explored.

The Mirror Weir

Afterwards, they put barriers along the edges of the bridge, high enough that you could no longer see the water and what lay beneath it. But that was afterwards.

Before, there was only a waist-high railing separating the edge of the footbridge from a ten-foot drop to the rapids below. The locals called it the mirror weir, because the water is so clear where it runs over the edge that, from the bridge, you could see yourself reflected in the shadow of the structures beneath. Some people saw other things besides, or so the rumour goes, and it was a convincing rumour because it answered questions that were otherwise unanswerable. Why so many deaths, decade by decade, year after year? How could you explain the strange behaviour that preceded them? And why that spot specifically?

Nonbelievers would say it's not uncommon for drunken students to fall into rivers, and that people are willing to jump off practically anything when given the opportunity, whether they're seeking clout or oblivion.

But this story isn't for them.

Fresher's week. In a university city, revelry abounds. The new crowd heads to the centre, untethered, drawn by the siren call of drinks offers and bright flyers that beckon them to the loud and easy places, where their shoes will stick to the floor and their drinks will be served in test tubes, jam jars or glow-in-the-dark shot glasses, depending on the theme. But the old crowd, the graduate students and third-years, avoid those haunts. They seek out quiet corners to catch up with friends they've already made, and with whom they stuck to those same floors in years past. They're the ones, jeans-clad and unkempt, who walk over the bridge and down the towpath to the tree-filled beer garden of the Water Boatman.

It's a nice pub. A little dated, perhaps, but that's part of its appeal. It serves beer and ale, scampi fries and peanuts. The wine list is two bottles long, and the closest you'll get to a cocktail here is a gin and tonic. It's a magnet for real ale purists, and dog owners love the beer garden, but for everyone else it's just a pleasant place to sit and watch the river while they enjoy their pint.

Martin is not a casual customer. He has picked his venue carefully. He knows that Laura is an aficionado of ale, that she likes to walk along the towpath at the weekends, and that she stops to say hello to every dog she passes on her way. He's been thinking about her all summer – her ruthless grammatical precision in tutorials, the satisfied curve of her lips as she pieces together a translation, the way the library lights pick out the shimmer of red in her otherwise brown hair – and he's decided it's finally time to take the plunge.

'Fancy a drink at the Boatman?' he texted earlier this afternoon. Casual, no pressure, chill.

'Sure,' came the response. 'Six-ish?'

So here he sits in the beer garden as sunset approaches, one pint of ale standing ready for her across the table as he nurses his own – truth be told, he isn't a fan – and waits.

And waits.

There's a bug in Laura's glass. Martin fishes it out, then realises he probably shouldn't have put his fingers in her drink, but surely that's better than giving her a pint with a bug in it and she'll never know and they're clean, he's sure, at least they were before he covered them in ale. It's running down his wrist and he can't hug her with a wet hand – what would she think? – so he wipes it on his jeans but he can *see* it there like a stain, even in the twilight, and now she's going to think he's pissed himself or got really sweaty or something awful and oh god he shouldn't be this nervous about having a quiet drink with someone he's been friends with for two years.

Six o'clock turns into quarter past, turns into half past. Martin's jeans have dried and the sun has gone. It's a moonless night, so the only light left comes from a few solar-powered lamps that mark the path, and whatever pours out of the pub's front windows, both sources reflecting off the river in a kaleidoscopic scatter.

He hears her laugh before he sees her. At first it's welcome, a relief to know she hasn't stood him up for this date that she doesn't know is a date, but then he realises what it means: she's not alone. As she rounds the corner into the beer garden, they lock eyes and he tries to smile, despite the crowd around her: her two housemates, Serena and Ruth, along with three of the guys from their tutor group. James and Murad are okay, but Martin is less than happy to see RJ at Laura's shoulder, leaning in so close he must be able to smell her hair.

'Martin!' RJ yells. 'Why are you sitting in the dark?'

He mumbles something about it being a warm night and watching the stars, despite the fact that there are none to be seen this close to the city, then he picks up his ale as the group ambles towards the pub's door.

'Is that for me?' Laura asks, smiling shyly at Martin as she gestures at the pint left sitting on the table.

'It was there when I got here,' he says, abandoning all attempts at charm, because what's the bloody point?

Then, without looking back, Martin follows RJ inside.

Laura isn't sure how things got so out of hand. Everyone was excited to be back here for the new term, excited to see each other, and somehow they all got scooped up in Martin's invitation to the Water Boatman. The moment she arrived, she knew it was a mistake. He'd clearly been in the mood for a quiet drink with a friend, and she'd turned up with half their tutor group and turned it into something raucous. Why did she keep making these errors in judgement?

And RJ. *Ugh*. RJ.

So obnoxious. So brash. So handsy, as though their misguided one-night stand at the summer ball gave him the right to fondle her forever. She should have pushed him off the bridge on the way over and been done with it.

'So,' RJ says, flourishing a penny between his fingers. 'Is everyone clear on the rules?'

They're sitting at a large round table in the middle of the pub, getting glares from the locals as they embark upon the third drinking game of the night. RJ has a bottomless repertoire, of course. The latest involves flicking a penny into a glass, then different people drink based on a complex system of nominations that no one except RJ seems to grasp. They all nod along nonetheless.

As with all the games this evening, somehow the rules require Martin to drink more and buy more than anyone else. Laura sees the vicious twinkle in RJ's eye and kicks him under the table. He takes this as a cue to put his hand on her thigh. She is in the process of extricating herself when Martin's head thumps down on the table top.

'Marty boy!' RJ crows. 'You're wankered, my lad.'

'And why do you think that is?' Laura asks, glaring at him as she finally eludes his grip. 'You've been fucking with him all night. Why can't you just leave him alone?'

'He's a big boy, Laura. He can look after himself. He just can't hold his drink!'

James and RJ laugh, drunk and manic, but none of the others are smiling.

'Come on, Martin,' Murad says, helping him out of his chair. 'Let's get you home, mate.'

'Yeah, it's late.' Laura stands and shrugs on her coat. 'I've had enough.'

'Hey, come on now,' says James. 'Why are we breaking up the party?'

'Yeah, come on, Laura,' RJ says, snaking an arm around her waist. 'Have another drink.'

'You know what, RJ?' Laura pushes him away, eyes blazing. 'Fuck off. Fuck *all* the way off. And when you've finished fucking off, fuck off some more.'

'Whoa,' RJ says with a laugh, 'calm down, love. Must be that time of the month. Am I right?' He sniggers and turns to James, who dutifully sniggers back.

Ruth glares at James. Serena calls RJ a sexist prick. Laura ignores them both and helps Murad get Martin back on his feet and out of the pub, with the other girls following behind.

When they reach the river, Laura is cuddled up between Serena and Martin. The towpath is wide enough for all five of them to walk abreast, clinging to each other for warmth and support.

'What the fuck was his problem tonight?' Serena slurs.

'RJ?' Laura murmurs back. 'He's just being a dick.'

'Because of what happened at the ball?'

Laura glances at Martin, but it's clear that he's not following their conversation, or any other conversation, for that matter. Instead, he's singing *Show Me the Way to Go Home* under his breath. Badly. He's cute when he's wasted, his mousy hair sticking out in all directions

as his glasses teeter on the very end of his nose.

'I guess,' she whispers to Serena. 'I don't know why I let him come. This whole night was a fucking disaster. Poor Martin. He just wanted a quiet drink. I don't know how I'm going to make it up to him.'

Serena smiles. 'I think I have some ideas.'

'Serena!' Laura fearfully glances at Martin again, but Ruth and Murad have joined in the song on his other side and the noise is easily muting their conversation. 'What are you implying?' she continues, more softly. 'Martin and I have been friends for years.'

'And whose fault is that?'

'I don't know what you're talking about.'

'Oh, come off it. You've fancied the pants off him since our first seminar.'

'Will you keep your voice down?'

'Oh, relax. He's away with the fairies. Besides, would it really be the worst thing in the world if he found out how you felt? One of you is going to have to make a move sooner or later. I'd say it's your turn. You kind of ruined his go tonight.'

Laura's feet stop moving. She only stays in motion because the others are pulling her along.

'You think he… Tonight?' she says after she's managed to pick up her feet and get them back in order.

'I'm pretty sure.'

Laura sneaks another look at Martin and smiles to herself, then she and Serena join in the song, letting it carry them along the river, across the bridge and all the way home. The girls don't look down as they cross, so they don't see the shape beneath the water of the mirror weir.

But someone does.

Still, there's no sign that anything is wrong until the next morning.

Laura's hangover is possibly the worst of her life, and she's had enough of them that she's created her own hangover measuring system. Today, it's a ten point five: head in the toilet, kill me now, should have made herself sick last night because it would have felt better than this unending torture. Just as well that lectures don't start until next week, because there's no way she's dragging herself out of the bathroom this Friday morning. She can only imagine how Martin must feel.

They left the boys in the sitting room last night, Martin curled up on one sofa and Murad on the other. Martin seemed coherent enough after the bracing walk back, if a little distant, so Ruth gave them each a bucket, just in case, and left them to it. Truth be told, they were all too drunk to worry much about how drunk their friends were.

Until now. Laura expects to find Martin in exactly the same place when she eventually descends to the sitting room in her pyjamas, but although Murad is snoring happily, the second sofa is empty.

'Ruth?' she calls back upstairs. 'Are you awake?'

'No,' a groan replies. 'Ruth is dead. There is no Ruth.'

'And no Serena either,' a second voice adds.

'Is Martin up there with you?' Laura calls.

'What? No!' Serena yells, at the same time Ruth says, 'Who the fuck is Martin?' which Laura takes as a no.

She searches the house without finding any trace of him. She wakes Murad and asks if he knows anything, but he's been sleeping like the dead all night. She texts Martin repeatedly, then gets desperate and starts calling him instead. Still, there's no reply. Eventually, she throws on some clothes and starts walking towards his house. The route takes her over the river, over the footbridge to the other side of town.

It's an overcast day, so cloudy that it makes the morning dark. Perhaps that's why the shine catches her eye.

There's a pair of glasses in the water.

And, beyond them, a face.

Laura startles, expecting blank eyes and lifeless limbs, but that's not what she sees. Instead, his eyes twinkle through the clear water. His lips twitch into a smile. His fingers curl in invitation, as though he's simply standing behind a window, beckoning her inside, and she has the sensation in that moment that he *knows*. After two years of dancing around the truth, they can be honest about how they feel. The gulf between them has evaporated, not only because they now understand each other, but because he's so close. There's no drop to the weir, no water between them, nothing between their lips except a few inches of air that she could do away with if she just leaned forward and let them touch. He's only a breath away.

'Laura?' The voice draws her gaze from the water and breaks the siren call. Serena is hurrying across the bridge towards her, a coat wrapped over her pyjamas. 'What are you doing? It's freezing out here.'

'Looking for Martin,' Laura says, blinking away her dizziness. 'I was going to go over to his place.'

'I've called. He's not there.'

'I saw—'

But when Laura looks back at the weir, there's nothing to see except the reflection of the two girls and the clouds above their heads. The water rushes ever onwards, down towards the lock.

That's where the police find his body, crushed in the mitre gates.

When RJ finally drags himself out of bed, he's filled with alcohol-induced regret. And real regret. God, he behaved like a prick last night. He's already thinking about calling Laura to apologise when James pushes into his room.

'Hey, how about knocking?' RJ yells. He likes to sleep in the nude, like a proper red-blooded man, but he is not cool with his housemates stealing a peek at his goods. Not the male ones, anyway.

'Have you seen the news?' James says, not slowing down enough to apologise.

'I just woke up. What do *you* think?'

'Martin's dead. They're saying he drowned.'

RJ's first thought – *good riddance* – does him no credit, but even he recognises that it's a shitty response to finding out a sort-of friend is dead. Instead of saying it out loud, he asks, 'Is Laura okay?'

'Not really.'

It's an understatement. She refuses to talk to him over the weekend, despite many attempts to contact her via text, email, voicemail, letter and shouting outside her bedroom window. Ruth and Serena are giving him the cold shoulder too. Apparently it's his fault Martin got drunk and went wandering in the night, but it's not like

RJ was buying the drinks, and it's not like it was RJ's sofa the idiot crashed on. RJ wasn't the one who left Martin unsupervised when he was completely off his face. Accordingly, he fails to see how the accident has anything to do with him. He'll say sorry anyway if it means Laura will talk to him again, but he can't get close enough to try. Monday comes, Tuesday and Wednesday pass, and still she doesn't turn up for classes.

Eventually, Serena sets him straight after Thursday's lectures.

'Leave her alone,' she says through gritted teeth. 'She doesn't want to talk to you.'

'Why not? What did I do?' He deploys his hurt little puppy dog eyes. For the first time in his life, they don't work. To his surprise, Serena doesn't melt. Instead, her eyes fill with tears of rage.

'You were a fucking prick to him!' she yells. 'All the time, every class, every time we hung out, every single moment. You couldn't leave him the fuck alone, and now you won't leave Laura alone either. If anyone's responsible for his suicide, it's you, and everyone knows it. So just fuck off and stop pretending you're the fucking victim, because it won't work.'

Ruth takes Serena's arm and steers her away, leaving RJ alone on the pavement outside the lecture hall, trying to piece together his next move. To his mind, his predicament boils down to one problem: Laura thinks he pushed Martin to suicide. He simply needs to find a solution to that problem.

It's possible she's right; Martin always was a weak excuse for a man. He was just the kind of pathetic boy who'd take a joke the wrong way and end up getting everyone else in the shit when they'd done nothing wrong at all and really it was just that Martin was too fucking wet to act like a grown up.

But maybe she's wrong. Maybe Martin didn't commit suicide at all. And even if he did, maybe there's a way RJ can throw enough doubt on the question to get himself back into Laura's good graces. And, if all goes well, her knickers too.

RJ decides to dedicate himself fully to this project, so he starts skipping classes, too. Instead of attending lectures, he hangs out by the river taking photos and noting down everything he sees: the dimensions of the weir, the distance to the lock, the marks on the standings that hold the bridge steady. He sees Laura there sometimes, standing on the bridge and looking down at the weir for hours on end, as though she's hypnotised by the rushing water. He says hello the first couple of times, but that sends her scurrying back home without a word, so he learns to keep himself out of sight beneath the bridge. He can watch her from down here, following the lines of her face for as long as she follows the lines of the water. She never sees him, but seeing her is enough to motivate him to keep going.

His absences get worse over the coming weeks. Instead of learning advanced grammar and vocabulary in his seminars, he spends his days in his room trawling through the internet for articles about deaths in the area. This takes him to the library's microfiche room, where he scrolls through old newspapers and finds an eerie number of suspicious deaths connected with the mirror weir. For a C student who's barely cracked a book since the end of the summer term, he does good research. It almost gets him the real answer, the one he isn't even looking for, but the library is closing and he packs up his bag just one screen before he reaches the story that would explain it all. It's unassuming: three short paragraphs in an ancient paper.

Clairvoyant's Ill-fated Love Affair Prompts Triple Suicide

But RJ doesn't see this. Instead, he goes home and falls down a rabbit hole on the internet: college students are drowning all across America, all in mysterious circumstances, and all linked by graffiti of a smiley face found at the scene. He pulls out his photos of the bridge, sees what might be a scrappy smiley face spray-painted on the standings, and sets the hare running through conspiracies of murder cults and schools for assassins.

This will be his story.

Martin – gentle, inoffensive, wet-behind-the-ears Martin – was the target of an international syndicate of hitmen who've been operating around the world. Here's the proof: the smiley face, the fact he drowned, the similar disappearances in America, all signalling clearly that this criminal network has been established in the U.K. for decades.

RJ doesn't believe it for a second, but maybe Laura will, if he can present her with the right evidence. And if he can prove that Martin was a murder victim instead of a suicide, that'll be his job done, name cleared, pathway to Laura's pants once again unobstructed.

So he gets to work, locking himself in his room for days to prevent any distraction from the task at hand. In this, his prime objective, he is motivated. He prints out the relevant bits from the internet, running through all the ink in his housemate's colour printer to get the photos sharp. Then he goes back to the river with his expensive camera and gets up close to the smiley face graffiti, comparing his angles to the print outs so he can make his own crime scene photos resemble the ones on the internet as closely as possible.

He's concentrating so fiercely on his task that he doesn't see her fall. He didn't even realise she was here. He hears the splash, though, and turns in time to see something drop over the edge of the weir. It looked like a shoe.

At first, he thinks it's nothing. Probably a branch. But then he remembers the way Laura has been gazing into the water and he starts to wonder.

He runs down the towpath, eyes scanning the point where the weir crashes down into the river and beyond, searching for any sign of a shoe, a foot, a body. There's nothing.

Starting to doubt his own mind, he runs back the way he came, cradling his camera in his hands, along the towpath and up the steps to the middle of the bridge, to the same spot where she has been standing, day after day.

He drops the camera to shatter on the ground at his feet. Taking the railing in his hands, he leans over to look down into the water, just as he has seen Laura do so many times before.

The weir is like a sheet of glass between them, cocooning her beneath its current as though she's surrounded by air, not water. It doesn't seem to move her at all. She looks like she's sleeping. Then her eyes open and fix on his. She lifts her hand beneath the water and waves. RJ would swear he sees triumph tilting the corners of her mouth, and he can feel her mocking him with her intention to go somewhere he can't follow.

He can't abide that. She can't drown. He hasn't won her yet. She's not *allowed* to drown. He won't let her leave.

So he jumps.

But RJ has been locked away in his room for days. He's out of touch. He doesn't know that Laura has been dead since last night, or that the police recovered her body from the lock this morning.

There's nothing in the weir but a soul waiting to be released; a role waiting to be filled.

In a university city, memories are short. Students move on, taking their stories with them, and people forget that more of them arrived at the beginning of term than left at its end. Twenty years on, the few locals who remember how many lives the mirror weir has taken are outnumbered by those who decry the way the new barriers block the view, or who argue that their height makes the bridge a hot spot for assault. It's not their fault. They mean well. They're not wrong, either, but they don't remember enough to balance the drawbacks against the danger they keep out.

In the end, they win.

The barriers are coming down next month. Beyond them, one soul has been waiting two decades for someone to replace him. He is unlikely to be kind to the one he takes.

Living Underground

He boarded the Northern Line at Bank station.

Normally I wouldn't have held that against him, but he was wearing a shiny, pin-striped suit in a cut that made him look like a mobile phone salesman and he brought with him a pervasive stench of stale, cheap, teenager aftershave. The footballer's knot in his tie was the final nail in the coffin.

He looked me up and down appraisingly, making no attempt at subtlety.

I practically sneered back. What a creep.

Consigning him irrevocably to the dickhead pile, I retreated back to the comfort of my Kindle, my spare hand wrapped lightly around the pole at the end of the carriage to stop myself from toppling off my modest heels as the train lurched forward on its journey south.

It had been a very, very long day. In fact, since it was now just past midnight, it had started yesterday. And nothing had gone right. From the delivery that had turned up four hours late to the total I.T. failure that was only solved after I'd already missed an immovable deadline, it had been a complete washout.

A strand of my hair fell across my vision and I blew it away ineffectually.

I was overheated and feeling antsy in the stuffy air of the London Underground's seventh circle of hell. It was grimy and sticky, the dirt in the tunnels settling inside the trains and onto the platforms in an indelible layer that left your skin tacky and coated the insides of your nostrils with soot. Blowing your nose after disembarking was always something of an adventure.

I didn't care how late it was when I got home; I was drinking as much wine as I could reasonably fit into my largest wineglass. I might even take it into the bath with me. And drink it with a straw.

I shifted my handbag up on my shoulder, wincing as tension twinged in my neck, and glanced across the carriage to where Mr Dickhead was lounging against the opposite doors (in direct contravention of the rules, I might add).

For the first time, I noticed that he wasn't the only passenger who had joined us at Bank. I performed a split-second assessment of the newcomer.

Interesting, I thought.

The moment I looked at him, he fixed his eyes on mine, the startling green of his irises trapping me in his gaze.

I realised I was staring and glanced down nervously, trained by years of tube travel to avoid even casual eye contact while the train was in motion, much less rapt attention.

While he had none of Mr Dickhead's sleaziness, he had been almost threatening in the surprising directness of his scrutiny, almost predatory.

Almost.

I could feel a blush warming my cheeks and lowered my head further to hide my face behind the curtain of my loose hair.

Now, why was I embarrassed?

I tried to read and failed, concentrating furiously on the page in front of me. I was ashamed that looking at him had had such a big effect on me, but I was unable to stop fixating on the memory of his face. Then I realised how circular and stupid that was, and started beating myself up for that, too.

God, I really needed that wine.

My eyes ran over and over the same line of text, but I couldn't even remember what book I was reading, let alone what the sentence said.

We pulled into London Bridge station seconds afterwards, but the doors stayed closed; no one getting on, no one getting off. No distraction to allow me a reprieve from my internal bully.

I risked a glance upwards, unable to shake the feeling that the newcomer was staring at me. In fact, his face was in profile now, turned away from me towards the other end of the carriage. So I cautiously took a moment to look more closely.

Dark, overgrown hair, pale skin, strong jaw line, full lips and fierce, and those piercing green eyes.

Black jeans, maroon T-shirt, dark trainers and a suit jacket.

No wedding ring.

Very interesting.

I looked away as he turned his head, pretending that I had been moving to put my Kindle away in my bag, and stared away down the train.

I decided that, with his colouring, he probably had an Irish name. The accent would suit him.

The carriage emptied out as we arrived at Borough, a good quarter of the passengers rising from their seats and leaving the train, led out onto the platform by Mr Dickhead. I waited for them to pass me, dancing around them in the limited space, then took the seat closest to where I had been standing, closest to the doors. I breathed a silent sigh of relief that Mr Dickhead was leaving.

The seat backs ran along the outside walls of the carriage, the lines facing each other across its width. I settled myself down with my handbag on my lap, pressed tight between the glass partition and an elderly woman who was sitting to my right. She was a large lady, taking up more space than her ungenerous seat allowed, so I pulled my elbows and shoulders in as much as I could, leaning forwards in my chair and towards the partition.

And there he was, sitting directly across from me, his green eyes looking straight into mine.

I flicked my gaze slightly sideways, staring fixedly at my reflection in the glass of the window behind him as we sped through the tunnel. I could see him in my peripheral vision, the stark contrast of the colours in his dark hair and his pale skin, and in his green eyes and his red lips, drawing my attention almost irresistibly to his face.

Almost.

Thankfully, the strobing of the lights on the tunnel wall quickly became hypnotic in my exhaustion, pulsing into my brain so forcefully that I had to close my eyes and turn away. Elephant and Castle passed by in a dream, my mind swirling with images of his eyes, his cheekbones, his lips... I felt an overpowering urge to open my eyes and check that they were just as I saw them in my head, that nothing had changed since my last glimpse.

It hadn't. And he was looking at me again.

I flashed a nervous smile, but his expression didn't change, remaining preoccupied and purposeful as he followed the tumbling line of my hair from my forehead to my neck.

It was unsettling.

Grasping for something to distract me, anything other than the man opposite me, I settled for reading the Tube map above his head. I'd travelled this route twice a day for three years, but I studied it like I'd never been on the Underground before.

The minutes passed in agony.

I chewed my lip nervously as the doors swooshed open at Kennington, disgorging my neighbour together with all but four of the other passengers.

I risked a look.

The Irish dream was still sitting opposite me.

I was feeling even more uncomfortable with fewer people in the carriage, but I couldn't work out whether it was because I wanted everyone else to leave as well, or because I wanted more people between me and the object of my distraction. A bit of both, perhaps.

I fumbled in my bag for my phone and pulled it out, flicking absently through my emails in an attempt to give the gesture validity. I wasn't sure why I bothered; this far underground there was no signal anyway, nothing new to read.

He'd know that, of course. But, then again, for all he knew I was reading something I'd already downloaded. That was believable, right?

God, I was being pathetic.

Oval station.

I put the phone back in my bag and watched with a mixture of horror and excitement as the remaining four passengers disembarked, leaving me alone with Emerald Eyes.

The door alarms sounded, signalling their imminent closure, and I started to panic as I realised I was going to be shut in alone with him. Would he say something?

He was looking at me with a determined set to his jaw as we pulled out of the station and into the darkness of the tunnel beyond. And then there was a smile, twitching with subtlety at the corners of his lips.

It looked like amusement, and I wondered about whether that was good for me or not, but there was no cruelty in his eyes. Just… something else.

I found myself unable to do anything but stare back at him as the seconds passed.

Wouldn't he say something?

The lights in the carriage flickered then went out, and my heart started beating at a million miles an hour. The darkness was broken only by intermittent flashes from the tunnel walls and by the light filtering through from the carriages to either side of us, which were still fully lit.

There was a soft, rustling noise to my right and I realised that he had sat down in the seat next to me. I had only split-seconds to take fright before he spoke.

'You remember.'

It wasn't a question.

Everything came rushing back with such shocking speed that it was almost physical, as if the train had swung a corner and thrown me back in my seat. I remembered his hands on my arms, his lips on my cheek and his body against mine. I remembered the soft, lilting accent in his voice, the scent of the rain on his skin and the rustle of his hair against my pillow. Most of all, I remembered the taste of his lips.

The sensation of the recollection was so familiar now that it barely threw me for a moment.

'Kieran,' I said.

He took my phone from my hands and put it carefully into my bag, which he lifted from my lap to the floor, then kissed me lightly on the mouth. I leaned into him, inhaling the familiar and earthy scent of him as I wrapped my hands around his neck and pulled him into a deeper embrace.

'Where have you been?' I murmured.

'It's only been a week.'

'Has it?'

'Yes.'

He pulled me across the seat and onto his lap, cocooning me in the warmth of his arms, and I finally relaxed for the first time all day.

'Well,' I said, 'I missed you. Are you hungry?'

There was a heavy silence. I pulled his jacket and T-shirt away from his neck and saw the fresh tracery of burns across his shoulders and his chest, the pale skin puckered and raw from the heat.

'She hurt you again,' I said.

'She always does, every day.'

'Then why do you go back?' I asked, although I already knew the answer.

He had no choice.

'You look tired,' he said, moving away from the subject. He looked so beaten that I accepted that for tonight.

'I'm fine,' I replied. 'I don't mind.'

I felt his fingertips brush my neck, pushing my hair behind my shoulder, and he lowered his head to my throat, the warmth of his breath sending a shiver through my body that awakened feelings in me that I knew we had no time for. Not tonight.

But then his lips touched my skin.

His teeth touched my skin.

His teeth broke my skin, and the endorphins flowed.

I gasped and wound my arms around him, into his hair, over his arms, up his thigh, over his chest, and back into his hair.

The doors to our carriage didn't open at Stockwell, leaving us sunken in darkness and ecstasy.

But in less than a minute it was over, his tongue licking the blood from my neck and sealing the punctures closed. He rearranged my hair over my shoulder, settling it back into its place, and the lights flickered back on.

I blinked blearily in the sudden brightness and

pushed my fingers through my hair, shrugging off the fog of euphoria.

Back to reality.

'I hate it when you come here,' I said. 'It's never long enough.'

'It won't always be this way.'

'Yes it will. You'll never leave her.'

'One day, I'll be free.'

I pushed myself out of his lap and back onto my own seat.

'One day,' I said, 'I'll be gone and it'll be too late.'

There was nothing for him to say to that, so he simply took my hand and kissed my palm.

'I'll see you on Saturday night,' he whispered.

'You remembered,' I said, surprised.

'I never forget,' he said, 'but you do.'

The motion of the carriage around me was rhythmic and soothing as we pulled into the station, the announcement of our impending arrival drawing me back into consciousness. I opened my eyes and pulled my head up, wiping self-consciously at the corners of my mouth in case I had drooled in my sleep.

I was the only one left in the carriage. I enjoyed a quiet moment of satisfaction at the fact that I was no longer sharing airspace with Mr Dickhead, who had clearly disembarked somewhere between here and Bank. Gathering up my bag from the floor, I hurried out onto the platform and into the night. My heels clicked as they ate up the short distance from the station to my flat, and within moments I was at my front door, key in hand. It didn't pay to hang around at this time of night, not in this part of the city.

The skin at my neck was itching and I felt it gingerly as I let myself in. Bloody mosquitoes again. They were going crazy this summer, and it was like I was some kind of magnet for them.

The hall light was on, but Dan would be in bed by now. Somehow, I didn't feel like I needed the wine anymore, or the bath. I was about as relaxed as I could be, and all I wanted was to curl up in bed next to him.

But I had a stop to make first.

I pushed open the door to my daughter's room as quietly as I could, not wanting to wake her but needing to see her, to reassure myself that all was well. Her messy, dark hair was spread on the pillow around her face, her eyes closed in sleep. She was growing up so fast that the guilt ate me upon evenings like tonight, evenings when I didn't even get to tuck her into bed.

She was turning six this weekend, my little Kiera, and she was already so beautiful that I almost couldn't believe she was ours.

Almost.

Last Christmas

The world used to be bigger. The land used to go on for miles, stretching into the distance so you could walk all day without ever getting your feet wet. There used to be people living here who didn't even know how to swim.

They're all gone now. All that's left are dregs and scavengers.

The ragtag group makes its way across the swampy ground from stream to pond to puddle. There are seven of them in all, an inauspicious number, but they don't care for superstition. They're opportunists, seizing on this chance to get in first, take what they can and get out again before anyone knows they've been here. Other people might worry about radiation and the uncovered remains of old munitions.

Mara does not.

She is approaching forty, with a striking combination of bright-blue eyes and brown skin. As far as she can remember, she has spent her whole life in and out of the water. She is in her element here.

'Time?' she says.

'Just before midnight,' one of the younger women replies. She's new to the group and Mara hasn't bothered to learn her name. She never will, since in fifty-four minutes' time the girl will be dead.

'Can you see anything yet?' Mara asks the man beside her.

Rui lifts the binoculars to his face and trains them on the centre of the lake. This whole area was underwater a week ago, but now the lake is all that remains of the sea that once covered this plain. The rest of the land has been reclaimed, pursuant to a pilot project that was the current government's ticket into power. But the earth is waterlogged and soggy, which is why it is also deserted. It will be some weeks before it hardens enough to support the construction vehicles that are supposed to be rebuilding the lost city.

Mara doubts the dams will last that long. She certainly has no intention of waiting.

'Rui?' she prompts him.

'Yeah, give me a minute…'

'Can you see it, or not?'

He pulls the glasses away from his face and glares at her. 'You do realise that it's pitch fucking black out here?'

It isn't, but Mara just nods and waves him back to his work. It's easier than arguing with him when he's coming down. They both know that he can see well enough; the moon is waning, but it's nearer full than crescent. They've travelled without lights from the stilt-borne slum where they gather in the evenings, so their eyes have adjusted to the moonlight. Rui is just frustrated and anxious that it's taking him so long to spot their target.

They all need this score, Rui more than most. He wouldn't have let himself go into withdrawal tonight, of all nights, if he could have afforded not to.

He is frozen, tense and still, scanning the lake while the other six stand at the edge of the water and watch it glint with waves. It's cold, but their wetsuits keep out the worst of the chill. A fish jumps out of the water, then flops back down into it, sideways. More follow, as though they're trying to escape the banks of the lake that now contain them.

Once they would have made the entire ocean their home, but even this last remnant will be drained soon. The fish jump as though they know they are on borrowed time.

'I don't like it,' says Osian.

'You never do,' Mara replies, which is an exaggeration, but not an unreasonable one. Osian is the eldest of the group by some five years, and it shows in his attitude. He is cautious, but it's difficult to discount his opinions on that basis when it has such an obvious benefit. He is old because he has been careful.

'I still don't like it,' he says. 'Look at the fish.'

Mara looks again. There is something in their movement that suggests urgency. If it had been only an hour or so since they had been trapped, perhaps that urgency would make sense, but it has been longer. Much longer.

Still, Mara laughs it off and squeezes Osian's

shoulder gently.

'You worry too much,' she says.

He pats her hand, resigned to being considered an old fool, then pulls away and walks to the water's edge.

'You don't remember it,' he murmurs. 'You don't know what it was like.'

But Mara has heard enough about the flood that a shiver of fear runs down her spine anyway. Still, it changes nothing. They need this, and she can't afford to spread doubt amongst their party.

'There!' Rui shouts, pointing. 'I see it. Off to the left, a little more than halfway across.'

'Are you sure?'

He hands the binoculars to Mara, looking over her shoulder to direct her to their target.

'There,' he says. 'You see it? There's a rod on top of it, sticking up from those rocks.'

The wind changes slightly, and Mara sees something move. She catches her breath.

'Is that… the weathervane?'

Rui grins. 'The Daggett Dragon.'

The four youngsters whoop and laugh, passing the binoculars between them until they have each picked out the tarnished gold dragon topping the structure that pokes out of the lake.

Mara meets Osian's eyes in the darkness.

There is no way around this now: they are going into the water.

Isaac scouts on ahead. His dark skin and suit render him practically invisible, so those waiting on the bank can only mark his route by the small splashes he leaves in his wake. He's halfway to the weathervane by the time he pulls himself up onto a rock, dangling his feet over the edge while he sits and waits for them to follow.

The lake is too wide to cross without a break, and he's picked a good resting point.

Mara checks through the binoculars then approves it, nodding to the others to push out the dinghy. Osian climbs on board, holding their equipment securely in place, but the boat is too small to carry anyone else. They swim alongside, pushing their cargo silently across the lake.

There's no talking now.

The breeze has died down, leaving the surface of the water as smooth as glass. The fish are no longer jumping, so there is barely a ripple in sight.

As they approach the middle of the lake, it becomes clear that Isaac is not sitting on a rock, but on a rooftop. Half-crumbled masonry peeks out from the water, the stonework pockmarked from where wood supports have rotted away. The roof has disintegrated in places, pulled apart so thoroughly that it looks as though it has been smashed through, but there's still enough algae-covered slate on top to provide a ledge for them all to rest.

They're within twenty feet of the resting point when it happens, far enough from the shore that there can be no turning back.

The new girl disappears.

She doesn't shout or splash or make any noise at all. She simply disappears.

No one notices until Osian turns around and sees that she is missing. She was swimming at the back of the pack, pushing the dinghy from behind, and now there is no trace of her.

'Stop,' he says. 'Wait.'

The others pick up on the quiet panic in his voice and start scanning the water, searching for whatever has alarmed him. Then they count heads and realise that five plus one does not make seven.

'What happened?' Mara asks. 'Where is she?'

The dinghy shunts forward abruptly, throwing Osian on top of the equipment and pushing the boat into the side of the roof where Isaac is waiting for them.

'Fuck,' Rui mutters.

Everyone else is too busy scrambling out of the water to make a coherent sound.

They line up along the slippery rooftop, wetsuits dripping dry as they stare at the water. It is empty and black, like a pool of ink beneath them. Nothing moves.

'Did you see what happened?' Mara asks Isaac.

His eyes are wide. 'I looked away from her, and when I looked back she was gone. I don't know. I guess she went under.'

They continue to stare at the water, because it means they don't have to look at each other and see their uncertainty mirrored back at them.

'Probably got her foot stuck in some weed,' Rui says.

'Or caught on a rooftop,' says Isaac. 'This isn't the only building underwater here.'

Mara nods, but not in agreement. It is a gesture of finality: the matter is closed. They will forget it ever happened, and that should be easy, because they all care more about the prize than they care about the girl. She was practically a stranger.

But her death still matters, not because they are kind,

but because they are selfish, and intelligent enough to know what this means for their own safety.

None of them can forget the way the dinghy slammed into the building.

Not one of them believes the girl drowned by accident.

They wait on the rooftop for half an hour. Mara allows them only that much time to refuel, because any less would leave them exhausted, but any more would be an indulgence. They're here for a reason. If they hadn't been willing to risk their lives, then none of them would have come this far.

But they're still reluctant to get back in the water.

Kemba, the youngest, is the first in. She needs this as much as anyone. The rest follow, but Caleb holds back. He joined up only a few months ago, blond and young and a little too full of wonder for Mara's taste. He's only here because of his proficiency with locks.

'It's just like the story,' Caleb says to Rui in a whisper.

'Don't be an idiot,' Rui replies, but he's whispering too. There's a shiver in his voice. Mara can't tell whether it's from the cold, the jonesing or the fear. Maybe all three.

'Come on,' she says to Caleb, raising her voice deliberately. 'Or do you want us to leave you behind?'

He jumps into the water, swimming fast so he isn't the one bringing up the rear. He has learned his lesson.

They swim quickly and silently. They don't need to keep their voices down – there's no one out here to hear them – but they do anyway. Instinct is working overtime. Their movements are economical and brisk: fast strokes, smooth kicks, minimal splashing.

It almost works.

Almost.

The building becomes clearer as they approach it. What looked like a hunk of moonlit rock from the shore is actually a two-storey structure of glass, metal and stone. Above them, the skeleton of the building overhangs its two wings, which fan out to make a U-shaped footprint. It must have been glorious once, large and grand enough to suit its owners, but now it is nothing more than a rotting wreck. The stones are slick with weed, the metal rusted and warped. One of the huge windows at water-level has shattered, leaving a cavity through which the tide laps into the shell of an entrance hall. It takes rubbish in with it: bottles, driftwood and the miscellaneous plastic scum of life before the flood.

No one has been here for thirty-five years. For thirty-five years, this room has been underwater.

A half-staircase rises out of the detritus. Osian heads there, dragging the dinghy behind him as he wades in through the window frame.

The others follow. Caleb is last out of the water.

He stumbles as he tries to haul himself over the ledge and into the building. At first it seems as though he is simply tired, that he hasn't kicked himself out of the water hard enough, but then he jerks backwards with a cry.

Isaac is closest to him. He turns and grabs Caleb's hand as he starts to disappear back into the water.

'Help me!' Isaac yells.

Kemba runs to hold onto Isaac, while Rui grabs Caleb's other hand. Between the three of them, they try to drag Caleb out of the water, but they can't shift him. He's stuck there, waist-deep in the water, screaming as his joints crack with the tension. Meanwhile, Osian is scrabbling in the equipment strapped to the dinghy.

'Hurry!' Mara says to him, gesturing impatiently.

'I'm hurrying!'

Eventually, he finds what he's looking for and shoves a weapon into Mara's hands, taking one for himself as well. He needn't have bothered, because Mara is already jumping into the water with her spear.

It's dark in the water, even darker than it is up above. The government's draining of the land has stirred up dirt and sand, and Mara struggles to see anything beyond the range of her own hands. It takes a moment for her to orient herself, to see the flash of silver glinting in the moonlight as the creature thrashes back and forth, trying to dislodge its prey from the shore. Its massive tail swirls and flicks, pushing Mara back while it drags Caleb down.

Mara darts forward, stabbing with the spear. It glances off the side of the creature, not drawing blood, but making it loosen its jaws. Caleb slips free. Then the creature turns on Mara, looking for a substitute. It opens its jaws, revealing a wide maw filled with teeth that seem to glitter through the murky water. With a final thrust, Mara wedges the spear into its mouth then kicks towards the surface with a desperate stream of bubbles following in her wake.

Osian's hands are waiting for her, pulling her from the water with a grip that squeezes hard enough to bruise.

Caleb is lying on his back in the shallow water beyond the window frame. Mara joins him there, collapsing as the adrenaline bleeds out of her and leaves her gasping for air.

'You alright?' she asks.

'Yes,' he says, but he's wincing. 'Did you see it?'

'Just a big pike,' she says. 'That's all. Big teeth, but just a pike.'

'Tell that to my leg,' says Caleb.

He's entitled to be bitter. There are gouge marks down each side of his calf muscle where jagged teeth have torn clean through the fabric of his wetsuit.

Mara tries to get up, but Osian pushes her back down. 'Rest,' he says. 'We'll unpack the dinghy.'

She doesn't argue, she just lies down next to Caleb.

'Don't tell me that wasn't real,' he mutters.

The others work while the two of them look up through the rusted girders above their heads, watching the wind change as the moonlight shines off the coiling weathervane dragon.

The Daggett mansion was placed carefully, high on a hill in the middle of the plain, lest any of the locals forgot who was lording his wealth over them. The building was visible for miles in every direction, so they were well aware of their subjugation. They knew who was gouging them for rent, who was poisoning their crops with his run-off, and who was water-logging them by pumping water from his land into theirs. When they got sick, the stagnant pools of standing water were usually the culprits. When injuries to feet and legs became infected so badly that gangrene set in, they knew who to blame. But blame was the only power they had.

Now the mansion sits empty, as ruined as the land that once surrounded it.

'It's huge,' says Kemba as they crest the top of the short staircase.

The steps lead up from the entryway into the first floor, such as it is. The struts supporting the floorboards have fallen away entirely in the centre of the room, leaving small ledges around the walls that are only just wide enough for Osian and Rui to negotiate with their bundles of equipment, but are too narrow for two people to walk side by side. Isaac has to carry Caleb on his back, with Kemba and Mara following on behind.

The upper floors of the building's wings would once have branched off from this room, but there are only uprights and scraps remaining. The sole purpose of the room now is to provide access to the staircase on its far side that leads down into the house proper.

'It's a good thing these steps are marble,' says Isaac as he and Caleb follow the others down into the room below. It's on the same level as the entryway, with doors on either side that lead into the ground levels of the wings. 'Is this floor safe?'

The water level sits half a foot above what might once have been carpet. Osian hangs his pack on an overhead girder and stamps on the ground a few times.

'Concrete,' he confirms. 'Solid.'

'Okay,' says Mara. 'Rui and Kemba, search the east wing. Osian and I will search west. Isaac, search this block. Caleb, stay here and keep your leg out of the water. I don't want you gunking it up and getting sick before we can get into the vault and get out of here.'

'But you're fine for me to get sick after, right?' Caleb says, settling himself onto the steps. 'As long as it doesn't interfere with the plan?'

Isaac cuffs him on the ear. 'You want us to leave you behind?'

'Ow,' says Caleb, rubbing the side of his face.

'Don't tempt me. I'm not looking for a reason to carry you back out of here.'

They search. Between the five of them, they wade through every room, pushing aside rotten furniture, opening cupboards, moving picture frames and lifting up carpets. For an hour they fill the air with sound of dynamo torches winding as they shine light into every corner.

'So where's the treasure?' Rui says when they reconvene. 'Where's the vault?'

'Downstairs,' says Osian.

Rui looks around the room, then turns back to Osian. 'What stairs? This is the ground floor.'

'There's always a downstairs. These people were rich. Really rich. They would have had a bunker.'

'No, they would have had a helicopter,' says Rui. 'Fancy place like this. They wouldn't have hidden in the basement, waiting for the water pressure to break the walls, waiting to starve. They would have gotten into their shiny helicopter and flown away somewhere better, probably somewhere on the continent where they still have more overground acres than they do people.'

Osian is feeling around along the wall under the stairs. He pulls off his gloves, going fingertip to marble until he finds the join. When he does, the door clicks open under his touch to reveal the contents of a shallow cupboard: an airtight metal hatch with a wheel in the centre to seal it closed. It resembles a bulkhead door, set a foot above the floor as though whoever designed it had predicted the maximum water level.

Wealth on the scale of the Daggett fortune could afford that kind of precision.

'Aha,' Rui says, walking towards the door, but Osian stops his hand before he can turn the wheel.

'Not yet.' Osian retrieves his bundle of equipment, then he fiddles with the seals and presses devices up against the metal. He listens. When he's satisfied, he drills through the door and tests the air that comes out through the hole he's made.

Finally, he says, 'Safe.' Then he turns to Rui. 'You can open it.'

But Osian's care has made Rui nervous.

'You first,' he says.

Osian looks at Mara for confirmation, then he spins the wheel. The door swings open easily.

'It wasn't locked?' Mara asks.

'Should it have been?'

'I guess not.' But Mara is uneasy. There's something about this place, about the way the moonlight catches the edges of its structure, that gives her the creeps. It's oppressive, like a memory waiting out of sight in the seconds after you wake up, a dread that builds in the moments before reality rushes back in. She is not sure how hard she wants to examine it.

The others seem to feel it too. A hush descends on them as Osian pulls the door wide. The air that rises up is dry, but surprisingly fresh.

'Stairs,' he says. 'Going down.'

'It's a bunker after all,' says Kemba. 'Do you think they're still—'

'No,' Mara interrupts. She doesn't want Kemba speculating, not when they're already twitchy.

That doesn't mean she's not cautious. She is not an idiot, but if there's any real danger then she and Osian are prepared enough for all of them. He steps forward, hand on the gun at his hip, with Mara following close behind. The others fall in line.

The staircase seems longer than it should be, descending deeper than a floor. Tension can distort reality like that. Mara knows this and slows her breathing, consciously regulating her intake. The air tickles the back of her throat.

'I don't know why you're all so worried,' Rui says, breaking the silence. 'I'm telling you, there's no fucking way they would have hidden in a bunker. They got out by helicopter.'

Osian has reached the bottom of the stairs. He stops walking, blocking the passage from view.

'No, they didn't,' he says. 'They never left.'

It happened quicker than you'd guess. People imagined it would take thousands of years to melt every piece of ice on the planet, hundreds for the water level to rise and swallow the coastal land.

It didn't.

Ironically, there was a snowball effect. It was compound, not linear, meaning that each melt encouraged another, bigger melt. The flooding that had started when Mara was a baby had reached its apex by the time she was three. By the time Mara was adopted aged five, there was no more ice left to melt. It cascaded across this plain, rising in waves that engulfed even the hill on which the Daggett mansion stood. Within minutes, it was all under water.

When people found shelter, they had to do it quickly.

But Mara remembers none of this. She is as much in the dark as Rui and his friends.

'Fuck,' he says.

There are two skeletons at the bottom of the stairs, propped up against the walls like gatekeepers. Their skin has mostly disintegrated and fallen away, but some parts of it have been mummified by the air conditioning.

'There's still power down here?' Rui asks.

'They must have a tidal stream generator,' says Osian. 'There was always water here, even before the mansion was built. They had a moat around this house once.'

'A moat?' says Kemba.

'There are photos in the library in Highridge. I used to work there.'

'Really?' she asks, impressed by his credentials. Rui scoffs.

'Really,' Osian confirms, ignoring Rui.

The library is a huge building on the cliff that overlooks the stilt-town. It's on prime land, staffed by the best and brightest for the benefit of the most rich and privileged. Getting a job there is remarkable, but it's even more remarkable that Osian managed to lose it. Once your feet are under the table, you're usually set for life.

'Tell her the rest,' says Mara, glad of the distraction. She kicks the skeletons out of the doorway as she pushes into the room beyond.

'He fucked a rich girl,' says Rui, following Mara in, 'and so she did what rich girls always do.'

He waits for Kemba to rise to the bait.

'And what's that?' she asks obligingly.

Rui smiles over his shoulder at her. 'She fucked him right back.'

They don't need the torches down here. The space is illuminated by low-level lighting set into the ceilings. Motion-activated emergency lights.

'It's dry,' says Kemba, surprised.

'And huge,' Rui adds.

He's not exaggerating. They've stepped out into a massive, multi-purpose living space. The ceiling is supported by regular columns that separate the kitchen from the dining room, the dining room from a seating area, and the seating area from what looks like a library. At the far end of the room, a corridor snakes back into darkness.

Maya wanders into the dining area, her rubber soles dragging against the deep-pile carpet.

'It's amazing,' Kemba goes on. 'All this time under water and it's not just dry down here, it's so dry that it doesn't even smell damp.'

'Did you want to move in?' Rui jokes.

But Kemba looks entirely serious as she replies, 'Yes. It's gorgeous.'

The table is laid. There's no food, but the cutlery, crockery and glassware is set for four. A centrepiece of pinecones and dried citrus is circled by Christmas crackers. The crackers are foreign to Mara, a legacy of a time when it was possible to keep them dry. Rui pulls one apart and gets a shock.

'Christmas,' Osian says. 'It happened at Christmas. I remember that.'

'This was what Christmas used to be like?' Isaac asks.

'No.' Osian's reply is quiet. 'Not for us.'

There's a tree in the corner, plastic so it hasn't shed, with coloured lights draped all over it. They're still twinkling. Ornaments adorn the boughs: shiny baubles, plastic icicles and wooden toys that look as though they were handmade by amateurs. They are the tradition of this dead family, but they hold no meaning for Mara. She takes one from the tree, a little angel with matchstick wings, and turns it in her fingers. It so fragile that if she applies too much pressure, it will splinter into pieces.

'Why's there no dust?' Isaac says, helping Caleb down the stairs and into a chair. 'Have you noticed that? It's like they only just walked away.'

Caleb snorts painfully, looking at the skeletons. 'They didn't walk anywhere. But I'd like to.'

Isaac takes the hint, pulling out the medical kit he snagged from the dinghy and getting to work on Caleb's wounds.

'He's right,' says Kemba, looking around the room.

'The place was sealed,' says Mara, not wanting them to get ideas in their heads. They're already spooked about the attack. 'There's no way for dust to form if the place is sealed.'

'But the bodies decomposed,' Kemba points out. 'And there's air-conditioning in here. See.' She points to a vent.

Mara shrugs, dismissing it. 'No one's been here for decades.'

Rui is already rummaging through cupboards, which is enough to distract Kemba from the weirdness of the bunker. She joins him, going room to room as they search for things they can sell. They're after precious metals and jewellery, because despite the state of the world, the things that were once considered precious are even more so now. So much was lost. Mara and Osian search for food, but they'll eat it rather than selling it. Their customers aren't interested in food. It doesn't matter to them that there's so little land left for sowing or grazing, because they reap everything it produces. The rest of the population are lucky if they can catch enough fish to live on.

'Leave the food,' says Rui as Osian carries more tins from the kitchen. 'We can buy whatever we like when we find the treasure.'

'Old habits die hard,' Osian says, going back for more. Mara joins him. They've emptied the cupboards by the time Rui and Kemba finish their search.

They've found nothing. Rui is not pleased.

'Then where's the damn treasure?' he says. 'If the stories were right about the dragon, then they have to be right about the treasure.'

'It was a big fish,' Mara scoffs. 'Hardly a dragon.' She can feel anxious sweat prickling under her arms, but Caleb doesn't challenge her answer.

'Just because dragons and treasure fit together in

stories, that doesn't mean they fit together in real life,' says Osian.

'Anyway,' Mara goes on, 'I didn't come here looking for a legend. I came here looking for the things that rich people leave behind. The rich people died here, so that has to be a good sign. It means they didn't have a chance to take anything with them. So stop worrying about treasure, and look for a safe instead. There has to be one around here somewhere.'

But another search of the rooms reveals nothing, and it's not long before Rui is kicking off again.

'This is bullshit,' he yells, pushing over a side table. 'It's just books and furniture and rubbish. Where are the fucking jewels?'

He picks up a book, ready to throw it at the television screen, but Kemba catches his arm before he can cause any more damage.

'Have they got LifeDrives?' she says, with the kind of patience that hints at them being more than friends. 'Did you check?'

'Fuck. No.'

Rui drops the book, rushes over to the television and opens the cupboard beneath it. He isn't careful. He pulls out wires and consoles, discs and data cards until he uncovers a box behind everything else, still active after all these years. There's a green light blinking on its face. Four slots are filled, one LifeDrive inserted into each.

They're still trying to record, even thirty-five years after the lives to which they're linked have been extinguished.

'Load one up,' Mara says, dropping into an armchair

opposite the screen. Osian takes the one next to her, while Isaac sits on the sofa where he's tending to Caleb's leg.

It takes a while for Kemba and Rui to find the right remotes and press the right buttons, but once they have, four photos pop up on the screen: a brown-skinned family. There's a name under each.

Veronique, under a picture of a stylish-looking woman in her thirties, tanned and lithe, wearing dark clothes and diamonds.

Paul, a stern face on top of a fat neck. He wears a suit and tie, and his face is thickly-lined. He looks about fifty, but it's difficult to tell whether his facial lines are wrinkles or just the result of his frown. He could be anywhere from thirty to sixty.

Tammy, a toddler with curly blonde pigtails.

And finally, *Eli*, a surly teenager with dark hair and flashing eyes.

'You pick,' Kemba says, handing the remote to Rui.

He picks Paul.

'I'm not doing this again,' Veronique says, looking straight into the camera, into Paul's eyes. 'I can't go through another Christmas dinner with the two of you at each others' throats.'

'He's out of control,' a disembodied voice says. Veronique continues to look directly at the camera, so the voice must be Paul's. 'How do you ever expect him to learn if there are never any consequences for his actions? He has to be taught. If you won't do it, then I will.'

'Any other day of the year,' she says, pleading. 'Any

other day, but not today. It's Christmas. Can't you make an effort?'

'I'm not the one who should have to.'

The image pans as Paul turns away.

'He's just a child,' Veronique begs from offscreen. 'You're the adult.'

'And in a year's time, he will be too. He's my son, not yours. He needs discipline. He needs to learn that if he wants to benefit from this family's wealth, then he has to earn it.'

'Rich people's problems,' Rui says, skipping ahead. 'Boring. Let's get to the part where he goes to the safe to bask in the warm glow of his vast piles of gold.'

'Wait,' Isaac says, snatching the remote before he can scroll too far forwards. 'I want to see what Christmas used to be like.'

Veronique looks at the little girl and smiles. Across the table from her, the teenager stares down into his plate, shovelling food into his mouth without making eye contact with anyone.

For a minute or so, the only sounds are the clink of cutlery on crockery and the chalkboard scrape of teeth on fork tines.

'Well,' Veronique says eventually, a rictus-smile fixed on her face. 'Isn't this nice?'

No one answers her.

The little girl seems worried, looking between Veronique and Paul, but the teenager just keeps on eating in silence, head bent over his plate.

'Answer your mother,' Paul says to him in a tone like

thunder.

'Paul—' says Veronique, but then she goes quiet, her smile slipping for just a moment.

'And you could try eating like a human being for once,' Paul says, turning his attention back to the teenager, 'instead of troughing away like a pig. If you want to eat, then you'll do it with good manners, or you won't do it at all.'

The boy pauses for a moment with his fork in the air, straightens his back, then starts eating again, more deliberately this time. He still doesn't raise his eyes. He is like a frightened animal, praying that if he doesn't look at the predator, then it won't see him.

'Shall we pull the crackers?' Veronique suggests.

'More plastic tat,' Paul mutters loudly. 'More rubbish we don't need.'

The family finishes their meal without saying another word.

Rui snatches back the remote and hits fast-forward.

'Satisfied?' he says to Isaac. 'Rich people are awful and they don't deserve their money. Enough said.'

'Wait,' says Kemba. If it had been anyone else asking then Rui would have carried on regardless, but he presses play for her, stopping the flickering time-lapse on the screen.

Paul is alone, sitting in a large room with a wall of glass. Beyond it is only water, a striking blue, cut through by intermittent washes of sunshine that filter down from above. He sits in a leather chair and watches the colours change.

* * *

'Where's that room?' Kemba asks. 'Is it here?'

'Not that I've seen,' says Isaac.

Everyone trades glances, but none of them recognise the place.

'Then there must be another level to this place, down below this one,' says Mara. 'A room we haven't found yet. A room with a window onto the moat.'

'Then let's spin on,' says Rui, trying to find the point in the recording where Paul enters or exits the room.

Mara is the only one who notices the flash of silver in the water before the picture speeds away.

She remembers the 'pike'. She remembers the way her spear glanced off its side with a jarring clang, as though it were made of stone, not flesh. She remembers the way its flanks shone, resembling nothing so much as a huge metallic snake, flying through the water on winged fins.

The Daggett Dragon.

When Paul leaves the glass-walled room, he goes from a dark space into the corner of the multi-purpose room. His family waits in the seating area, all except Eli, who is already walking towards him.

'You can't do this,' he says. The boy's face is contorted in anger, but his tone is one of disbelief. 'Do you know how many lives you're ruining? Do you have any idea—'

'You don't know what you're talking about,' Paul says, walking past him to where Veronique and little Tammy sit on bright white sofas.

Eli follows him.

'*I'm not an idiot and I'm not a child,*' he says. His voice is shaking as he speaks, as though he has been fearfully repressing the words for so long that now they've started coming he can't make them stop. '*It's all about you, isn't it? All you care about is getting more of everything, even if it leaves nothing for anyone else. When will you have enough? Never. You'll just keep taking and taking.*'

There is a pause in which time seems to stop.

'*You have no comprehension of how the world works,*' Paul says, slowly, dragging out each word in perfect control. '*Do you know what's coming? What will you do when there's no land left, no food? You'll be thanking me then. You'll be grateful that I, at least, have the capacity for good sense.*'

'*You're wrong,*' Eli says. '*You're miserly and elitist and wrong.*'

The screen goes perfectly still, so still that it looks almost frozen, but there are slight points of movement: the flames waving in the fireplace, the rise and fall of Eli's chest, and the fear flickering in his eyes.

All at once, the camera rushes forward and a hand wraps around Eli's upper arm. He struggles, but then a second hand flashes into view, blurring across the screen and leaving a trail of blood dripping from Eli's nose.

'*Do you know what I've done for this family?*' Paul says, his voice eerily calm. '*Do you have any concept of how hard I've worked to give you a home, an education, and all the security you could ask for? You're a selfish, ungrateful child.*'

'*You're calling* me *selfish?*' Eli spits back, spraying

blood into the air. 'I never wanted this. I never asked for it, and I don't want anything you can give me. I'll take my chances out there on my own.'

'No, you won't, my boy.'

The camera pans as Paul drags Eli towards the corner of the room. He opens a cupboard door and rolls back the carpet covering the floor to reveal a hatch. He spins it open with one hand and throws Eli into the room below with the other, stomping on the boy's hands and legs to shove him through the hole.

There is a sickening thud as Eli hits the ground in the darkness. Then nothing.

'You'll stay down there until New Year,' Paul yells down, then he closes the hatch and locks it in place with the wheel.

When he turns back, Veronique has moved away.

'We're leaving,' she says. She has Tammy in her arms, even though the girl is really too big to be carried on the hip. 'I told you I wasn't going through this again, and I meant it.'

'Really?' He laughs. The adrenaline has tinged his voice with hysteria. 'Where are you going to go?' He takes a step towards her and she flinches back. 'You have nowhere to go, Veronique. You have no money. No family. No friends that aren't more my friends than yours. Do you think it'll be easy to give all this up?'

She's backing towards the door, towards the staircase that would take her up into the main building and out.

'I can't live like this,' she says, cradling the girl closer to cover her ears. 'I won't do it, Paul. I'll take her away with me. Away from you. You just watch me.'

The camera's focus moves to the little girl,

bewildered and frightened in her mother's arms, then back up to Veronique's face. When Paul speaks again, his voice is softer, calmer. The excitement has passed out of it.

'I didn't mean to upset you,' he says, holding out a hand to his wife. 'You know what it's like with teenagers. He knows exactly what to say to rile me up. He'll be gone next year, away at university, and that'll be the end of it.'

Veronique doesn't move.

'Come on,' Paul goes on, gesturing with the hand he is offering her. 'Don't get taken in by his dramatics. Let's not let it ruin Christmas.'

Veronique wavers, but she doesn't seem convinced. Then Tammy reaches out to take Paul's hand, her little fist wrapping around his fingers, and Veronique lets herself be pulled along in their wake.

A few minutes later, the family goes to bed. There's a short sequence of half-lit movement that is impossible to make out after that, then the screen goes black.

There is nothing else.

Osian finds the hatch in the bottom of the bedroom wardrobe, exactly where the LifeDrive showed it would be. It's been carpeted over, but all they have to do is roll it away, and there's the metal door, locked down and watertight.

'Me first,' says Rui.

He's getting desperate now. There's sweat rolling down his face. Mara is dreading the idea of the journey back across the lake, because whatever they find in this place, they'll have to get back home and sell it before

Rui will be able to get his hands on what he needs. He's going to be a nightmare for the next few hours, and she's the one who'll have to manage him. She always is.

He spins the wheel and yanks the hatch up and open, but Osian stops him before he can jump down.

'Wait,' he says.

Mara remembers that he hasn't yet drilled and tested this door like he did the previous one. At first, she thinks that's what is bothering him. When he rummages in his pack, she assumes it is to pull out the equipment he used earlier. Then she sees the guns in his hands. He passes them out, one each. He hesitates before giving one to Rui, seeing the way his fingers are twitching from withdrawal, but something overrules his caution. He hands over the gun.

'Expecting more skeletons?' Rui says.

'Shh,' Osian replies, nodding towards the hatch.

Then Mara notices it too. The hatch doesn't open from the inside. If the LifeDrives recorded the last moments of Paul's life accurately, then he died in his bed the night he threw Eli down this hatch.

'You think the boy's still down there?' Rui whispers.

'Shh,' Osian says again. 'Look at the light.'

It's bright downstairs, brighter than it is up here, and there's a sound: a low rhythm, as though someone is softly playing music. The smell that wafts up to them is not dry and sterile, but fusty and stale. It smells lived-in.

Mara and Osian exchange glances, then she settles her gun on her hip and says, 'I'll go.'

This was her idea. It's her job, her dream score, the

prize she's been obsessing over her entire life. She considered diving down to it when she was younger, that's how much the Daggett treasure called to her. When she heard that the government was draining the land, it was Mara who gathered the crew and made the plan.

Now that she's here, she will see it through to the bitter end.

The room she drops down into is very different from the one they saw on Paul's LifeDrive. The glass wall is still there, cold and imposing, but almost everything else is different. Every piece of furniture has been moved, every ornament rearranged, and the carpet is worn and dirty. Everything is dirty.

The noise is coming from a corridor leading away from the glass.

Osian drops down silently behind her, followed by each of the others. Despite their protests, even Caleb insists on joining them.

'I want to see it,' he whispers, lowering himself awkwardly through the hatch. 'I want to see the treasure.'

They're all catching the fever.

Unfortunately, Caleb's landing is far from graceful. He crashes to the ground with a hollow thunk that announces their presence better than any fanfare.

'Shit,' Mara mutters.

The music goes silent. They all freeze, guns raised. A few seconds later, there is the sound of a shotgun ratcheting. Rui jumps about half a foot in the air, and Mara worries that he's going to squeeze off a shot without meaning to.

'Is there anyone here?' Osian calls out.

The man who steps out from the corridor is old. His face is even more deeply-lined than Paul's was in his picture on the LifeDrive, but he is thinner.

And he is angry.

'Calm down,' Osian says, raising his gun to point it at the man. 'We're not here to hurt you.'

'You could've fooled me,' the man replies. His voice is soft and rough from disuse.

The safe is open on the other side of the room. Seeing that Osian and the others have the man covered, Isaac doesn't waste any time. He rushes towards it, scooping handfuls of banknotes into a duffle bag.

But the man doesn't hesitate either, swinging around the muzzle of his gun to track Isaac's movements. He fires only one cartridge, but it detonates in a spray of shot that practically cuts Isaac in two. Everyone starts shooting then. Rui is peppering the walls with bullets. The man gets off one more round, hitting Kemba in the stomach, before Mara's pistol takes him down.

'Fuck,' Rui says from behind Mara. She rushes forward to kick the shotgun away from the man's outstretched hand. 'Fuck, fuck, fuck.'

He isn't dead yet, but he's not far off.

'You fool,' she says to him. 'You should've just let us take the money. Is there anyone else here?'

But the man doesn't reply. Instead, he squints up at her and says, 'Mara?'

She freezes. She is sure that no one has said her name since they entered the house.

'Come closer,' he whispers. 'Please, Mara.'

Please, Mara.

Something cracks open inside her, something so painful that she shoves it away again before she can recall what it means. Nonetheless, it draws her closer. Without any conscious thought, she finds herself crouching on the floor next to the dying man.

His hand touches her cheek, then goes still. 'You came back,' he whispers. 'I always knew you'd come back.'

His hand drops from her cheek to the floor. Mara looks at it, then at him. He has her dimpled chin, her brown skin, her own blue eyes, though his are staring at the ceiling now, sightless.

You came back.

'What the fuck was that all about?' Rui says, staring at Kemba's body. The gun is shaking in his outstretched hand. He's losing it, his voice a broken soundscape of yells and whispers.

Caleb moves over to Isaac's body, walking with an uneven gait that favours his injured leg. He bends down. Mara thinks he's mourning for a moment, but then the boy pushes Isaac's body off the bag of money and goes back to filling it, as though nothing has happened.

'Fuck,' Rui says, laughing and crying at the same time.

There's a tapping from the glass wall. A few of Rui's wild bullets have hit it, and now lines are snaking out from the impact points as it bows under the pressure of the water.

'Hurry up,' Osian says to Caleb, watching the wall.

'How long have we got?' Mara asks him.

'Not long.'

Rui shoves the gun into his belt and goes to help Caleb. That's when Mara sees it: the flash of silver in the black. It's hard to pick out, because the bright lights in the basement room reflect awkwardly from the glass, but it was there. She is sure.

'Did you—' she says to Osian, but now he is staring at the glass in horror.

There is a thump from beyond it. Water is starting to trickle through the cracks in the weakened glass, encouraged by the press of an enormous body on the other side of the wall.

The Daggett Dragon.

It is five times the length of a man, half fish, half snake, with silver-scaled coils that screw through the water, propelling it into the wall. Fins spread out like wings behind it, fluttering with the grace of toile in the wind. Its jaws stretch wide, displaying rows of teeth as sharp as daggers. It roars soundlessly, pushing bubbles from its throat. It is so beautiful that Mara finds herself frozen, captivated by the way the moonlight shines off its skin.

Then it breaks through the glass, and time back rushes in. Water rushes in too, sweeping the banknotes into a tsunami of paper, but that lasts for only a second before Mara and Osian are hurled against the opposite wall with the force of the incoming wave.

The dragon comes with it, an articulated monster of silver plate and blades.

The water is already rising to the ceiling, kept out only by the force of the air that is trapped inside. Soon the pressure will equalise, and the entire building will flood.

Mara forces her eyes open in the stinging gloom. They have to reach the hatch.

The creature goes for Caleb first, finishing what it started when they first crossed the lake. It takes him in its jaws and bites him in two, then spits out the pieces. When it turns back towards Mara and Osian, its tail catches Rui across the chest, slashing open his stomach. He will not be coming out of the water.

Meanwhile, Osian has found the hatch. He grabs Mara's shoulder and drags her up out of the depths, hauling her towards their only way out. There is just a foot of air left between the water and the ceiling.

They both have one hand on the ladder when Osian disappears, tugged down and out of sight as silent as a breath. Mara dives down after him, sees the end of the dragon's tail curled around his ankle, and points her gun.

The shot ricochets off the scales, but it distracts the dragon enough that the creature lets go of Osian. Mara pulls him to her, shoving him towards the ladder, interposing herself between him and the dragon.

It turns to look at her.

She's expecting a strike, expecting that it will dart forward and snatch her in its jaws, but it doesn't move. Instead, crammed and coiled in the remains of the room, it fans its fins out behind itself and watches, statue-still, as she sculls backwards to the ladder. It is a sunken relic, motionless and haunting in the dark water. Blue light glints in the depths of its eyes, familiar and chilling.

Osian grabs her collar, pulling her back up to the

surface. Only a few inches of air remain now, but they're academic because Mara's hands are already on the rungs of the ladder, climbing automatically towards the air-filled room above.

When she's through, Osian reaches up to catch her hand. She manages to drag him through the hatch before the watch level rises beyond it. They slam it shut and spin the wheel, sealing the water beneath them.

They are both soaking wet and filthy, and Osian is bleeding from a deep graze along his arm. Some of the glass must have caught him when the wall burst in, or maybe it was the point of the creature's tail.

Mara doesn't have a scratch on her.

'Daggett Dragon,' she says, rolling onto her back. 'Damn dragon is real.'

But Osian isn't interested in the fish creature.

'Mara,' he says, his voice shaking. 'How did he know your name?'

'Who?' She is out of breath.

'What do you mean, *who*? That man. That man we just killed.'

There is a long pause as they each count the bodies that are floating in the water beneath their feet.

Rui. Kemba. Caleb. Isaac.

Eli.

She killed Eli.

'I don't know,' Mara says eventually.

'I don't believe you.'

They look at each other for a long moment before Mara pushes herself to her feet and walks over to the television. She pulls her waterlogged gun out of her belt on the way, dropping it onto a side table, then sits down in one of the armchairs. With trembling fingers, she picks up the remote and selects a different LifeDrive on the screen.

Eli.

The screen shows an enclosed space, dimly illuminated by one emergency light.

The little girl's face is in the middle of the picture.

'We're going to leave this mausoleum,' the boy says to her. 'Pack what you need, but nothing more than you can fit in your rucksack, okay?'

'Eli—'

'You can do it. All right?'

The little girl nods seriously.

'Okay. Now, do you think you can turn on the power for me? Dad's revoked my permissions.'

Tammy turns to a box by the wall and, with Eli's help, pushes her tiny thumb up against the sensor. It flashes for a second, then turns green with a quiet click. The screen above the sensor reads: Thumbprint recognised: Daggett, Tamara.

The overhead lights come on, flooding the room. In their reflected glare, the water beyond the glass wall is black, black, black.

Now that the power is on, Eli opens the safe with a code that's written on a scrap of paper he produces from his pocket. The lock glows green. He swings the door open, then starts pulling out banknotes and jewels.

'Go,' he says to Tammy, pushing her in the direction of a side corridor. 'Hurry. Get what you need.'

By the time she returns, Eli has filled his entire bag with riches, so much that he can barely zip it closed, but there's still plenty left in the safe.

'Ready?'

The journey up through the silent house is mostly too dark to see on screen. It's only once they reach the entrance hall, where wall-to-ceiling glass frames the door, that moonlight picks out the edges of the picture once more.

Eli and Tammy creep out of the front door hand in hand, rushing for the bridge that will take them over the moat and out to freedom.

Then something goes wrong. Tammy is running ahead over the bridge, little feet tapping on the wooden slats. Eli is lagging behind, waving her on, because he can't stop looking over his shoulder to check on the house behind him. It is still and peaceful, so unthreatening that Eli's obsessive checking seems strange.

The danger comes from the other direction.

There's a crash. The image on the screen shudders then drops, and for a moment the only thing visible is the wood of the walkway. Eli is down. The duffle bag falls from his hand, then rolls over the side and into the moat.

'Eli?' Tammy asks. She turns and moves back towards him. She's confused, because she didn't see what happened. She thinks Eli has just fallen over. She doesn't realise there's something more sinister at work.

When the second strike comes, propelling silver jaws straight through the wood, snatching for Eli's legs, the impact is enough to send Tammy to her knees as well.

She screams.

Eli doesn't wait for the next hit. He scoops Tammy

into his arms, leaving her rucksack discarded on the bridge, and runs straight back to the house. She is crying on his shoulder. When the camera pans down towards her, the only thing the screen shows is the top of her head.

'Why?' Tammy murmurs. 'Why would she attack us?'

'Not you,' Eli says. 'Me. Dad removed my permissions, remember? We'll have to reset them.'

Tammy looks up with wide eyes. 'Go back downstairs?'

'I'll go. You stay here.'

Eli goes back into the house alone, but by the time he opens the hatch door leading down to the living space, Tammy is standing beside him.

'I said to wait,' he whispers.

'I'm coming for Mummy,' she says firmly. 'Mummy will come with us.'

Eli doesn't argue. The moment he steps through the doorway, they're in the dark again.

There are a few seconds of silence, then there's the sound of a gunshot. A light at the bottom of the stairs. Muzzle flash.

The sound of a scuffle follows, then another shot in the darkness.

The lights flick on.

The screen is filled with Eli's blood-covered hands, one of them holding a gun. A pistol, small, pocket-sized. A weapon small enough to fit in a stylish handbag.

Two bodies are sprawled at the bottom of the stairs, two steps beneath Eli: Paul and Veronique. There's a lot of blood. Paul is dressed in his pyjamas, but Veronique looks as though she was on her way out. She has an overnight bag next to her, her handbag slung over her shoulder. She is still breathing, her exhalations rattling and final. Her lips part in bloody gasps.

'This is your gun.' Eli says to her in disbelief.

'He had to die,' she gulps. 'You understand. Don't you?'

Eli drops the gun.

'I didn't mean to take it from you,' he says. 'I didn't mean to... I thought you were him.'

'I'd already dealt with him.' She smiles, rueful. 'I was following you.'

Behind Eli, Tammy says, 'Mummy?'

'An accident, darling,' Veronique says as the girl reaches her side. 'Go with Eli.' She can't get any more words out.

Eli scoops Tammy up into his arms, steps over the bodies and runs into the house. Tammy is crying by the time he has carried her down into the glass-walled basement, but even though she kicks and screams, he doesn't release her.

'We have to get out of here,' he says. 'You have to turn off the dragon so it'll let me over the bridge.'

He finally puts her down beside the control panel. She is shaking, but she nods and turns to do as he asks. He leaves her there, returning to the safe to fill another bag. This time, the banknotes are tinged red.

'How are you getting on?' he says after a moment, but Tammy doesn't answer.

Eli turns.

Tammy is already at the top of the ladder that leads out of the hatch and up to the floor above.

He abandons the bag and runs, but he's too late.

She's already out. The hatch is already swinging closed as he climbs up behind her.

The door slams shut. There is the sickening sound of the wheel turning on the other side.

'Mara!' Eli yells through the sealed hatch. 'You can't leave me here!'

The voice that comes back is faint, but defiant. 'You killed Mummy.'

'It was an accident. I didn't mean to. I didn't mean to do it. You know I didn't.' He thumps against the hatch with his fist. 'You can't leave me down here, Mara. Please.'

There is no sound from the other side.

'Please, Mara,' he says softly. 'Don't leave me.'

Mara turns off the LifeDrive and sits back in the chair. She doesn't need to see any more. She remembers now.

Osian is staring at her, his eyes wide.

'Is it you?' he asks. 'Did you know?'

She doesn't answer, she just walks over to the door at the foot of the stairs and pulls open a panel. Inside is a screen like the one they just saw on the LifeDrive recording, a keypad with a sensor built in.

She presses her thumb against it.

The screen reads: *Thumbprint recognised: Daggett, Tamara.*

Then all the lights come on, spinning up systems that must have lain dormant for years while Eli was trapped downstairs. Music floods the room, the same song that Eli had been playing when they arrived.

A computerised voice cuts through it.

'Welcome home, Tamara. And Merry Christmas.'

Osian laughs bitterly, wiping the blood from his hands onto the white sofa.

'Sure,' he says. 'Merry Christmas.' His eyes are wet. 'Merry Christmas, Tamara Daggett.'

How the Other Half Lives

Veronica Harcourt suffered from the affliction of older brothers. She described them this way not because they were particularly unkind to her, but because she was forced to follow in their footsteps. Perhaps it would have been easier had the boys not been identical twins as well as overachievers. It was as though their parents, having created the perfect mould for Harcourt Child A/ B, were reluctant to make any adaptations for Child C.

Unfortunately, Ronnie – as her family insisted on calling her – was not turning out quite *right*.

She tried to fit in. She really did. Sometimes it was not by choice: she wore her brothers' hand-me-downs, went to the same clubs – football, swimming, Scouts – and read their old adventure books. But she willingly spent her young summer days barefoot, trailing after them along the hedgerows with jars full of ladybirds and worms, trying to love insects and grubs as much as they did. She even made friends with their friends in the village. Almost. It was less that they were friends and more that she took her knocks silently when the local boys allowed her into their games. They liked that.

Friends of her own were harder to come by. After the boys left for boarding school – Langburn College, on full scholarships – Ronnie was alone. She'd been looking forward to coming into her own, as her brothers had promised she would, but it simply wasn't happening. At her own school, she was too masculine for the girls, too feminine for the boys, and not smart enough for anyone to want to copy her homework. She had no friends who deserved the name, no one who bonded to her fiercely in the way that people attached themselves to her brothers, as though they were stars at the centre of their own galaxy.

Without them, she had no gravity.

Perhaps it was inevitable that she would end up at Langburn eventually. A scholarship was out of the question, but her parents went to great pains to secure her a bursary, as they told her often and at length. She was expected to live up to her potential, they said. The school relied on her being as exceptional as her brothers, they said. She'd have to pull her socks up, they said, or she'd embarrass Thomas and Edward. Mustn't let the side down.

And so, when the summer was over, to Langburn she went.

Never to return.

The college was not what Ronnie had expected. It was a huge complex of old buildings set in acres of woodland

and sports fields. That much she had expected, but that September was the first year it had accepted girls as pupils. It was not ready for them. The toilet stalls were too narrow for bins, the shower drains clogged with hair by the end of the first week and there was only a single mirror in each shared bathroom. As often as not, the bathrooms hastily designated 'female' were so busy that the girls resorted to using the boys' anyway. But not Ronnie. Having grown up in a house with two brothers and a mother who was not interested in the feminine arts, she found the girls' morning routines fascinating. They cleansed, they scrubbed, they applied lipstick and kohl that were forbidden by the school's uniform policy and would have to be rubbed off again by break time, then reapplied at lunch. Ronnie used those bathrooms every time just to watch them, even if it meant queueing.

The girls paid her no attention at all. Ronnie wasn't even sure they realised she *was* a girl. As new additions to the school, they had the choice between wearing skirts or wearing trousers like the boys. All of them wore skirts and black heels. Ronnie, typically, was in her brothers' hand-me-down trousers and flat shoes. They pinched her toes and blistered her heels.

The bedroom situation didn't help. Ronnie had won a single room in the dormitory lottery, a luxury in a school where even her brothers shared a twin. It was a relief not to be thrown to the sharks in the main dorm, but at the same time she felt singled out. Denied the opportunity to socialise with roommates, her isolation seemed doomed to continue indefinitely.

Until she met him.

Ronnie had never been good at sports. She should have been. She was nearly as tall as her brothers, lean rather than lanky, with a tightly muscled core that promised power. Unfortunately, she had little speed and her hand-eye coordination left much to be desired. Because there were so few girls at the school they all played with the boys, but even years of practice with her brothers couldn't make up for Ronnie's natural inability. She took a hockey ball to the shin and a football to the stomach in the first week, but it was the rugby ball to the face that finally defeated her. Blood spattered down the front of her jersey and sent her from the pitch in disgrace as the teacher muttered, 'Why can't you be more like your brothers?'

Ronnie had been asking herself the same question for fifteen years.

She was expecting to make the long trudge across the playing fields to the san on her own, since she did everything at Langburn on her own, so when she heard footsteps behind her, it was a surprise.

'Want some company?'

He wasn't handsome, not exactly. His features were a little too sharp, his hair a little too fine and his eyes a little too strange. But still, there was something about him, a promise hiding in the mischief playing across his lips. He was the first boy Ronnie had really *noticed*.

'Shouldn't you get back on the pitch?' she asked. 'I don't need a guide. I know where I'm going.'

'I know a shortcut.' His smile was impish and irresistible, it was a very long walk to the san, and she was inclined to trust a fellow pupil. Especially one who looked like him.

Ronnie let him lead her off the path and into the trees that crowded at the edge of the playing field. The light was different here. It had been grey on the playing field, overcast and relentlessly cold, but there was warmth in the embrace of the boughs. There were evergreens here and there, but mostly the woods were filled with oaks and beeches whose leaves were now descending through yellow, orange and red to the ground. The litter cracked and crinkled beneath Ronnie's plimsolls.

'Is it far?' she asked.

'Barely a dream away.'

That was no kind of answer, but perhaps the boy was an aspiring poet. He had the look of it. He was walking ahead of her, leading the way through holly and bracken, trailing his fingertips through the leaves despite their spines. It was only then that Ronnie realised he wasn't wearing the school's rugby uniform.

'Did you forget your sports kit?'

'For years now,' he said, weaving through the undergrowth. 'You should try it.'

Ronnie turned back to see how far they'd come from the playing fields and saw nothing but trees. She felt a prickle of unease.

'Are you sure this is the way?'

'Of course,' he said. 'I'm the one who made the path. Just around this corner, just a couple more steps and…' He pulled back a sprawling elder sapling from a mass of trees and bushes that divided the woods like a living wall. 'Here it is.'

Ignoring the blood smeared across Ronnie's fingers, he took her hand and drew her through the branches.

Into another world.

* * *

'This,' Ronnie said, 'is not the san.'

Which was quite obvious and didn't need saying, but it was the least weird of all the thoughts that were floating around in her head at that moment, so felt like the safest to verbalise. Commenting on the sudden dusk, or the bronzed branches above them, or their foil leaves, or the twinkling lights that skipped around them like fireflies, only seemed likely to invite further impossibilities.

'Welcome to my home,' the boy said with a bow.

'You live in the woods?'

'These aren't the woods that you know.'

She could see that for herself. The copper-coloured trees arched their boughs together overhead to make an avenue that shone and twinkled with reflections of the moving lights. Leaves had dropped to make a carpet beneath their feet that glowed with gilded warmth. Everything at the tunnel's end called to Ronnie's senses: the jumping firelight, the thud of drums and footsteps vibrating through her chest, the babble of conversation, the scent of sugar and spice. It was so inviting that she couldn't resist its pull, drawing her step by step through the canopied passage until it opened out into a clearing surrounded by buildings carved from the living trees.

There were hundreds, thousands of people. Their clothes were bronze thread and black lace, their skin bronze and jet, their hair bronze and so white it had no pigment at all. The dancers around the fire – just a small portion of the crowd – were moving in a synchronised pattern that was almost hypnotic, staring into each other's eyes as they moved from partner to partner. Without thought, Ronnie stepped towards them.

'Not for you,' the boy said, catching her by the wrist. 'Look at the dancers' feet.'

She had to squint to see through the twilight and movement. Half of the dancers seemed fine, but the other half wore shoes soaked with crimson. Their leaps and twirls spread the colour in smears up their calves and the ground around the fire was bloody with their footprints.

'If you join them,' he said, leading her away, 'you won't stop dancing until your shoes have rubbed the nails from your toes and the skin from your heels. There are other, safer things to entice you here, I promise. Now, let's get you cleaned up.'

He was the one who washed the blood from her face and hands, weaving through the crowd and the trees to a dark pool rimmed in mossy stones. It was fed by a rill that burst from the rock at its head. He cupped handfuls from its clear stream, holding them to her face with one hand while he held her cheek in the other. She'd never known that cold water could heat so fast between fingertips and lips.

'Who are you?' Ronnie breathed.

'Now is not the time for names. I won't ask, and you won't tell, not to me or anyone else. Not yet. Deal?'

Ronnie smiled at the game. 'Deal.'

He led her away from their quiet corner to one of the nearby tree houses. There was a gaggle of voices inside, light with excitement. Through the doorway, Ronnie could see spills of colourful fabrics.

'Ladies,' the boy called. 'I have a guest in need of a

dress.'

One head peeped out of the trunk, then a second, and a third, until five beautiful faces were looking Ronnie up and down with delighted intrigue. They ushered her in with smiles and happy murmurs.

'For now,' the boy whispered to Ronnie before they hurried her away, 'just call me the boy who brought you through the woods. And please don't forget about me.'

He'd changed in the embrace of this bronzed bower. The cold daylight outside had leached the colour from him, making him thin and washed out, but in the firelight she could see the shine of his hazel eyes, the gold in his hair and the richness of his skin. Her gaze followed him as he took his leave. It seemed impossible that she should ever forget him.

'Come on,' one of the girls said as she dragged Ronnie inside the room. 'Let's get you sorted.'

The space carved out between the tree's roots was warm and earthy, and filled with cupboards and mirrors.

'Your mouth was hanging open, you know,' a girl said to Ronnie, but her tone was surprisingly warm. She was a portrait of shining hair and smoky eyes, exactly the type who usually ignored Ronnie, but now she was looking straight at her with friendly interest.

'Was it?'

'Don't worry,' the girl continued, holding various dresses up to Ronnie's body. 'If it wasn't mutual then he wouldn't have brought you here.'

'Excuse me?' Ronnie was horrified. 'What kind of place is this?'

The girls all laughed, but the cruel edge she was accustomed to hearing from her peers was unaccountably missing.

'*Don't worry*,' the first girl insisted. 'It's nothing like that. Aha!' With a triumphant flourish, the girl grabbed an armful of material. 'This one, do you think?'

With a chorus of agreement, the girls crowded around to manoeuvre Ronnie into the dress.

'Close your eyes,' said one of them, wielding a pot of something shiny. Her fingertips on Ronnie's eyelids were feather-light.

'What *is* this place, then?' Ronnie asked.

'It's a sanctuary,' one of them replied. 'A time out of time. Enjoy yourself. You're safe here.'

'Just don't dance,' another said.

'No,' the first agreed. 'Don't dance. Now, what do you think?'

She turned Ronnie to face the mirror, a mirror from which a stranger looked back. Ronnie had never worn a dress before. Ever. Now she was draped in a tumble of autumnal tulle that made miracles from her chest and cinched at the waist to display her stomach. The only blemish on the outfit was her dirty plimsolls, peeking out from beneath the frothy fabric; the girls had no shoes in her size, and she didn't want to brave the forest floor unshod.

But her make up more than compensated for her footwear. There was extravagant iridescence around her eyes and her lashes were lined with shadows that brought something sultry to her gaze.

She had never felt beautiful before.

She didn't want this to be the last time.

'Show me how,' she said.

So, smiling and laughing all the time, they did.

When Ronnie emerged from the tree roots, the boy who brought her through the woods was not the only one waiting for her, dressed in bronzed finery, offering her his hand. But his was the hand she took.

'It's magical,' she whispered, as multi-coloured lights rose to the treetops like fireworks.

He smiled. 'You bring the magic with you.'

But to Ronnie, the magic was *here*. They watched dancers and tumblers, drank and ate concoctions so exquisite she was sure she would never taste their like, and all the time she was overwhelmed by laughter and joy and the gentle press of the boy's hand in hers.

She never wanted to leave, but knew she must.

'I need to get going,' she said, when the weight of her conscience grew too heavy to bear. 'They'll miss me.' Maybe. More probably, no one would even notice she was gone until they checked the rooms at lights out, and surely it couldn't be that late.

'You don't need to worry about that,' he said. 'I've taken care of it.'

'How?'

'Haven't you worked it out yet?' he asked with a hint of a smirk. 'There's a little bit of magic in me too.' As he said this, he clicked his fingers and the leaves at their feet swirled up around them like a twirling curtain of bronze.

Was this romance? She wondered, and wondered again as he fetched her cups of sweet cider, leaves filled with sugared nuts, and bronze feathers to adorn her hair. They didn't dance, but they did talk about the darkness and the light, and the beautiful and deep, in all the urgency and earnestness of hours stolen.

And she wondered.

When the sky finally grew light and he kissed her hand in farewell, his breath danced across her skin like the brush of a butterfly's wings.

There was no music at Langburn. It was quieter than a school had any right to be.

When Ronnie stepped out of the trees, the wind was freezing and the dawn light stripped the bronze from her gown, tearing through it like fire through spider gossamer. Within seconds, she found herself standing in her bloodstained rugby kit at the edge of the playing field, as though no time had passed at all.

It had, though. Back in her room, the days, weeks and months had been torn from her calendar as far as December. She might not have believed it, but the clock confirmed that the mornings had darkened, and there was more work in her room than she had thought she would complete in a lifetime.

Worse, there was a changeling in her bed. It had her size, her shape, her colour and scent, but when she threw open the curtains to get a closer look it dissolved in a shower of bronze light.

But it had been there. She knew that for a fact, because during her three months in the other place, everything about her life had been changed.

That morning at breakfast, Ronnie discovered she was now popular, but not as she would have wished to be. The scholarship boys called her over to their table, quickly crushing her frisson of delight when she realised they only wanted to review that weekend's rugby match in minute detail. She played on the first team now, apparently. She was on the track for a scholarship herself next term. Her brothers were proud to the point of envy.

It was everything her family had ever wanted for her, yet she couldn't stop her eyes from straying to the table where the girls sat together, splashes of colour in a sea of grey. Even when she discovered that since her return she was just as good at sports as everyone now believed her to be, her eyes lingered elsewhere.

It was everything they had ever wanted, and it was nothing but dust to her.

She tried to go back. She walked through the woods every morning, every evening, sneaking off during lessons so she could be sure that she had checked every time of day on every day of the week, in case that was the key to the magic. But the light wouldn't change for her. The living wall and the elder sapling that formed its door, they were both gone. She began to wonder whether the whole adventure had happened only in her head.

Until the last week of term, in the middle of a snowstorm, when she saw the boy who brought her through the woods in the middle of her geography class. She blinked a few times to be sure it really was him – in truth she had been nodding off – but even pinching herself didn't banish him from the old disused fireplace where he crouched, holding out a hand towards her. She didn't hesitate for long.

As the false back swung open behind the grate, Ronnie snatched a look over her shoulder to see if anyone had noticed her escape. As it happened, there was nothing for them to notice. If, like her, they looked at her desk, all they would see was her perfect changeling, looking attentively at the blackboard and taking careful notes.

Ronnie followed the boy into the tunnel as the hidden door clicked shut behind them.

Let her doppelgänger learn geography. Ronnie had other lessons in mind.

She followed the boy down a dark passageway that seemed ancient, but was clean of cobwebs and had rock walls that were dry to the touch.

'I wasn't sure you were going to come back,' she said, not wanting to show quite how miserable she'd been in his absence.

'The doors don't open very often.'

'Oh.'

There was an awkward pause, their footsteps reverberating around the stone tunnel. It was getting lighter now, as though they were approaching its end.

'I wanted to come,' he said. 'If I could have come for you again the day you left, then I would have done, though you probably would have thought me unbearably intense. But time moves differently here, as you will have noticed. It wasn't as long for me.' He looked over his shoulder at her and smiled, a little shyly. 'But I missed you anyway.'

He turned away too quickly to see her smile back, but she smiled anyway. Couldn't stop smiling, in fact. After weeks of waiting, she was back. It felt like coming home.

She was expecting to follow the tunnel into the woods, to come out in the same place she had before, but this time it was different. Instead of a walkway of bronze leaves, their path was marked by silver trees that pushed their way out through the walls until, by the end of the corridor, there was hardly any stone to be seen at all. Diamonds dangled like icicles from the branches above their heads. While the boy walked on ahead of her, she reached up to snap a twig from above her head. She stowed it safely in her pocket, a tangible reminder for her future self that she really had been here, that it wasn't just in her head.

When they reached the end of the path, Ronnie found herself in a huge hall filled with people dressed in finery of silver and white fur, and edged with stalls and tables laden with food and drink. Doors opened here and there, revealing further delights. Silver ivy and birches erupted through the stones of the walls and floor into the space, bringing the outside in with them. Birds swooped, rabbits scattered around her toes and snowflakes fell like confetti. Except in the centre, where a roaring fire was the focal point for the dancers. She could already see their bloody footprints in the snow, but they smiled and danced on nonetheless.

'It's completely different,' she breathed, turning in a slow circle as she tried to take it all in.

'It always is,' the boy replied. 'Look around. You're safe here. Just don't—'

'Join the dance,' she interrupted. 'I remember.'

'Good. Well. The ladies of the wardrobe are on the other side of the fire, waiting to help you dress. I'll be by the bar.' He waved vaguely in the direction of laden tables and steaming cauldrons. 'If you want me.'

He walked off before she could reply. When she

found him again – once she was newly-clad in a warm silver dress even more beautiful than her last – he was wearing a jacket that seemed to have been spun from spider silk. He looked unaccountably relieved to see her.

'Did you think I wouldn't come back?' she asked.

'No,' he laughed. 'No.' But he was still smoothing the worry from his face as he spoke.

It was the last time that evening that he seemed concerned. They walked every inch of the massive hall, exploring each corner and stall. They ate, they drank, they held hands as they dragged each other from jugglers to musicians to fireworks unconstrained by the hall's towering ceiling. And in the quieter moments, they sat and spoke.

Ronnie had something on her mind.

'How did you get here?' she asked the boy who brought her through the woods.

'The same way that you did: I wandered off the path.'

'But you stay here. You can come and go. I tried, but until you came to fetch me…'

'It's different for me,' he said.

'Why?'

'Because it is. But I can never go back, you know. I gave up my place in that world. The person they sent to take my place, he's out there now. That's the cost of the magic. I've become…' He gestured at his face, at his too-silver eyes that changed with the season, at the frost in his hair. 'I belong here now.'

Ronnie could see that he wasn't the only one. On her last visit, she had been so overawed by the surroundings, the joyful surge of the music, the glitter of the leaves and bodies, the perfume of fruit and sweetness, that she'd not paid attention to the things that differentiated one person from another. To her, they had simply been a crowd of glorious colour. She could see it now, though: most of them were like the boy was, twinkling and bright and otherworldly, but a few of the revellers looked out of place and slightly… dull. Some of them were like her.

'I want to be like you,' she said. 'Tell me how.'

He smiled ruefully. 'I can't.'

'It must be possible. You did it. There must be a way.' Feeling daring, she reached up and put her fingers to his cheek. He shivered at the contact, but he didn't move away. 'I don't want to go.'

'You should.'

'I won't.' She snatched her hand away, pouting like a child. The boy just shook his head and smiled at her sadly.

'You can try,' he said.

And she did. Until the dawn came, she ate and drank and laughed and talked to every person she could meet, marvelling at the tricks each could do. They were filled with all the colour and noise and feeling that she had missed in the weeks since she had left, filled to the brim. She never wanted it to end.

But, soon enough, her eyelids began to droop. One moment she was sitting beneath the silver trees with her head pillowed on the boy's shoulder, and the next she was waking up in the fireplace of the classroom, freezing cold and covered in soot. The twig of silver and diamonds was nothing but dust in her pocket.

* * *

It was worse the second time. The longer she spent away from it, the more unrecognisable her life became. In the night she'd been absent – the *months* she'd been absent – the changeling had become everything she was supposed to be. It had followed her brothers into the Army Cadet Force, so now her spare time was spent marching in polished boots that constrained her feet, rubbed her skin and made them bleed. Apparently the assault courses were supposed to be fun. Ronnie found no fun in them, so was angry that she found them easy. If she'd had no talent for such drudgery, she could have bowed out gracefully, but now it would be a waste of her potential to quit.

She'd never wished so hard to be a failure.

It wouldn't be long, she promised herself. Just a few weeks. That was all it had been before.

Just a few weeks.

But the summer term had nearly ended when he finally came for her again, the boy who had brought her through the woods. This time, he caught her hand as she walked out of the dining room and rushed her through a door that opened into the cellars. Their labyrinthine path took them past wine bottles, then discarded barrels, then forgotten boxes, and on into a tunnel carved from the earth. After a while, it pitched upwards, and they were climbing as the walls changed from dirt to sap-wet wood. When they finally emerged, they were in the treetops, surrounded by canopy walkways that stretched in every direction through leaves that glittered with gold. Red and green gems hung from the boughs like ripe fruit, glittering and inviting.

'This way,' he said, leading her across bridge after

bridge, hand in hand, until they converged with the rest of the crowd at the centre of the forest. The tree there was enormous, hundreds of years in the making, and a large platform had been built at its crown. As they climbed the weaving walkway up to it, surrounded by partygoers on every side, Ronnie felt light-headed. Something was about to happen. She could feel it in the thrumming of her blood.

'Why is it different for you?' she whispered to the boy. 'What did you do to stay? How did you become part of the magic of this place?'

'I can't tell you that.'

But there was a reason. There had to be a reason that he could live within the magic while she was ejected from it. She scrutinised her surroundings for a clue as they walked out onto the platform, but then she saw the rooms built between the branches at the edges of the space, and the fire burning impossibly at its centre, up here in the treetops, and she forgot herself. It was only once she was with the wardrobe girls, being draped in waves of shining gold material, that she recalled her mission, and then only because the answer was staring her in the face.

A different girl applied her make up this time, a girl she almost recognised, but who seemed somehow different. She was one of them, her hair threaded with natural gold and her lips the colour of rubies, but…

'You've changed,' Ronnie said to her. 'You weren't like this last time.'

The girl smiled, but started to move away.

Ronnie grabbed her wrist. 'No, wait. Please. How did you become one of them?'

Quickly, so quickly that Ronnie almost missed the gesture, the girl glanced through the doorway at the fire.

'You were…' Ronnie searched her memory, desperately trying to place her. 'Dancing,' she whispered finally. 'You were dancing. Barefoot.'

The girl leaned in and, looking at Ronnie's hand-me-down shoes, whispered, 'You won't need those.'

Ronnie's grip slackened and the girl slipped away.

When the boy met her outside, now dressed in a shirt that glittered like the sun, she knew exactly what she had to do. Taking his hand, she started to lead him towards the fire.

'Wait,' he said, seeing her destination. 'Are you sure? You have to be sure.'

'I am.'

And she was. The changeling could have her other life, with her blessing.

But before she could lead the boy any further, he stopped her with a hand on her waist and pulled her close.

'Give me your name,' he whispered.

'You first.'

He breathed it into her ear like a promise, and in return she gave him her own name, her true name, the one that sang in her heart. Then with the flames leaping in the impossible fire at their backs, their lips met in a kiss.

Finally, she kicked off her shoes, took her lover's hand and joined him in the dance.

Her unencumbered feet never bled again and, for all I know, the two of them are dancing still.

The Forest at the End of the World

In the middle of the forest at the end of the world, there's a boneyard where old things go to die. Creatures collect under its trees in piles of bone and sinew, each one the last of its kind. They walk their final steps into the shade to lay themselves down amongst skeletons of animals so odd and forgotten that nothing now living would recognise their form. They're relics, memorials, repositories of the past waiting to be rediscovered. That is the fate of all living things. When we are distilled beyond the point of worthlessness, rendered obsolete, the forest will be waiting for us too, bony arms outstretched.

But that isn't the folklore Zuri knows. The story her father tells goes like this:

In the beginning, there was a fire in the forest at the

end of the world. Before the fire, the forest was empty. There were trees, and plants, and rain, and earth, but nothing with a heartbeat or a conscience or a soul. When the fire came, it burned itself into the world and left seeds of itself behind, little sparks of consciousness that woke and grew and spun themselves into something new.

That's where we come from, Zuri, he would say. We all came from the fire, and one day we'll go back to it too and be reborn.

Zuri knows this is true, because it's happening now.

In the middle of the great continent, fire is falling from the sky. From the ground, it seems almost as though the clouds are combusting and breaking away from each other, like flaming chunks of cotton wool igniting in the hot air. They fall hard and far, not stopping when they reach the ground but instead burning straight through the earth and into the rock beneath, on and on, turning underground rivers into steam as they blaze their way toward the mantle, seeking common heat. If you could get close enough to them, you'd see the spots where the fire falls become craters filled with lava that bubbles up from under the surface. But nothing can get that close; the falling flames are so hot that they eat the air for miles around as they descend, ripping moisture and oxygen from it as they strip all vegetation from the landscape. Any creature that sees the impact is conscious of little more than a distant brightness before the searing wave takes them.

From beyond the next valley, so far away that the view is lost over the horizon, Kade watches the smoke and steam rise. He sought this vantage point in the hope of running, but in what direction? He can look to all four points of the compass and see something that worries him. To the north, east and west, smoke turns the skies dark. To the distant south, past the rolling hills and valleys, the salt pans reflect so much sunlight that it threatens to blind him, and beyond them the desert waits. Surrounded by so much heat, there is no good option.

'South,' says Ama, his wife and the mother of their child. Zuri is just three years old and too small to climb up here on her own; for the moment, she has been left behind in the care of their township in the valley below. Her parents don't want her to see their worry and despair, though she will see far worse before this is through. With forty residents in the township and food enough for only a week more, she has seen worse already as they have been forced to cut and cut. They were once more than two hundred.

Kade knows they must move now, even if he cannot see what lies beyond the smoke. He doesn't want to. He is attached to his home, though it is not what it once was. The river has dried to a trickle, the crops turned yellow and brittle, and the animals so emaciated that they have long since been butchered for their meat. But there are other colours in the township beyond the sepia tones of endless summer, like the walls of the house he whitewashed with his brother and the blue glass monument that marks his father's grave, the spot where they burned his body to ashes and turned them in the earth. The trees might be dying and the ground reduced to nothing but baked clay, but he loves it still, loves it so much that he has never imagined he might end up be elsewhere. The thought of leaving it behind cuts deep, as though he's excising a piece of his soul to cut the bond between himself and his past. To him, they are the same thing. He might as well cut himself in two.

And yet.

The animals have been moving south for days, fleeing through the valley on their way to a promised land that may not exist. The animals move because there is nothing left to eat where they are, because the ground is cracked and empty, not because they think there will be more elsewhere. Kade knows this and takes no comfort from it. Why move at all if there is nothing better over the horizon? Why not stay in their homes and die in their own lands?

He doesn't have to put these questions to Ama, because he has done so enough times over the past two days that a look is all it takes for her to know his mind. She is more practical than he is, more resolute, more energetic. She will keep walking until she can only crawl, then crawl until she can only pull herself along the ground, will only stop moving when she is dead if that is what it takes to win even the chance of a future for their daughter. Kade is not like Ama. After years of praying and striving, only for the land that he lavished with attention to fail him, he is tired. He would lie down right here and wait for the end if only she would let him.

'South,' she says again, and that is the end of the discussion.

The township packs up quickly; there isn't much left to take away. Each family carries their own ration to spread the load and the risk of loss. They each carry their share of grief too: the loss of their homes, the futures they had hoped for, and the family members that have been left behind. Not everyone is fit enough to make the trip. Ama's mother is amongst that number, a woman as determined and merciless as Ama herself. With few years left ahead of her, she insists that she will slow them down, and she isn't wrong. She walks with a stick when she walks at all, which is rarely these days. They leave her in their house with a small store of food, a stack of books, their love and their memories. Ama cries, but only until Zuri comes to say her own goodbyes. Then her tears are wiped away to reveal a smile so genuine that it is hard to spot the force behind it. Kade does, though. He always can with his wife. This is how he knows her strength, by the way she smiles through her pain for the sake of their daughter.

'I'll see you soon,' Zuri's grandmother promises, showering the little girl with kisses. 'After your trip, we'll be together again.'

The words might hold more truth than the old matriarch would wish.

The rain starts the moment they reach the top of the fell overlooking the valley, and it feels like an omen.

It rains through the night. The caravan planned to travel in darkness so they could sleep through the scorching days in whatever shade they could find, but the downpour makes the ground sticky and slippery at first, then turns well-worn hill paths into torrents that force them into the spiky undergrowth crowding on either side. It's impossible to navigate, impossible to find a footing as the moon hides behind the storm clouds, so they shelter under the drought-stripped trees as best they can and try to sleep. When they wake in the morning, all trace of the rain is gone, but so are two of their number, along with their packs. Whether they continued in the night without stopping – either unwilling to stick with the others or unconscious of their decision – or whether they were carried away by the storm, no one knows. The wandering township now numbers only thirty-two.

Worse, despite the heavy rain, there is no water to be found. The lakes they pass on their way to the salt pans remain stagnant and almost empty, the streams still dry, and not a single puddle remains on the ground. The cracks in the earth start to steam as the sun hits them, burning and softening the feet of those without shoes until they are forced to stop and fashion some from their clothing or risk laming themselves with blisters. The rest of the caravan waits for them this time, but they know that sooner or later they will leave more people behind. When the group finally moves off, the smoke coming from the north chases them on their way.

Despite the rain, the fires still rage behind them. That scares Kade; there must be something supernatural about a fire that can't be quenched by a storm so strong.

'Tell me a story,' Zuri says as he carries the shoeless girl on his shoulders.

'I can't think of any.' After a sleepless night and a meagre breakfast of dried meat and fruit, Kade feels barely strong enough to keep the child aloft. He wishes he could pass her to her mother, just for a little while, but Ama is at the front of the line directing their route.

'So tell me an old story.'

He thinks of the burning at the end of the world, then, and wonders if this is it. But that won't do at all. He scrambles for a different tale.

'Tell me the one about the founding,' Zuri suggests.

She is asking him to break his heart open. Since leaving the valley, he has gathered the memories of his home in close and locked them away for a day when they are less raw, less urgent. He spent the night trying not to imagine the deluge bringing the roof of the house he built down onto his mother-in-law's head, trying not to picture his last stringy crops washed away with the bones of their last goat, his father's glass grave marker toppled in the mud.

He pulls it all inside and seals it shut.

'Why don't you tell me a story instead?'

The little girl hums in thought, then jumps as the air cracks with thunder. The wanderers look up, hunching their shoulders to keep their heads low. Dark storm clouds are gathered above them, but there is no more rain. It feels too hot for it, as though the water would evaporate before reaching the ground. Kade slides Zuri down from his shoulders just as the first lighting bolt forks across the sky and grounds itself on a withered tree to their right.

Like all the vegetation around them, it isn't a large tree. Not big at all. Not much taller than the height of his little girl on his shoulders.

That's when Ama calls another halt. They have no choice but to crouch in the scant cover of the brush and wait for the lightning to pass.

* * *

The storm goes on too long, for days. Summer storms in the township are usually brief affairs, cathartic breaks in the sky that douse the land with water and quench the heat. This one is different, and they can all feel it. It's not natural for weather to hang in one place for so long, cracking above their heads, strobing light across the cloud-shaded landscape, circling them like a starving dog circles a lame deer.

When the rain finally comes, it does so meanly, in short showers of miserly drops that barely wash the dust from their skin. Hours of frantic labour with bowls and oilskins net them four litres of water. It's only a fraction of what the delay has cost them from their stores, and even the most optimistic amongst their number knows it won't be enough to get them all safely down the hills to the border township that waits on the edge of the desert. There are wells there. Those sunken stores have been the hope that burned in all their chests as they made this hopeless march out of their valley, that have sustained them through the blazing days and torrential nights. The rain might not settle in this cracked-clay, hilly region that was once their forested paradise, but all that water has to collect somewhere, doesn't it?

Kade is starting to question even that. The land and skies he once knew have turned on him, and their trust is broken. It bewilders him to see the familiar turned foreign, the reliable turned unpredictable. He is used to the gentle vagaries of nature, but this? Fire falling from the skies while rain steams up from the ground? There is nothing natural about this.

Ama leaves the group of matriarchs and seeks him

out. She has been doing this sometimes, rarely, when she needs comfort more than advice. To Kade, it's just another sign that things are terribly, terribly wrong. He knows this before she speaks a word, by the silence in which they sit side by side, watching their daughter pick through the spongy dirt to find treasures of glass and wire. Usually Ama would stop her, afraid she might break her skin on the sharp points, but now they simply watch as lightning reflects off dangerous remnants of the world that came before them.

The reminder is bleak.

Ama's words, when they finally come, are bleaker still.

'Only half of us will make it to the desert. At best.'

'At best?' Kade glances at Zuri as he speaks, but their voices are low and the girl is absorbed in her digging. She hasn't heard, he is sure.

'At worst, maybe ten of us. Maybe five. Maybe none. Either we brave the storm or we huddle here and die of thirst.'

Kade looks out at the path. It winds down and then up again, down and up, tracing the undulations of the diminishing valleys on the way to the salt pans. He expected that portion of the journey to be the difficult one, the dry march into the desert, not this faded green portion so close to home. It's only now that he can see the danger. As the height of the hills decreases, so does the height of the vegetation. The wanderers might be safe to walk for the moment, if they crouch, but very soon they'll be too exposed to hope that anything more than prayers might save them from the lightning. There are already fires burning around them from the strikes, and all the while more and more smoke drifts down from the north.

'We're moving, then?' He tries to keep the tremor from his voice.

'Some of us.'

They put it to a vote in the end, those who wished to press on to the border township against those who would rather wait here for the storm to pass. At least, those were the choices presented, though it was clear to everyone that the latter was a death sentence.

The vote was not truly calling for opinions. It was calling for volunteers.

Those left behind knew this when they raised their hands. They knew this when they surveyed their wrecked feet, their stiffening joints, or their tired lungs. They knew this when they paired their farewells with bundles of food and water, promising they had plenty for themselves while leaving their own packs empty. The spirit of the township they had built together was strong. They wouldn't see it die with them.

Kade feels the weight of their trust as he walks away with just ten others, hand in hand with his daughter.

His feet are cracked and blistered. His joints are agony. His lungs rattle wetly with every breath.

He keeps walking not because he is strong, but because he is too weak to admit that, sooner or later, he will slow the others down.

Through the morning haze, with the desert behind it, the border township looks like a mirage. It's circled with high mud walls, but the many buildings inside poke above the edge, promising the kind of comfort the travellers haven't experienced since abandoning their homes weeks ago. The sight and smell of cooking fires draws them on.

They've left the storm behind them, but it has not been an easy journey. Their backs feel permanently damaged from holding their bodies bent below the height of their surroundings. Kade has been shaking so much that he couldn't carry Zuri, did not even dare to hold her hand in case he was struck and passed the charge into her tiny frame, so the days have been filled with her cries and complaints. She's too small to understand that he loves her too much to hold her close.

She's quiet now, though. They all have been since they lost their leaders.

The two women were walking at the front of the line, blazing the trail through the increasingly featureless landscape – no trees, no bushes, just salt beneath their feet – when the lightning struck. It had been striking all morning, a mile away, two miles away, but this time it zeroed in on the women's heads as though it had been directed there. They were dead before they hit the ground.

Ama, previously only a member of the council, now leads the ragged remains of their township: their family of three, two teenaged brothers, a young couple, a middle-aged man and one last matriarch. Nine altogether.

They would have fallen to pieces without her. She was the one who knelt before the singed bodies and tried to revive them, who pulled their cloaks over their faces and stripped the ceremonial beads from their hair. Metal. Perhaps they should have thought about those earlier, the clicking relics of the past that marked their office, but also drew the lightning to them. That's what Ama said when the brothers began babbling about fate and god and the hopelessness of continuing. She offered them science, kept them walking, kept them focussed, and stopped them from panicking.

Even now, approaching the border township beyond the salt pans without knowing what might lie within, she has a calm about her that Kade can't replicate. He's tried it before while soothing Zuri, but he just can't lull her the same way. It's magical, the way Ama channels her serenity out to others and takes their anxiety into herself. Kade is the only one who sees beneath the surface, sees her own insecurity and pain. She makes sure of that. To everyone else, Ama is invincible.

Even now, as the arrows fall.

They are unfletched, unworked, just dry twigs tipped with sharp things dug from the ground. They don't fly true, so it's more by volume than by skill that they hit their marks.

'Back,' Ama orders, her voice loud but flat.

It's too late for the matriarch and the young couple. They lie in a field of arrow shafts, unmoving. To Zuri, it looks as though their bodies have sprouted growth, as though they are turning into trees in front of her eyes and might lift their branches from the ground at any moment to send out shining bright leaves. Her father has told her stories about the cycle of life, about green things springing from the earth, about the verdant forests of his youth. She wants to see the magic for herself, but he holds her back.

One of the boys has a cut on his leg. It's bleeding, but

it doesn't look deep. A graze, nothing more. The flies will find it soon though, even as quickly as the blood will dry in this heat, so he wraps it tight.

Kade is the only one who realises there has been another injury. His eyes always go to Ama when things go wrong, as though the mere sight of her face will soothe him, so he saw the slight jerk, the falter in her step as she backed away from the border township. She keeps watching its walls now, putting herself between them and her family like a shield. Kade can see her elbows working as she worries at something by her hip. A drop of blood spatters to the ground, then a twig broken into several pieces follows it. Throughout it all, she keeps her back turned to her people.

Six now.

They are too distracted to notice, but Kade has seen and can't pretend otherwise. When Ama finally turns, their eyes lock for a second before his gaze drops to the blood on her hands. With fierce eyes and a tiny shake of the head she makes her will known: he will say nothing.

Nothing at all.

The stragglers sleep on the salt through the heat of the day in whatever shade they can create, then at nightfall they return to the border township. Ama directs their path, leading them in a route that is beyond bow range. They never get close enough to find out whether there's water in the wells or food within the walls. The bodies of their fellows are gone though, which feels like answer enough to the second question.

They move on: Ama, Zuri, the brothers and Kade. The other man wandered away while they slept, leaving his pack behind. Those remaining didn't bother looking for him – if he had been within two miles of them, they would have been able to see him on the shining plain that surrounded their campsite. Sending out searches would have been a waste of time and resources, so instead they took his supplies for themselves and followed Ama into the unknown.

And to them, the desert really is unknown. They don't know anything of this place. It's only now that they are discovering that it's not really a desert at all; the ground looks like sand but feels like rock. Occasionally, back in Kade's younger days, someone from their township might have ventured as far as the border looking for trade or adventure. That hasn't happened for decades now. People stopped coming back from those trips, and Kade suspects their recent encounter might explain why. Zuri keeps asking him where they're going, but he has no answers for her. He's too scared to ask Ama what waypoint she's fixing on in the distance, because in this clouded moonlight he can't imagine that she would have an answer for him either. There seems to be nothing ahead of them except the dark, the rustle of the dirt and the steely conviction of their leader.

They don't stop for comfort breaks because they can't afford the time. Instead, those who need to empty their bladders – a rare enough occurrence when they are all so dehydrated – simply step off the path and catch up afterwards. Zuri needs breaks more often than the rest. It's not just that she's small and doesn't have their endurance, it's also that Kade has been giving her more than her ration by sacrificing his own. He's so thirsty that he's dizzy with it. In these circumstances, it was perhaps inevitable that they would get separated from the others.

Kade doesn't understand it.

He had his eyes on Ama and the brothers. They were walking all together when he split off with Zuri, clumped together as though for safety, too tired for conversation and too scared for songs. One moment he'd been watching Ama's back, her pale hair cascading down her shoulders and clearly visibly despite the darkness, and the next she seemed to blink out of existence, as though she'd never been there in the first place.

Kade gathers Zuri into his arms and runs around frantically, unable to remember in which direction the travellers had been moving. He squints into the dark, scans the ground for tracks, even appeals to Zuri's younger eyes, but there is no trace of the rest of their party and, worse, he has let himself become disorientated in his panic.

He breathes. He must calm himself. He must put them back on the right path.

'It's okay, Zu,' he murmurs softly into her ear. 'I'll work out which way they went and we'll catch up in no time.'

Unfortunately, that's easier said than done. He thinks of the fires, the only feature by which he might navigate in the clouded night, but to no avail. Up until now they have managed to keep the smoke at their backs, but suddenly it seems to surround them. It's so pervasive that every direction in which he turns could be north. He wastes his energy walking and sniffing, running and scanning, straining his ears for the slightest noise.

Nothing moves. No one calls for them and his own calls go unanswered.

Kade has no choice but to wrap his daughter in his arms and wait until morning.

The smoke makes sense, then. Kade can no longer see the border township. Instead, there is smoke engulfing the horizon where it once stood. It's so thick even here, miles from the place, that the sunlight is hazy and the ash burns his eyes. The phlegm he coughs up is black and red. Using a small measure of their precious water, he wets a rag and ties it over Zuri's mouth and nose. The moisture will bake away quickly, but hopefully not more quickly than he can get them out of the worst of it.

Putting the sun on his left, he cradles the girl to his chest and runs.

The conditions get better over the next week, but not by much. Less smoky, more desperate.

And still there is no sign of the others.

Their supplies are low, very low, and Kade is fading faster than he realises. The walking feels easier because the weight on his back is lighter, but that's only because they have so little left. They got lucky after the separation, stumbling across a large pack that someone had dropped in the middle of nowhere, filled with water and food. There was a marker flag in the ground next to it, a red bandanna tied to a stick, so Kade assumes it was a stash for someone who never made it this far. Their loss was Zuri's gain.

But water doesn't last long out here and Kade knows

they'll never get so lucky again. He's long since given up on any hope of wells or springs; the ground is dry and unyielding beneath their feet. The clumps of grass they see now are more bone-coloured than yellow, as though as the pigment has been leeched and bleached from them, leaving just husks in their wake. Kade feels the same way, though he is far from pale: his skin is a mottled pattern of tan and red that peels and bleeds. It's all he can do to keep Zuri wrapped up and safe from the sun, so there's little fabric left to shield his own hide.

But he can handle the pain. It is more important that he is sparing with everything. He knows that what they have now is all they will ever get until the end, however that comes.

He wonders about that more and more. They came out here because they were running away from something, not towards something. They have no destination. As far as Kade knows, there is nothing waiting for them at the end of the plain. The only reason to carry on in this direction is that he believes his wife will be doing the same. If it were up to him, he would already have stopped. He would stop here right now, but what would he do with Zuri? He couldn't just sit and watch her die of thirst and starvation. The kindest thing would be to kill her and himself, but that would require positive action, and he isn't brave enough for that. He can't make that decision. It's too hard.

But he's so tired.

A desperate hope keeps him going: they will be reunited with Ama, she will have a plan, and she will save them all. Just like she always does.

In the end, they find her by following the carrion birds. It is less of a surprise than Kade expects. He knew she had been bleeding when he'd last seen her, trying to hide her limp. The only real surprise is that she made it this far.

'Mama?' Zuri says.

They're still fifty metres away, but Kade knows the bundle on the ground is his wife. He can see the teal of her skirt beneath the mud, the blonde of her hair beneath the blood, the curve of her cheek beneath the crow's claws.

Kade walks on, cradling the child in his ever-weakening arms.

'Is that Mama?'

'No,' Kade says, and it doesn't feel like a lie.

Ama wasn't the body behind them. Ama was the spirit that is filling him now, pouring strength into his weak and lazy limbs. He will keep walking until he can only crawl, then crawl until he can only pull himself along the ground, will only stop moving when he is dead if that is what it takes to win even the chance of a future for their daughter.

Because that is what Ama would have done.

It takes three more days.

Kade has given up on a regular sleeping schedule. Instead, he walks when he can and sleeps when he can't. He carries Zuri constantly, because she is tired and he is desperate to rebuild her strength. She has to be able to walk on her own. Soon she will have no choice.

Eventually, he spots a feature ahead on the unbroken flat of the plain. That's the direction in which he crawls when he can no longer walk, with little Zuri riding on his back. By the time he can no longer crawl, the feature is clear enough that he can see, unbelievably, that it is a forest, not more than a mile away. He is so close.

It's come too late for him, he knows, but they are not the only ones heading for the trees. He can see movement in the distance, animals and maybe people too, all making their way towards sustenance and safety.

But not him.

'Do you remember the forest at the end of the world?' His voice breaks into croaks and whispers.

'No,' Zuri says, but Kade knows she just wants to hear the story again, one last time, so he tells it as he ties their last supplies into a bundle and slips them over Zuri's shoulders.

'In the beginning, there was a fire in the forest at the end of the world. The fire made all the living creatures that exist, our flame from its flame. We're all born from the fire, and one day we'll all go back to it and be reborn.'

'Is that the forest?' The little girl's eyes are opened wide and fixed on his.

'Maybe.' He can feel his lips cracking as he smiles. 'You could go and explore it. Find out whether it's true or not. Then, when you're older, you could come back and tell me. Okay?'

'You'll wait here?' she asks, uncertain.

'I'm not going anywhere. Promise.'

Satisfied, she takes her pack and strides away with steps that are too big for her stature. Long after she has disappeared into the woods and out of sight, Kade feels the splash of raindrops on his skin. He turns onto his back and lets them fall into his mouth. His lips taste of blood.

In the distance, thunder rumbles. One second passes – he counts it – before lightning forks down onto the highest tree in the forest at the end of the world. It passes fire among the tinder-dry branches, engulfing everything in slow and painful minutes.

Lightning strikes again, hurrying the flames. In the negative that is burned onto the inside of his eyelids, Kade sees the phoenix in the shape of its fork. He sees the raised head, the feathered wings, the triumphant resurrection of bones from the ashes, and in the spread of its light he feels that this is not the end.

This is just the beginning, again.

SnapShot

When the alarm goes off, I know I've fucked up properly this time. I've known it for hours, since the moment Rich locked me in, but until the beeping started I was still hoping I'd pull through somehow.

It was always a futile hope. Rich doesn't make mistakes.

Neither do the timekeepers.

'Sarah Castell.' The woman's voice comes from the watch welded shut around my wrist. 'You have violated your curfew. This is your third infraction. You are being reassigned.'

I was so close. My hand is already outstretched in front of me, reaching for the scanner that would admit me into my block. I wave the watch across its face once, twice, a third time, but the red light is constant and mocking.

It's too late.

I'll never see daylight again.

It started a month ago.

I probably should have woken with the sun, but I actually woke to the sound of my watch alarm. I wanted to sleep later – I've never been a morning person – but the monitor would have recorded my idleness. It would also have recorded that I was in perfect health. Without a good reason for staying in bed, I'd find my account docked tomorrow, and I couldn't afford to lose another credit.

I dragged myself through the shower, six scant feet away from my bed, then to the corner of my room that passed for a kitchen: coffee maker stacked on microwave stacked on fridge. They were the small luxuries that made life worth living.

There was the shadow of a dream in my head as I brewed up the recycled beans. My dreams usually flee the moment I wake up, but this one was lingering with remarkable persistence.

I had been walking up a wide staircase to a building covered in ornate blue tiles. The patterns they made were intricate and beguiling, carrying my gaze in swirls across the face of the structure. The sun glinted off the polished glaze. I'd never known stone and ceramic could be so beautiful.

It was the kind of dream you want to recapture, so you can slip back inside it. I knew it was useless, but I closed my eyes nonetheless, trying to conjure up the feeling I had lost.

My watch pinged at eight o'clock precisely, snapping me to alertness.

'Your assignment has been delivered,' said an automated voice. 'It will take thirty-two minutes to reach your destination.'

It wasn't so much a prediction as an order; if I arrived any later than 8:32, my account would be docked. If I turned up looking less than presentable, my account would be docked. In fact, if I did anything that wasn't to the liking of the sector manager, my account would be docked.

I checked the address on my watch, abandoned my coffee, then walked straight out of my room and into the lift, taking it down ten storeys to the street. Far beneath me, the D-Defs of my block were getting ready to sleep. Since they're never awake during the daytime, they don't need to live above ground. Officially, they're called Moonlighters, but no one ever uses that term. We call them D-Defs instead – Vitamin D-Deficients – even though the name isn't strictly accurate. They spend most of their working time under UV lights strong enough to counteract the effects of their nocturnal existence. Still, it's not much of a life.

'The A91 will arrive in thirty seconds,' my watch announced.

I ran to the stop, then hopped aboard the high-speed tram and took a seat at the front, one of only a few left empty. At this time of day, all of us Sunshiners were on our way somewhere, smiling and chatting as we followed our watches. Well, the others were smiling. They were probably of a higher rank than I was.

I turned on my phone and forced my attention towards the details of today's assignment. I almost didn't bother, because I knew what it would say. I'd be cleaning dishes or packing rations or sorting recycling, just like yesterday and the day before and the day before that. The work was always menial and always inside. I might as well have been a D-Def.

It hadn't always been this way. Once upon a time, I'd been given assignments picking fruit, or waiting tables, or – for one glorious summer a decade ago – gardening in the prettiest park I'd ever seen. But every moment of noncompliance, every second of lateness, had been tallied up against me over the course of my working life until I found myself at the bottom of the pack. There was no way for me to climb back up.

Which is why I was surprised when I opened my assignments app to find that I would be working as a museum curator that day. It wasn't a prestigious assignment, because it wasn't outdoors, but it wasn't menial either. I looked around the tram. Was this some kind of mistake? Had I received someone else's assignment instead? But that was nonsense; it had been sent to my phone. That couldn't have happened by accident, and this was definitely my phone. It was keyed to my wrist watch in the same way that everything else in my life was.

There was only one explanation: overnight, a whole block's worth of people must have been demoted below me. It was the only way I could have been bumped up so high so quickly. I hadn't thought that there was a Sunshiner rank below mine – the really awful jobs go to the D-Defs – but apparently I had been wrong.

Well, their loss was my gain.

Museum curator.

Even the sound of the words in my head made me

more cheerful. Maybe it would turn into a permanent assignment. Maybe, if I did well, they'd let me stay. Maybe they'd issue me with a suit as my uniform. I couldn't remember the last time I'd worn a suit. How long ago had my last office job been? Three years? Five years?

I opened the photo vault on my phone. I knew I had a picture of me and Clara in the sector's central office, taken one evening after work. It would be dated. I didn't look at the photo often, because that night was the last time we ever saw each other. The very next day, she was promoted and I was demoted, which took us out of each other's orbit for good; socialising outside of your rank is not encouraged. With my meteoric race to the bottom, I had shed all of my friends along the way.

But I never got as far as the photo I was looking for. When I opened the app, it showed me the latest photos it had captured. For the most recent two, I had not been the photographer.

The first was a picture of a man leaning in a doorway, smiling. I didn't recognise him.

The second was so familiar that it turned my stomach.

It was the building from my dream. I don't mean that it looked similar, or that it reminded me of that building, I mean that it was identical in every respect. It wasn't just the shape of the structure, either; the camera angle and the light made for a perfect replica of the image I'd seen in my sleep. It was as though the picture on my phone had been lifted straight from my head.

Was I still asleep? I pinched myself, hard, but I didn't wake up. Everything felt real, but then dreams could be so deceptive.

Maybe it was just a glitch with the phone. That would explain why I'd received such a plum assignment. I turned the phone off and on again, waiting out the nervous seconds until I could open the photo app again. When I did, the images were still there: the man and the building.

A picture I didn't recognise, and a picture I knew only from my dreams.

Both were impossible.

The night isn't what I expected it to be. I thought being a D-Def would be just like being a Sunshiner, only with muckier jobs and in the dark. It's actually a thousand times worse.

My wrist watch directs me to my new room in my new block, twenty storeys beneath ground level. It's deep enough that at first I thought I was on the very bottom floor, but the noise that filters up from below is enough to prove me wrong. I can hear voices and thumping from the cells that surround mine, but nothing like the moaning and screaming that comes up from the lower storeys. It's probably just children playing, or something similarly innocent, but the insulation of the earth around us makes the noise echo eerily. I don't like the stairwells, where the sound is amplified, but there's no way to avoid them. The lifts that serve the block don't go beneath ground level.

I hold my wrist up to the scanner outside cell -2089. It flashes green and the door swings open.

The doors are close together on this floor, so I wasn't expecting much, but the cell beyond is only half the size of my old room. There's a mattress on the floor, a toilet in the corner and a tiny sink above it. No shower. No fridge. No electricity except whatever's powering the single bulb set into the ceiling. The only other furniture is a small cupboard above the bed, stuffed full of basic ration packs. I guess that's what I'll be eating from now on.

I rinse my hands in the sink. Even after the water runs out, they're bloody and torn. I broke more than one nail prying apart the chainlink to get out of that alley. Now the cuts around my cuticles burn with infection, sending shocks of pain up my arms. All for nothing, because I missed curfew anyway.

I wish I'd never been sent to the museum.

I wish I'd never met Rich.

After I found the dream building on my phone, I couldn't stop shaking. I told myself it was because I'd missed my caffeine hit that morning, but in truth I was spooked.

I hopped off the tram at my destination – the buzzing of my watch prompting my exit – and stepped out into an area I'd never been to before. Like all the other habitation blocks, my home sat in the hinterland between one city and another. Usually, my work took me from one hinterland to another, but that morning I had been deposited in the centre of Legacy A, one of the largest and oldest cities on the Island. And when I say it's large, I mean *large*. Just because the Island is technically an island, that doesn't mean it's small. There are billions of people here, and the cities are proportioned accordingly, even though only a small segment of the population gets to see them.

It was a special kind of privilege to walk these streets, and one not usually extended to people of my rank. That was what cemented my conclusion, more than my new assignment, more than the prospect of a new suit: I must have been promoted to be allowed into a city centre, especially one this ancient and revered.

There were buildings everywhere, but not the right-angled structures of the blocks. Every single one was different from its neighbour. They leaned towards each other as though they were sharing confidences, crowding close like friends. None of them rose more than five storeys, but they were so intimate and the road was so winding that each time I turned a corner I came across another unexpected treasure.

My watch buzzed to signal my arrival just a split-second before I turned into the tiny square and saw the museum. It was circled with other structures and a few trees in full blossom, but still the sun glinted off the tiles and the intricate patterns drew my gaze.

There was no mistaking it. It was the building from my dream. The building from the photo. The building that was right in front of me now, covered with staircases and steep-roofed towers and draped with flowering creepers.

I was here. I was really here, mounting the steps to the beautiful blue entrance, just like I had in my dream. It was so much like sleepwalking that I felt dizzy with the unreality of it.

'Sarah, right?'

I looked up to see a man at the top of the steps, standing by the door. He had blue eyes, and blond hair that shone in the sun, the kind of hair that was washed regularly with genuine shampoo. He was about my age, but clearly well above my rank, someone I would never have come into contact with in my day-to-day life. And yet I felt that I had. Recently.

I furrowed my brow at him for a moment, trying to work out why his face was familiar. Then he leaned against the doorframe and it hit me: he was the man from the photo on my phone.

'I recognise you,' he said, taking the words right out of my mouth.

'Excuse me?'

'My name's Richard. I'm the museum director. And I know you, don't I?' He looked at me, his eyes searching my face for something: a clue, a memory, an answer. I knew this, because I was busy searching his face for the same.

'Have we met?' he asked.

Had we? I didn't think so, but if that was the case then how had his picture ended up in my phone? How had the picture of the building ended up in my phone? How was any of this possible?

I couldn't admit the truth, not when it might cost me a cushy job in this gorgeous building, so I plastered on a smile and said, 'I don't think so. Sorry.'

He blinked. With the blink, his brief disappointment was erased, as though it had been nothing. But I'd seen it, that moment of thwarted expectation.

'Oh well,' he said brightly. 'My mistake. Come on inside. Let me show you the ropes.'

He held the door open for me and I passed beneath the blue tiles, into the cool marble hall beyond.

* * *

Someone's hammering on my door.

I check my watch, but it's still early in the evening. I'm not expecting to get my next assignment until eight.

'Who is it?' I yell.

'Who do you think?'

I jump up from the mattress and practically rip the door open, leaving smears of dried blood on the handle from my torn fingers.

'You,' I say, crossing my arms over my chest. 'What the hell are you doing here? How did you even find me?'

'I followed you,' Rich says. 'Can I come in?'

I widen my stance to block the door. 'No.'

'Sarah…' he says, his tone pleading. Then I look at him properly for the first time. It doesn't look like the past twenty-four hours have been any kinder to him than they were to me. I can see the terror in his eyes. His hair is dishevelled, his face is dirty, and he clearly slept in that shirt.

I step aside to let him in. He doesn't speak until the door is closed behind us, and when he does, it's a whisper.

'I think I fucked up.'

'You *think*?' I ask him, looking around pointedly at my new room.

'No, not that.' He dismisses my misery with an irritated glance. 'I mean this.'

He holds up his wrist so I can see the face of his watch. At first, I don't notice anything wrong with it, but then I see that the numbers are ticking down rather than up. I don't know what it means, but it doesn't seem like a good thing.

I look him dead in the eye.

'What did you do?'

'I don't know!' He runs a hand back through his hair, leaving a greasy mess in its wake. 'Do you remember anything?'

'What are you talking about?'

He moves closer. The cell is so small that one step brings him into my personal space and up against my defences. I put up my hands to ward him off and he catches one of them in his.

'Do you remember?' he asks again, looking into my eyes.

'Remember what?' My voice comes out low and broken.

'Why do I know you, Sarah?' He lifts one hand to my cheek and strokes his thumb over my skin. 'Why do I feel as though this is the most natural thing in the world?'

I push him away gently, not because I'm scared of him, or because I don't want him close, but because he's clearly too upset for this right now. He doesn't resist.

'I just don't understand,' he says, sitting down on the mattress with his head in his hands. 'I don't understand what's happening. I don't understand why I feel as though I've known you my whole life. I don't understand any of it.'

I sit down next to him.

'Did you get reassigned?' I ask quietly.

'I guess. Maybe. I don't know. What do you think this means?' He lifts his wrist, flashing the watch face towards me. Whatever it's counting down to, it's going to happen in a little over two hours.

'When did it start?' I ask.

'This afternoon.'

'At the museum?'

His lips flatten into a tight line for a moment, then he says, 'No. Not at the museum.'

'You missed your assignment?' I feel like the room is spinning. 'Were you sick?'

'No.'

He doesn't volunteer any more information, so I prompt him. 'Was it a reward day?'

'No.'

'Then what the hell, Rich?' I'm suddenly on my feet, pacing the three square feet by the door. 'Are you trying to get yourself busted down to D-Def? Is this what you want?' I gesture at the filthy mattress, the flickering bulb and the steel toilet. 'Because this is what you'll get.'

He looks down at his wrist, where the numbers continue to tick down. I realise we're both thinking the same thing: he's probably in line for something much worse.

'Are you sure you're not sick?' I say, offering him an out. 'You look sick.'

He takes my hand and pulls me back down next to him.

'I'm not sick,' he says quietly. 'I'm busted.'

The museum was a dream job, which I supposed was fitting given how I first saw the place. My assignment was to patrol the corridors, along with a few other

Sunshiners, and make sure that no one touched the exhibits. Which were fascinating. I'd never had much interest in life before the Division, because it seemed so remote that it had no bearing on my life, but now that I was surrounded by artefacts from a time before Sunshiners and Moonlighters, it was impossible not to be intrigued.

There were books in dead languages, clockwork devices with unknown uses, and pieces of pottery telling stories that no living person recalled. The mystery of it thrilled me.

After a week, I was starting to believe it might be a permanent assignment after all. For the first time in ages, I was actually happy. There was even a uniform, a real suit. It lived in the changing room at the back of the museum, waiting for me to arrive and slip its tight-napped wool over my skin every morning. It was a beautiful creation, and I revered it so much that I took it off before my lunch break every day, so I wouldn't sully it by sitting outside in the sun for half an hour.

Even though the incident with my phone's photo vault still disturbed me, the museum was magical enough to win me over. You'd think it would have given me the creeps, but it didn't. In fact, it was quickly becoming my favourite place in the world.

'You've found the most valuable piece we have on display,' Richard said one evening as he locked up.

I was peering into one of the glass exhibit cases, fascinated by the filigreed metalwork within. The artefact was about the size of a dinner plate, but petalled like a daisy with overlapping ovals of metal.

'They don't know what it was for?' I asked him.

'Does it have to have a purpose?' he replied. 'Can't it just be beautiful?'

'I don't know. I think things are more interesting when they serve a function.'

'Maybe its function is to make you question that.'

I laughed. 'Now I understand why you're the director here. You have an answer for everything.'

Then he smiled the strangest smile at me, a half-smile that held a perfect balance of amusement and confusion. I'd thought the comment was innocuous enough, but apparently I'd said the wrong thing. It embarrassed me, so I said my goodbyes quickly and fled back to my block, my single room and my microwaved dinner.

But when I arrived at the museum the next day, he was waiting at the door.

'Good morning, Sarah,' he said.

I returned the greeting, but cautiously. He had a determined expression that told me he had something on his mind. I wasn't sure I wanted to find out what it was.

'Would you come up to my office, please?' he asked.

I panicked.

'Have I done something wrong?' I didn't want to lose this assignment.

'No, nothing like that.' His tone and his words were reassuring, but his expression was not. 'I just need a moment of your time.'

I followed him up the marble stairs to a breezy, sun-filled office at the back of the building. The double-doors were fully glazed and gave me a clear view back into the main gallery, but I still felt trapped when they closed behind us.

'This is going to sound strange,' he said as he sat behind his desk. He gestured me towards the chair facing it, which I took, despite my urge to flee. 'The thing is,' he went on, 'I'm certain that we've met before. It's driving me crazy. Your face is so familiar.'

He put his elbows on his desk, then leaned forward and looked at me. Really looked at me, as though he could see straight into my soul.

Without even meaning to, I pulled my phone out of my pocket, opened the photo vault and slid it over the desk towards him. There had been no more photos since the last two: the museum's blue facade and Richard leaning in its doorway.

'What's this?' he asked. 'Have you been taking stealthy photos?'

'Look at the date stamp.'

He did. Then he checked the calendar on his desk before looking back at the phone.

'Your date stamp is wrong,' he said eventually.

'It's not.'

'But I wasn't even at the museum that day.'

I reclaimed the phone. 'Neither was I. The night before I started here, I dreamed about walking up the steps outside. When I woke up in the morning, these photos were waiting for me. They were apparently taken the previous day. When I was halfway out towards Legacy B, repainting a fire-damaged block.'

He went still.

'That's not possible.'

'I know,' I said. 'But that's what happened.'

To my surprise, he believed me.

* * *

'They came to the museum,' he says. He's holding my damaged hand as we sit side by side on the mattress.

'Who came to the museum?'

'The timekeepers.'

I go still.

I've never seen a timekeeper in my entire life. Even though I've frequently been busted down from rank to rank, every punishment I've suffered has been enforced by my wrist watch. Since it determines where I'm allowed to go and tracks every second of insubordination, there really isn't any need for human intervention. If I don't do what I'm told, I lose privileges, or the food items sent to me through my room's delivery chute are lower quality, or my assignments become worse, or I get moved into a shithole like this cell. The whole system is automated.

So for the timekeepers, real-life human timekeepers, to come to the museum for Rich… It's something I can't even imagine.

'What did you do?'

'I slipped out the back. What else could I do?'

I look at him incredulously. 'Are you crazy? They'll track you here! You've just screwed us both.'

'Of course they won't. I'm not an idiot, Sarah. I disabled the wristband weeks ago. It's sending a false feed.'

'Excuse me?'

I didn't think such a thing was even possible. The watches are made from a single piece of metal with shatterproof glass set seamlessly into the face. There's no way to pry them open. If you try to cut into them then they send out a tamper alert. Or just detonate. It happened to a guy in one of my old blocks. He took out three of the surrounding rooms when he went up in smoke.

'There's a lot more in the museum than the attractive art we keep on display,' Rich says. 'There are tools. Books. Things you wouldn't believe. I've been making use of them.'

'What? Why? Do you know what you're risking—'

'Do you know how many people die every day in this city? Because they're rebellious, or outspoken, or just in the way of someone more powerful? Our world isn't a fair place. I tried to make it better. I guess I failed.' He holds his head in his hands. 'I wanted to save lives, to change the system. But whatever we try – and we've tried basically everything we can think of – everything just goes right back the way it was. It's so static. It's impossibly static. Things should be able to change. The fact that they don't beggars belief. And the thing with the photos and your dreams…'

'It doesn't make sense.'

'Right.' He sighs the word, and I can hear the relief in it. 'It doesn't make sense.'

'So what is this?' I say, grabbing his wrist to angle the face of his watch in my direction. The countdown is still going, relentless.

'I don't know,' he says. 'I've never seen it before.'

'Well, can't you just remove it? If you have all the tools—'

'Not on my own. I can't do it on my own.'

Our eyes meet.

I say, 'I think you need to tell me exactly what you

did.'

For a while, everything seemed normal. I'd started to think that maybe I'd imagined the whole dream thing. I was wilfully ignoring the photos that were still stored on my phone, as though they no longer existed if I wasn't looking at them.

But then, about ten days later, something strange happened.

I had just walked back into the museum after lunch when Richard came out of his office and started striding towards me. He wasn't wearing his suit. I'd never seen him without it before. I almost didn't recognise him in jeans and a purple henley shirt, and yet somehow he looked more himself than ever, as if I knew this version of him better. It was obvious just how much muscle had been hidden by tailoring. He wasn't built like I'd expect a museum director to be.

'Come on,' he said, looping my arm through his and turning me back towards the front door.

'What? What's going on?'

'We're taking a reward day.'

'But that's not what my assignment—'

'Check your phone.'

I did, and he was right. Where previously my assignment for the day had been listed as the museum, it now said *reward day*. A genuine half-day off, fully approved by the sector manager.

'I haven't had a reward day in years,' I said. The only time off I'd ever taken was on national holidays. 'How did this happen?'

'You've been working hard,' Richard lied. All I had

been doing was wandering around the museum, looking at the exhibits and smiling at the patrons. 'I thought we both deserved a break.'

He obviously had a clear plan for the day so, still reeling from the novelty of it all, I let him lead me wherever he wanted. I trusted him implicitly. I couldn't explain that.

'Have you checked your photos this morning?' he said as he guided me along the streets.

My teeth ground together. 'No.'

He asked me the same question at least once every couple of days. While I'd been trying to dismiss the whole incident, Richard had been doing the opposite. He wanted to crack open the mystery and solve it, whereas I just wanted to pretend it had never happened.

'Check your phone, Sarah,' he said.

I sighed, but did as he asked.

There was a new picture, a selfie this time. Richard and I were sitting next to each other somewhere high, smiling at the camera as the sun went down behind us.

I stopped dead in the middle of the road, feeling sick to my stomach.

'How did you know?' I asked.

He opened his own photo vault and showed me the exact same picture.

'I found it this morning,' he said.

'So that's why you put in for the reward day?'

'It's one of the reasons.' He looked away. 'I know where this is.'

'So you want us to go there?'

'I think we should. If this is what I think it is, then I'm not sure what will happen if we don't.'

'What do you think it is?' I asked, though I was scared to hear the answer.

'There's only one explanation, isn't there? Time travel.'

Time travel?

'But that's not possible.'

He laughed. 'I've been thinking that a lot myself recently. It doesn't change the facts. But we'd better hurry up – the mountains are a while away. Will you come?'

I didn't feel as though I really had a choice.

It was a long journey on foot, but I was used to it. A couple of hours' walking took us through the city and out to a rarified area that looked like something from the films we projected onto the museum walls. There was green everywhere, surrounding a forested edifice that rose from a sea of block buildings in irregular, craggy peaks. It was so strange to have the earth beneath my feet, the smell of greenery surrounding me, and the insects buzzing close to investigate Richard's purple shirt.

My life was concrete and fleas. The mountain was flowers and bees.

We were about three-quarters of the way to the top when I looked over my shoulder and saw the ghost of the photo in the view behind me.

'Richard—'

'We're not at work, Sarah,' he said, walking on without looking back. 'Call me Rich.'

I could feel the blush burning my cheeks and I hated it. It was out of place, deviant even.

'Rich,' I said, calling him back. 'Wait. Look. I think

this is the place.'

He pulled his phone out of his pocket and held it up in front of him, checking the photo against the view.

'You're right,' he said. 'This is it.'

It was a nice spot. There were a few boulders clustered at the edge of the path that made a comfortable seat. As I looked at them, I could see the photo in my mind's eye. We would have sat there as the sun set, me on the right and Rich on the left, and we would have smiled for the camera.

'So,' I said, 'what now?'

'Now,' said Rich, taking his seat in exactly the right place, 'I guess we wait.'

'I need to get back before curfew.'

'I'll call us a car.'

I stared at him. I'd never been in a car before. My sole methods of transport were the tram and my feet.

'Okay,' I said, downplaying my excitement. 'I guess that would be fine.'

So we sat and watched the sunset, both of us waiting for a dramatic revelation.

But nothing happened. We checked against the photo, waiting for the precise moment that it pictured, and it came and went. We didn't smile. The sun set.

We had trekked out here for nothing.

By the time we got back to the street, it was already too late. We'd lingered too long on the mountain, waiting for an epiphany that never came. It had been almost pleasant, spending that time with Rich, until I realised what it would cost me. The glamour of the car ride home – leather interior, seat belts, chauffeur – was all eclipsed by my agitation as I watched the numbers rising on my watch screen.

19:45

19:52

19:56

When it reached eight o'clock, my watch screamed at me.

'Sarah Castell. You have violated your curfew. This is your first infraction. You have fifteen minutes to return to your block.'

'I told you I needed to get back,' I said, a quiet accusation.

'You can earn it out,' Rich said. 'It's no big deal.'

Curfew infractions are expunged after three months' good behaviour, but good behaviour is an elusive concept. It was a small thing, but a thing that would niggle at me until I had erased it from my record.

'Why isn't your alarm going off too?' I asked irritably.

'My curfew's not till nine.'

'Nine? How did you manage that?'

'I'm a popular guy.' He grinned, as though daring me to contradict him.

I smiled back, despite myself. 'I believe you.'

'No,' I say, pushing him away. 'I don't believe you.'

'It's true.' I'm expecting him to boast, but he doesn't. He sounds resigned, and a little despairing. 'I've been helping the resistance, working with some friends of mine to remove the wristbands, but we got caught. Half of them got off the Island. Half of them… Well, I guess you know.'

'D-Def?'

'Not all of them. Some got their ranks dropped to the Sunshiner basement. Others got D-Def. The leaders just… disappeared.'

We sit in silence for a few moments as that sinks in. I don't know what happened to those people, but I can take a wild guess. Rich must have come to the same conclusion.

'That's why so many people got downgraded last month,' I say eventually. 'That's why I was promoted to the museum.'

'I suppose so.' He looks uncomfortable.

'Rich,' I say. 'What aren't you telling me?'

He looks at me for a long moment, his gaze flicking from my eyes to my lips, my mouth, my hair, as though he's searching for the traces of someone else in my features. Or for the person he thinks I once was, the person that he'll remember.

'It was you,' I say, as the realisation finally dawns. 'You're the one who assigned me to the museum.'

He laughs wryly. 'You think I have the power to do that?'

'I think you know people who do. You're the museum director.'

He's still trying to laugh it off, but then he looks at my face. Whatever he sees there convinces him that it won't work. He sighs.

'I saw you,' he says. 'I was going back to my block – it used to be across the street from yours – and I saw you getting off the tram. I knew you, Sarah. I still can't explain that, any more than I can explain the photos on your phone, or on my phone, but I *knew* you, and not just your face, but every part of you. I knew the way you raise your eyebrow when you're irritated. I knew the little mole behind your ear, and the way your hair frizzes in damp weather. I knew that you have a scar on your right hip—' I reach for the spot involuntarily. '— and, god help me, I knew that you'd giggle if I kissed it. How do I know that? Tell me how.'

I can feel my cheeks burning with my blush.

'I don't know,' I say, but I can feel the ghost of his lips on my skin. I know what it feels like to be kissed there – the gentle rasp of stubble on tender skin – even though I've never been that intimate with anyone in my whole life.

'Something's wrong in this place. That's the whole reason I got involved with smuggling people off the Island. But whatever this is, this thing between you and me, it's different. It was real once. Maybe not here. Or maybe it's been taken from us somehow. But I remember it. Don't you?'

I do. But I don't know what it means.

After our day in the mountains, Rich had become philosophical.

He had started abandoning his office to walk the corridors of the museum with me, talking to me about every aspect of our society: the curfews, the ranks, assignments, penalties and resources. It always riled him up.

'People aren't good at obedience,' he said to me one day. 'Have you noticed that?'

'People?' I asked. I was startled because I'd thought it was only me who struggled with the rules.

'And yet our lives are structured around a system that

demands obedience,' he went on. 'Miss a curfew, and the infraction is noted. Sleep in too late, and your accounts are docked. Annoy the wrong people, and suddenly your food supply is gruel instead of bread.' He spoke about these things as though he'd experienced them himself, which I knew couldn't be true, not in his position.

'What do you want me to say? Are you expecting me to be impressed that you sympathise with the struggles of us low-rank Sunshiners?' I wouldn't have been so short with him last week, but our daily conversations had eroded some of my barriers. I trusted him enough to be honest.

He shrugged. 'Even I have my little deprivations.'

'Oh? Chauffeurs not polite enough?' I teased. 'Champagne not cold enough?'

'Look,' he said, brushing off the joke, 'this is my point: why is it so rigid? Humanity isn't rigid. So why are we penalised for not acting like automata?'

'What does it matter?' I said. 'It is the way it is.'

But it bothered him. It continued to bother him for the rest of the week.

Then another photo appeared my phone. It had also appeared in my dreams the previous night. Given the content of the picture, seeing Rich the next day was always going to be awkward, but having the dreamed experience in my head made it worse.

'Hello,' he said as I walked in the door. He'd been waiting for me in the main hall, which was enough to tell me that the photo had appeared on his phone as well.

'Hi,' I said, then I ducked past him, making a beeline

for the changing room.

He followed.

'Sarah—'

'I don't really want to talk about it,' I said.

'I think we should.'

'I don't think it'll help.'

'So you're just going to ignore it? We can't pretend it didn't happen.'

'But it *didn't* happen,' I said, turning to face him. 'It happened to some other version of us in the future, or in another world. But it didn't happen to us. That wasn't our yesterday.'

He didn't reply, but his eyes were mapping my face. Without really meaning to, I found that I was looking at him in the same way. I liked the line of his jaw, the way his eyes were just starting to crinkle in the corners, and the softness of the skin on the apple of his cheek, above the beard line. I shouldn't have known that the skin there was so soft. How did I know that?

'It could be us,' he said.

I hesitated before replying, and that hesitation was enough. He went to the front door. For a moment I thought he was leaving. I was about to go after him when he locked it from the inside and turned back to me.

'It wasn't our yesterday,' he said, leaning against the door. He looked relaxed, but I could tell from the tension in his jaw that he was not. 'It could be our today. If you want.'

I didn't know what to say. I walked to the side of the room, to the exhibit case that held the petalled metal artefact I loved. I could hear Rich approaching, but I stayed where I was and got out my phone.

The photo was haunting. The light was the pale white of morning, filtering through the high windows that surrounded us. It glinted off the petalled artefact, catching on the pieces of filigree in exactly the same way that it did now, in real life. The picture could have been taken in this moment.

Except we were alone here, standing shoulder to shoulder. In the photo, we were face to face, toe to toe, mouth to mouth, while some unseen third person took our picture.

We looked happy.

Rich reached out and took my hand.

'I don't know how to explain it,' he said, 'but this is right.'

When our lips touched, it felt like a reunion.

The moment my watch reads eight o'clock, we leave the cell and hurry out onto the street. We got lucky: my assignment this evening is in the right direction, so my monitor won't detect any problems until we get off the tram two stops early. That should give us the time to do what we need before the timekeepers find us.

We hope.

On the journey, Rich is tight-lipped and pale. Despite the heat of the evening, he's pulled on a long-sleeved shirt so no one will see the countdown on his wrist, and he's checking his phone obsessively, as though he's willing a new photo to appear and show us what to do next.

'It doesn't make sense,' he whispers. 'The photos, your dreams…'

'It's just that everything's happening out of order,' I say. 'Time travel, like you said. My phone and my dreams are running a day ahead of reality, right?'

'Or you're running a day late.'

I shudder.

'But it doesn't explain why I knew you without ever having met you,' he goes on, 'or why I know that everything in the world is wrong. It doesn't explain why I've tried so hard to change it, even though the system benefits me. I'm not a selfless person, Sarah. Never have been. But this…'

'Maybe you're less selfish than you thought.'

He shakes his head, unconvinced, and turns his attention back to his phone.

He taps my arm when we reach the right stop and the two of us disembark quickly. It takes a moment for my watch to register that I have not moved along with the departing tram, but when it does the beeping is an insistent rebuke. When I check my account tomorrow, I'll be surprised if there's a single credit left in it.

The workshop is close. It looks like an abandoned block. I'd guess it was condemned because of a roach problem; they are all over the floor. Now the place is being used to dismantle the Island from the inside, one wristband at a time.

'Here,' Rich says, beckoning me over to a workbench. He has to sweep the roaches off the surface to make enough space to open the toolkit that sits on it. 'I'm going to do the tricky bit, but I need you to clamp the bracelet in place. Can you do that?'

I nod and start adjusting the tabletop vice, familiar from a brief cleaning assignment at a carpentry workshop. It's the only thing I know how to work; the tools Rich pulls out of the kit are oddly-coloured and strange. One of them lights up when he presses the buttons. It looks like an archaic version of my phone.

I fasten the vice around his wristband and close it tight.

'I'm going to disable the monitor,' he says, 'then as soon as it's safe I want you to cut through the band with this electric hand saw. Okay?'

I'm terrified, but I nod and take the instrument he offers. It's a single-edged blade, which he directs me to put on the inside of the bracelet rather than the outside, so I'll be cutting away from his wrist. It's a tight fit.

'When I say go, just press this button.' He takes a deep breath. 'Okay. Ready?'

I can feel the sweat soaking into the underarms of my T-shirt. 'Ready.'

He starts typing on the phone-like device while I stand, poised and waiting, with the electric saw.

The device beeps. It beeps again. After another minute or so, it starts beeping endlessly.

'Is that good or bad?' I ask.

'Bad,' Rich says, pushing the device away dismissively. 'Really, really bad. You may as well release the vice.'

'What?'

'It's not coming off, Sarah. It's locked into self-destruct.'

My mind races. 'So what do we do now?'

'Simple,' he says. 'You leave.'

After the kiss, everything was suddenly too

complicated.

Every look between us felt loaded, every accidental touch felt deliberate, and it was all coloured by the ridiculous strangeness of the situation. We had been brought together by an impossibility. It might crumble into nothing at any moment.

So I kept my distance. Or at least, I tried to, until Rich stopped me one evening as I was on my way out.

'Let me take you somewhere,' he said.

'Where?'

I was suspicious. There had been no more photos, no more dreams, and no more kisses. I was doing a very good job of pretending that none of it had ever happened. My promotion to the museum was an opportunity I'd promised myself I wouldn't waste.

'I want to show you something.'

'Rich, I thought we'd agreed that this was a bad idea.'

'It's not about that,' he said, ducking his head in an attempt to hide his blush. 'I'm not trying anything. I promise. I just want to show you something that I think will change your mind. About the way the Island works.'

'Rich…'

'Please?'

I wanted to say no. I wanted to walk away and go back home to my cosy room with its fridge and its microwave and its single bed. But, for some unknown reason, it was difficult for me to refuse him anything.

'An hour,' I said. 'Then I'm leaving.'

He smiled. 'You won't regret this.'

In the end, it took us forty-five minutes just to get to

the place. It was over the other side of Legacy A, practically out in the blocks, and Rich insisted that we travel by foot.

'What is this place?' I asked as the building came into view. It was nothing like the leaning, organic structures at the centre of the city. Instead, it was a thirty-floor monstrosity of gleaming glass and metal. It belonged in a newer city, something built after the Division. Here, it was a straight line in a world of wavy ones. It didn't fit.

'It used to be a central office,' Rich said. 'Closed down and used for file storage.'

'What? We shouldn't be here.'

'Calm down. I have a friend who works on the cleaning crew. The timekeepers will never know.'

I was surprised that Rich had friends who were low enough in the rankings to be cleaners – maybe that was where his empathy was coming from – but I didn't question it. I didn't want to be discovered hanging around on the street outside an official building when I should have been on my way home. So I followed Rich to a door at the back that had been propped open with a dustbin.

'In here,' he said.

When I hesitated, he took my hand in his and pulled me in behind him. I let him, because the alternative was waiting outside alone, and that wasn't any more appealing.

'Do you know where you're going?' I whispered.

'I've been here before. Trust me.'

Irrationally, I did.

After a few twists and turns and a couple of flights of

stairs, Rich led me into a large office where plans and charts were strewn across the tables. On the walls, bright screens displayed rolling stacks of names in a variety of colours.

'What—'

'Just watch,' he said.

For once, I did as I was told. After a few minutes, I worked out what it meant. My mouth dropped open.

'What is this?' I asked, looking for confirmation.

'The rankings feed from the central office. Still functional. You're watching a corrupt system at work. A system that needs to be changed.'

Over the course of the next hour, we both watched as name after name was demoted or promoted. The reason for each movement in the rankings flashed up beside the relevant name for a few seconds before the next name was considered. Sometimes the reasons were infractions or rewards, but sometimes they were simply marked *Potential Dissident*, *Insubordinate* or, most ominously of all, *Request from Councillor.*

'The illusion of accountability,' Rich said. 'Just enough information to satisfy the monitors, and nothing more. I managed to get my hands on some of the print outs. Did you want to see your file?'

'No,' I said, but he was already holding it. He'd prepared for this night. *No* was not an option.

I took it from him and spread the pages across a nearby table. The recent entries were what I had expected: infraction for breaking curfew, idleness, lateness. Every error of my years had been catalogued and deducted.

Then I got to the less recent history: four and a half

years ago, when I had been working in the central office with Clara. There was a note next to that assignment: *Adept and intelligent, but insubordinate. Displays undesirable levels of curiosity. Demotion recommended by Councillor Vickers.*

Clara's surname was Vickers. Councillor Vickers, her father, had found her the assignment at the central office. Then apparently he'd engineered a reason for me to be demoted, to clear the path for her.

'Are you angry yet?' Rich asked.

I was, but I was more angry at myself than anyone else. For believing. For trusting. And for letting Rich convince me to come here in the first place.

The alarm in my wristband went off when I was still twenty minutes from home. I imagined my name flashing up on that list and wondered how far it would fall as a result of this transgression. How much farther it would fall if they ever discovered what Rich and I had been doing tonight.

Curfew infraction number two. Now both infractions would stay on my record for six months. I could still earn them out, but if I incurred another in that time then I'd be done. Out. Finished. D-Def.

And if I kept hanging out with Rich, with his rebellious tendencies, chances were it would happen sooner rather than later.

The stakes were too high.

I needed to put him behind me. I needed to leave this assignment.

'You need to leave,' he says. 'Get to your assignment. Pretend that none of this happened. Pretend that we never met.'

'What? You can't seriously expect—'

'There isn't any time. There's no way to reverse this. What's the point in us both dying? You need to get out of here.'

There are tears in his eyes, but they're not for himself. He's frantic, desperate for me to leave. He puts his arm around the small of my back and ushers me towards the door.

The intimacy of his touch reminds me of the kiss.

And then, somehow, it reminds me of a million other kisses, kisses that we've never shared in this life, but that I remember in the same way that I remember the smell of coffee, the taste of oranges, and the feel of sunshine on my skin.

I grab his hand and hold it on my waist, pressing his palm into my side. It feels so familiar and comforting that I never want to let go.

'You're starting to remember, aren't you?' he says.

I am. I remember his face. I remember the weight of his body on mine and the scent of him in the morning, even though – to my knowledge – we've never woken up together.

He hesitates for a moment, then puts his hand on my stomach.

'Do you remember this?' he asks.

It's as though something has slammed into my chest. The force of it is visceral, even though it doesn't move me an inch. I remember.

I was pregnant, once upon a time. Or at least, I have the memory of being pregnant. I remember wanting it so much, but being afraid that I wouldn't be able to keep it. And then I remember it being gone, ripped away from me without my permission.

I feel like I'm going to be sick, but at the same time I'm crying, the tears streaming down my face.

He pulls me into his arms.

I remember how it feels to be held by him.

Or maybe it's not a memory, but a premonition. Maybe everything I feel when I'm with him – the comfort in his intimacy, the knowledge of his touch – is just an echo of something that is yet to happen. Maybe this really is time travel. Maybe we have a whole, long life together ahead of us, presented to us in snapshots that stretch years into the future.

Or maybe we have no more time at all. Maybe this is all we get.

There are only a few seconds left on his watch.

I had only a few minutes left. If I didn't leave soon then I was going to miss curfew, but Rich was still at the front of the museum, fiddling with his keys.

'Richard! Come on!' I yelled at him through the back door.

There had been a special event that evening: the unveiling of a new exhibit. It was my last day here – Rich had arranged a reassignment at my request – but I had agreed to stay late to help, on the proviso that he would get me home before curfew. He was coming dangerously close to breaking his promise.

'I'm coming,' he said, hurrying towards me. He had an armful of leaflets from the exhibition, which had some pretty inflammatory content. Rich's political agitations were starting to spill into his work.

'Why are you bringing those?' I asked.

'I thought I'd do some flyering on the way home.'

'Are you kidding me? They'll rank-bust you for sure.'

The audience tonight had been select, specially chosen to include like-minded Sunshiners only. They were all interested in how things used to be, before the Division, and were willing to support Rich's ambitions to change the system.

But the majority of the population wouldn't think that way. They, like me, were already in too precarious a situation to invite scandal. They needed to keep their heads down and stay out of trouble. If he went out throwing those pamphlets around, he'd be reported to the timekeepers in seconds.

'It's worth it,' he said as he locked the back door. 'I can't just sit and do nothing.'

'Why not? It's exactly what you should do.'

He stopped walking. We were in the short alley that led from the back of the museum to the street, so close to the car that I was tempted to manhandle him the rest of the way. I couldn't afford another infraction.

'Rich, please. Come on. Curfew. Remember?'

'Curfew is why I'm fighting this. I'm not going back, Sarah. Not after everything I've learned. They'll make me D-Def, I know that, but I'm doing it anyway.'

'You *want* to be D-Def?'

'Of course not. But that's the point. No one wants to be D-Def. Why do those who are have to put up with it? What did they do to deserve it?'

'They probably missed their damn curfews!' I yelled, frustrated. 'Now take me home.'

But he wasn't listening.

'I'll risk being D-Def, if that's what it takes. No one deserves that life unless they choose it. Isn't it worth fighting to change things? I thought you'd understand that. I thought you'd want to join me.'

'I want to go home.'

'Fine,' he said, striding along the alley ahead of me. But when he got to the end, he stopped just beyond the gate, blocking the path to the street.

'I'll prove it to you,' he said, slamming the gate shut in my face. The lock clicked home. 'You need to be outside the system to see it clearly.'

'Rich?'

'I'm telling you, Sarah. The world isn't what you think it is. I know I'm right.'

'Stop messing around. Where's the key?'

'I don't have it.'

A chill ran down my spine.

'What do you mean, you don't have it? I have to get out of here.'

'I mean I don't have it.' His expression was unreadable.

'Rich, come on. My curfew's in thirty minutes. I have to get home.'

'I'm sorry, but this is for the best,' he said. 'I know you won't understand it now, but I'm doing this for your own good. For both of us. To get us out.' Then he turned and started to walk away.

'Richard!'

I pummelled the chainlink with the sides of my fists, but it wouldn't budge. The building's back door was locked behind me – solid steel – and the alley walls and ceiling were concrete. There was no way out.

'Richard, you bastard!' I yelled at him. 'Get back here! You can't leave me here like this!'

But he just kept on walking into the night.

I open my eyes to a tiled ceiling, but it's not the blue tile of the museum, or the concrete of my cell. Instead, it's a white drop ceiling in a space that hums with air conditioning. I'm on a gurney.

I push myself up onto my side and see Rich watching me from a twin gurney next to mine. It all comes flooding back.

We have lived those lives already. We have had decades together: romance, marriage, dreams of children, all of it taken away by the state. This is the end.

'We broke the simulation,' I whisper.

The simulation we built together. Without the benefit of our memories, we've been working to dismantle it from the inside, without ever knowing what we were doing.

'It glitched on its own,' Rich says. 'It started messing up the simulation content, delivering it randomly as dreams, memories, photos—'

'Then we have to fix the glitch and get back in there. Try again. We have to prove that the Division will work. Without the photos on my phone, on your phone, without the time error, it would've worked. It was working.'

'It wasn't. You know the glitch wasn't the problem. You were losing rank like crazy and I was actively helping the rebels. The Division was unstable. People can't live inside such a rigid system.'

'Then maybe we need to change the parameters,' I say, desperately searching for another solution. 'Larger rooms, more storeys to the blocks, a different hierarchy, some other kind of assignment system, more socialisation—'

'Sarah,' Rich interrupts.

I rub at my eyes, pushing back tears of despair. He's right, as usual.

'It didn't work,' I say.

He nods to the space behind me. I turn.

There are other people in the room, about twenty of them, but none are looking our way. They have their backs to us while they stand clustered around a screen, transfixed. The sound is low and the pictures are shifting, but I can't see clearly with the crowd in the way. All I can see is ticker text across the top of the screen, a scrolling harbinger of bad news.

Redistribution of resources... All sectors of zones L-Z... Remain in your homes... Council directive enacted... Repeat, remain in your homes...

I can hear screaming. At first I think it's on the screen, but then I realise that it's coming from outside. People aren't obeying the Council directive. They're on the streets outside the university, running for zone K.

'It's too late,' Rich says.

The simulation project has failed.

We've tried endless permutations, countless models, and still we have no answer. There's no way to save the Island, no way for so many people to live safely in such a small space. And while we've been trying to come up with a solution, the International Council has pressed ahead with its depopulation agenda: eradicate the most populous areas – the poorest areas – and leave more land, more food, and more of everything else for the few who are left.

No wonder people are screaming.

The missiles are already on their way.

Rich reaches over to take my hand.

They'll be here in 3, 2, 1—

A Quiet Life

I don't remember the first time I saw Elias.

Perhaps you think I should, but do you remember meeting your childhood friends? I don't mean the ones you went to school with, or the ones who came into your life as tweens. I mean the kids who lived where you lived, who hung around in your neighbourhood, who squabbled over the same swing set and dug in the same sandpit. Elias is one of those kids, someone who's been in my life peripherally for so long and so constantly that, as we both grew into teenagers, it became natural to stop and chat for a few minutes if we bumped into each other in the street, but not about anything in particular. The weather, a new haircut, his latest songs or my latest sketches. We'd talk about ourselves with no context, pretending that we were grown ups, and that our homes and our families didn't exist. Of course, he wasn't pretending about that last part.

When I was younger, I fancied him without ever really thinking about it, because everyone fancied Elias, but he didn't do anything about it. My feelings for him were simply a true fact, one I accepted without acting upon it. There was a kiss in our younger teens, one that he seemed to regret almost immediately. Neither of us have mentioned it since, and we've gone straight back to being rather distant friends. That might sound cold, but it's weirdly comfortable.

So when I see Elias hanging around outside the shop one summer night, I stop to talk like it's the most casual thing in the world, because it is.

'You're coming home late,' he says.

'Yeah, I stayed behind at college for an art class. What are you up to?'

'Waiting for you.'

Now I feel distinctly *un*comfortable. We never meet up with any intention. We're not supposed to seek each other out; that's not the way it works.

If you force fate, it fights you back.

'Well,' I say. 'It was nice to see you.' I give him a little wave and carry on walking, hoping to dissuade him from what he's planning to do.

'It's Midsummer,' he says, following after me. 'It's time.'

'Not this year,' I say, whispering as though being quiet about it will make the words he's spoken disappear. 'It can wait another year.'

'It can't. You'll be eighteen next year, and so will I. It has to be this year.'

'Then you can take someone else,' I say, walking

faster so he has to trail behind me like a comet. 'Annabel would say yes to anything you asked her to do. Or Mariella.'

'No,' he says, grabbing my wrist to stop me from walking on. 'It's you, Salie. It has to be you.' There's electricity in his touch and I know from that – even if I didn't know it in my heart already – that he's right.

'Now?' I ask, praying for a delay I know isn't going to come.

'Now,' he says.

Fuck.

I do remember the first time I saw Diane.

I was getting a coffee from the grotty little cafe in town. She was behind the counter, serving people with an attitude that was brisk to the point of surly. Between that, her turquoise hair and the hand-painted T-shirt she was wearing, I was a goner from the moment I walked in the door.

'What do you want?' she asked.

I wanted to say *your name and number*, but I have never in my life been that brave or that corny, so instead I asked for a latte and watched every deft movement of her hands while she made it for me. Her nails were painted in neon, a different colour for every one, making a rainbow of her fingertips. She sang as she worked, loudly and off-key, as though daring someone to tell her to stop.

I tried to screw up the courage to talk to her, but the moments passed quickly and before I knew it she was handing over the cup and looking to the next person in line for their order. I only managed to murmur a thank you before shuffling away.

It wasn't until I got home that I realised there was something written on the cup.

Diane, and a telephone number.

The name doesn't suit her.

I call her now, in Elias's car on the way to the bridge. She doesn't pick up.

'You'll have to leave that behind,' he says.

'I know.'

No phones, no speakers, no electronics of any kind. Those are the rules on the other side of the bridge. It's been so many years since I was last there that I'm not sure I know how to live without those devices anymore, but then life on the quiet side of the bridge is different. Over there, they don't call friends or sing along to music or do video challenges on social media. Over there, they understand the language of gesture and touch, thought and feeling, peace and reflection. They don't know what it is to feel the tension building in your chest until all you can do to break it is scream. Or they know very well, and just push it all down. I'm not sure which would be worse.

When we reach the bridge, there are four other cars parked up on the scrubby patch of earth by the river.

'Busy night,' I say, playing for time that I know we don't have.

Elias gives me an odd look, because of course it's a busy night. Everyone's here for the same reason we are: the Homecoming.

'Is that Abel's car?' I ask, naming one of the guys I went to school with. I know he's a casual acquaintance of Elias's too.

'Yes.'

'I didn't realise he was—'

'He is. The year after us.'

'Oh.'

Elias has parked up and is already halfway out of the door. I haven't even unbuckled my seatbelt. I feel like I'm stuck to the seat.

'Come on,' he says. 'We're going to be late.'

'Yeah, okay,' I reply, but I'm still not moving.

'What's wrong? Don't you want to do this?'

'No, I do,' I say, because it's what's expected of me. This is supposed to be the most magical day of our lives, in lives that are pretty full of magic already, but the truth is that I'm not sure I want this at all. 'Just nervous, I guess.'

They're the last words I'll ever speak to him. Uninspiring, aren't they?

He smiles. 'I'll be with you.'

I don't find this as reassuring as he seems to think I should, but I can't put it off any longer.

I get out of the car and take his hand. We both leave our shoes behind.

It's been years since I last stepped through the water, but it's not something you forget how to do: five wet steps into the middle of the stream, then flip everything upside down until you're standing in a quiet mirror of the world. It's easy, really, but if you don't know how to do it yourself then there's no way I can explain the process that will let you copy it.

Maybe it's something innate, because I swear I

remember flipping my way onto the loud side of the bridge when I was in my mother's womb, ready to be delivered to the family waiting for me. There are no babies on the quiet side; they're too noisy, too ungovernable. We only return when we've learned how to mute ourselves into compliance. Apparently, I should have done that by now.

The years we live on the loud side of the bridge are supposed to make us appreciate the value of silence. After suffering so long in the deafening noise of the loud side, we're supposed to return with nothing but relief. Instead, when Elias and I emerge into the quiet side, I'm afraid. With everything so still, with no sound of singing birds or laughing people or leaves rustled by the wind, the place sounds dead and empty. There are twenty people or more arrayed by the gateway to meet us, but I can hear nothing from them, not even the sound of their breath. They smile as though they are pleased to see us, but the silence makes it sinister.

We follow them to join the other returners in Homecoming Hall by the riverside. It's dark now. It's always darker on the quiet side. I don't know why. Maybe it's something about the inverted geography of the place, or maybe the sun doesn't think it's worth illuminating a land whose people are so grey. Whatever the reason, as we process solemnly through the tall, dark grasses – they're never cut, for the noise it would make – night is falling with a speed that feels unnatural.

The hall is made of stone, though I'm not sure how, because how do you hew and build things from rock without making a noise? The building is white, shining in the twilight, drawing us into its orbit like moths around the moon. Beside me, Elias is moving in a jerky fidget that betrays his impatience. I'm worried that he'll miss his step if he doesn't calm down, and if he does then I'm standing so close to him that the Librarian might take both of us.

The name is a stupid joke, one we imported from the loud side, a tame moniker for the terrifying magic that rules this place. No noise, not a sound, or else…

Elias saw it happen, once. He, of all people, should know to be more careful.

'She fell,' he said, back when we were still on the loud side. I'd bumped into him after school, the way I often would, and stopped to talk. He was the only person that I knew for sure was also from the quiet side, so he was the only person I could talk to when the questions started coming thick and fast.

Why can't we stay with our real parents?

Why can't they visit us?

Why do we have to be quiet on the other side?

His parents had died when he was younger, during one of his infrequent visits to the quiet side. His mother tripped and fell into his father, and they'd both gone down to the ground in a clatter of limbs and a snap of broken bones. He'd been playing at their feet when it happened.

It had been his fault.

It was enough to make me glad that I wasn't allowed to visit my own parents. None of the girls are; the families we go to on the loud side might be temporary, but when we leave our quiet families we do it for life. For seventeen years, we have no real family at all, then we have our Homecoming and join the family of our Pairbond. It makes things simpler.

At Elias's Homecoming, with his parents dead, I didn't know where he and his Pairbond would go.

'It was like this.' He clapped his hands in front of my face, loudly enough to startle me. 'There was the noise of the fall, and then it was like a window opened up in the air and sucked them both away with a sound like something zipping up, you know?'

'The Librarian makes a *noise*?' I asked, horrified and fascinated.

'Weird, right? But it was instant. I mean, one noise and they were just gone. So be careful on the quiet side, Salie. All right?'

'I know.'

'But really,' he said. 'You have to promise.'

'I'm not an idiot,' I laughed. 'I don't want to get sucked into oblivion.'

'Promise me,' he insisted.

'Okay,' I said. 'I promise. No noise on the quiet side.'

He looked at me for a moment, as though satisfying himself that I was taking the promise seriously, then nodded and said, 'Good.'

When we finally make it inside Homecoming Hall, the others are already there. There are perhaps a dozen more couples like us in the centre of the room, half that number of elders arrayed along the front – all men – and a crowd who've come to watch the show. In room full of a hundred people or more, there is no sound above the gentle inhalation and exhalation of breath. I'm not sure how it's even possible, but there are no coughs, no sniffs, no shuffles and no sneezes. This is a congregation in perfect control.

My parents are somewhere in there, probably. I hope so.

For a moment, I wonder whether they're the couple in the front row who are smiling at me and Elias, but then I realise they have his features, not mine: blond hair, green eyes, ears that come to tapered points that are just a little too sharp to pass for human. Like Elias, they wear their hair long to cover their ears, but in this place they part their locks around them to show off their definition. It's a point of pride for some, apparently. At least, Elias always thinks its worth boasting about.

They can't be his parents, because his parents are dead. An uncle and aunt, perhaps?

What happens next passes in a series of intricate gestures from the elders that are meant to dictate our actions. I follow them shakily, trying to remember what each means. Some are clear: *go over there, stop, stay there, move forward, turn around,* but others are communicated by quick movements that I don't quite follow. Fortunately, Elias does, so when we're told to take our partners by the hand and step up to the line to wait our turn, he leads me.

When Elias turns his dark eyes on me in that spot, there is a thrill in the way he looks at me. I can feel the intensity in his gaze in a way that I never have before. I realise then that he's doing this not because he has to, or because he wants to, but because he *needs* to. I should be looking back at him with the same need, but I'm not thinking of him at all.

I'm thinking of her, and what I've left behind.

* * *

Our first date was in the mountains, as far from the river as we could possibly get. I didn't plan it that way, but Diane suggested a hike, and I was more than happy to oblige. I couldn't think of anything better than climbing out of the valley, out of the darkness, and into the sky with her at my side.

When we met in the car park at the bottom of the range, I felt so nervous I thought my stomach might flutter away on its own. I was second-guessing everything I was wearing and everything I'd packed in my rucksack, which was a whole other question on its own. Who wears a backpack? Plus, to top it all, like an absolute dork, uninvited, I'd packed a lunch for both of us. Then Diane arrived in a kaleidoscope of colour and sound and I discovered that she'd done exactly the same. This grumpy, multicoloured barista had made me a sandwich, and I'd made one for her.

We laughed. It was nothing, just a stupid mistake, but we laughed so hard.

We resolved to make a feast of it all and trekked up to the top of the peak in a raucous exchange of stories and campfire songs. When we sat down to eat and she asked, 'What do you want?' in the same surly tone she used at the cafe, I laughed at the ridiculousness of it and leaned over to kiss her, and she kissed me back, and that was the beginning of the best, brightest, loudest year of my life.

I could see our future stretching out ahead of us, one in which I forgot what I was supposed to do and instead stayed here, maybe helping out in the cafe, maybe going to university, maybe travelling around the world and seeing what joy we could find by losing ourselves in the noisy crowd. I wanted to spend my life making sound and colour with this girl who laughed, dressed and loved too loudly. I wanted her to deafen me with her voice.

I could imagine that future of excess so clearly that I could almost hear it.

I don't know what real life looks like on the quiet side. Like all babies, I was born on the loud side, and my few visits here since I was a child have been simple walks along the river with Elias, just for a few minutes, to remind me of its peace, and nothing more. I don't have the faintest idea what a normal quiet-side day would be, or how you're supposed to do anything at all without making a sound.

I suspect Elias knows. I suspect all the boys do. The way they're communicating with the elders by shorthand gesture suggests to me that they've spent time with these men. The elders act in a way that's familiar and genial, as though they recognise these boys as their future inheritors. Perhaps they will be exactly that. Perhaps I should be proud, but I don't feel like I have any claim on Elias at all.

Then things start happening.

Elias puts one arm around my shoulders and grasps my opposite wrist, holding me against his side by locking my arm across my stomach. Then he reaches his free hand across his body and takes my other arm, his fingers fastening around my second wrist like the links in a chain: *clink, clink, clink.* Is it wrong that I like how it feels? With each constriction, there's a little release in my chest that makes me wish he'd hold me tighter, closer. In this uncertain room, he feels like a point of safety. As though he can read the thoughts in my head, he starts squeezing so I can feel his grip, bone to bone.

I'm not so sure I like it anymore.

Looking along the line, I can see the others are holding their partners the same way. I open my mouth to ask for an explanation, but Elias hushes me before I can say a word.

It's the way things are done, he says, his words appearing silently in my head. It's a talent he has on the quiet side, that all the boys have, but that I lack. *It's tradition,* he says as his grip tightens, instead of saying that he's sorry.

I realise then that he has never said those words to me, not when he dragged me here with him, not when he hit me in the face with a tennis ball when we were seven, not when he knocked me off my bike when we were ten, not when he kissed me on the day I turned thirteen then ran away as though my lips had burned him.

I can feel his warm breath on my neck, ragged despite his attempts to control it, and I know he wants to burn again.

Follow me, he says. *This is a test, so concentrate, and get it right.*

I do, tracing a path across the floor to the beat of music I can't hear. I want to ask him what kind of test this is, and why we're taking it, but he doesn't explain, nor does he look again at my questioning eyes. He looks like he's counting steps in his head, his full concentration fixed on passing whatever this test is with flying colours. He spares no attention for me at all.

The other couples are moving too, with the same choreographed grace. I already had the feeling that things were happening beyond my control, but now I realise that there is a whole world of communication occurring that I can't access. The boys look at each other as they guide their paths, as though they are exchanging words. Meanwhile, all the girls can offer is blank confusion, cut off from the voices of everyone but their partner, and denied voices of their own.

We don't dance with steps, because the fall of our feet would be too loud. Instead, our bare feet shuffle in whispers of movement across the floor, so it feels like nothing so much as skating on a frozen lake. There are monsters circling under the thin ice beneath my feet, because if I make one wrong move, utter one word, create one jarring noise, then my life will be forfeit.

Somewhere in the twirling slide of the dance, I spot a face I recognise: Aiden. I used to play violin with him in the school orchestra, though he was a couple of years behind me. He was a virtuoso, a real genius with that thing. I would never have pegged him for one of us. I wonder if he approached today with the same reluctance that I did, knowing that he'd be leaving his music behind at the bridge.

I look for him at every turn after that, trying to find his feelings on his face. I'm so focussed on that task that it takes me a while to realise that his partner is familiar too. Stripped of her hair colour, her painted nails and her attitude, she's practically unrecognisable.

Diane.

She snaps her head around to face me as I spot her, almost as though she's heard me speak, but I swear my lips haven't moved. She smiles then, her perfectly uncouth grin, and I want to cry because condemning her to this dark and silent place feels like the worst kind of cruelty.

I didn't realise she was one of us. She shouldn't be.

She deserves to live a life out loud.

'What do you want to be when you grow up?' she asked me last month.

We were in the mountains again, lying on a towel with our tops rolled up and our socks rolled down, soaking up every last bit of sun. It was starting to dip towards the horizon, making a violent palette of the sky in reds, oranges and purples that tinted our skin weird shades of pink and brown.

'I'm already grown up,' I said.

'Fuck off you're not. I mean, when you're proper grown up.'

'I want to be happy,' I said, turning my head to the side to smile at her. 'I want to be yours.'

'Euch,' she grimaced, poking me in the ribs. 'Don't make me sick.'

'All right, fine, what do *you* want to be?'

'A singer.'

'Um.' I didn't know how to break it to her, so I just decided to come out with it. 'I love you, but you really can't sing.'

'I know. I want to do it anyway. Maybe I can be a novelty act: the singer who can't sing.'

'Or you could be a drummer?' I suggested.

'Yeah, I could hit stuff with other stuff,' she mused. 'It doesn't look so hard.'

'Only you have no sense of rhythm.'

'This is also true. So maybe not a career in music?'

'Maybe not,' I conceded. 'But I'll always listen to you sing. I'll even sing along if you like.'

'Promise?' she asked, rolling onto her side to face me.

'Promise.'

She kissed me, her lips on mine a perfect cacophony of sensation. Then, with the sunset rolling above us in the empty hills, we made some noise together.

I can't imagine a world in which we can never do that again.

Before long, by some silent consensus, the dancing slows and stops. Elias has been holding me so tightly in his grip for so long now that I can't feel my hands. I wonder if this is intentional, so I won't feel the Pairbond when it joins us together. The other boys seem to be holding their partners the same way, all except for Aiden, who's always been soft-hearted. I can see even from a distance that his hands are linked only loosely around Diane's wrists.

I'm glad that he's kind to her. At least she'll have that. After all that's happened tonight, I'm no longer sure that Elias will be kind to me.

They line us up again, the boys leading with their fierce grip on our wrists, then one of the elders approaches the first couple in line. I recognise the girl: her name is Bela. She's a friend of a friend from school. The boy is a stranger to me, but I realise he must be her boyfriend, Abel. I should have guessed from their names that they were both from the quiet side, but I didn't know Bela well, and I'd been trying not to give this place, or Homecoming, any thought at all.

The elder raises both of his hands in front of the couple, palms up, then mimes the placing of one hand in another. At this sign, Abel releases Bela's wrists and takes a step away. Slowly, he reaches his hand back towards her, inviting her to take it. She doesn't hesitate for long. When her hand touches his there's a flash of light that binds their hands together in a swirling mass of brilliance, which finally mellows into a glow, as though they've trapped a firefly between their fingers in the dark. Once the light has settled, the elder nods to Abel and then gestures something odd. It's as though he's miming a voice emerging from his throat, unfurling his fingers beneath his chin as he opens his mouth. He nods at Bela, then gestures again.

He can't be asking what I think he is. Can he? In this place where a single sound means death, he's asking Bela to sing.

There is a silent conversation between Abel and Bela, or from Abel to her, at least. Her eyes are urgent and scared, her head shaking as he holds her firmly by the hand and gazes intently into her eyes, communicating the fact that she *must*.

Finally, tentatively, Bela opens her mouth. After a moment, she closes it again. Then she opens it, touching her throat, starting to panic now because there's no noise coming out and she can't work out why. Her lips are moving, forming soundless words as she shouts and cries, but where there should be the horrible clash of terror and misery there is nothing but silence. She turns to the elder with tears running down her cheeks, but he's already moved on to the next couple. Their hands are already joined. Another girl is about to discover that she's just been robbed of her voice.

I turn to Elias, but he stares back at me impassively.

I want to ask him: Why? Why would you bring me here, knowing what they would take from me? But I have no power in this place. If I stay here, I will lose a piece of myself, but I can't run because Elias's hands are shackles around my wrists. If I shout for help, if I make any noise at all, I will die.

I try to pull Elias away with me, to get out of this place before it's too late, but his voice is in my head immediately, saying, *What are you trying to do? Do you want to end up like my parents? Because that's what'll happen if you keep struggling. We'll both die. Do you want to kill me, Salie?*

I shake my head, not in answer but because I don't want this, I don't want any of this.

It's the way things are, he says. *The sooner you accept it, the better.*

Then the elder is next to us and it's our turn and Elias is reaching out his empty hand towards me, urging me on with his eyes and the words he puts in my head. My hands are so numb that I didn't even realise he'd released me, but now, unbidden, my own hand reaches to meet his. I can't seem to control it. We're going to touch, and when we do, we'll be sealed together just as surely and irrevocably as Bela and Abel.

I want to scream. I can feel the riot building inside

me. Either Elias is going to take my hand and quiet me forever, or it's going to come out. I don't know which is going to happen first. My lips are already straining to part and if they let the messy noise out before Elias touches me, the magic of this place that abhors sound is going to crush me into oblivion.

At least it'll be quick.

Then I feel something in my other hand, something soft and familiar and so welcome that I could cry. I turn away from Elias to see Diane standing behind me. She's snuck her hand into mine while everyone was looking at Elias.

What are you doing? I think.

Getting us out of here.

When I hear her voice in my head, I realise that she's heard mine as well.

Our hands are glowing with the light that binds us together.

Elias looks outraged. The elders around the circle look appalled. I am elated.

It shouldn't have worked. These things are destined and prearranged, by everything from the families we're placed with to the names we are given before birth. She shouldn't be able to take my hand at Homecoming and make us belong together.

I changed my name on the other side, she says, seeing my confusion. *To Alise. I hoped it would be enough and... well.*

She looks down at our joined hands and smiles, the great wide grin I know and love.

I adore you, I think.

Good. Those are the last words you're going to say to

me in silence.

I mean to leave with her, but Elias gets in the way. He does not look pleased. What happens when someone breaks a fated Pairbond? What happens to the person left behind? I don't know, and Elias surely is not eager to find out. I can tell he's trying to speak into my head, because he's giving me that intense look, but I hear nothing except Alise's soothing voice.

I shrug at Elias.

He tries again.

I shrug again.

He reaches out, but Alise gets in the way, stopping him from touching me. Her face communicates her intentions so clearly that she doesn't need words.

Then Elias loses it. He shouts, 'No! It doesn't happen this way!' like a toddler who's been denied his favourite toy.

Out loud. For everyone to hear.

We all freeze. We're watching Elias in horror. All the women look as though they're anticipating his immediate demise at the hands of the Librarian, scared and strangely transfixed, but the men just look angry.

'I knew it was a lie,' Alise says. 'I knew there was no such thing as the Librarian.'

'There is too,' Elias replies, but it's too late.

Alise kisses me quickly, then drags me towards the door, still holding my hand. We don't have to push our way out; the horrified congregation clears a path for us, as though they're worried they might catch whatever we've brought into this sacred and – until now – immutable ceremony. We run past the elders, past the other Pairbonds, and past the older couple who are – I am increasingly certain – Elias's parents.

Of course they didn't die. Of course this place doesn't have the power to crush anyone who makes a noise within it. It has only the power that men bring into it, and the power we let them take from us.

They're not going to take it from Alise and me.

I can hear them trying to organise themselves behind us, but we're not stopping to give them time to realise they shouldn't let us leave with their secret. There are other noises, too: shouting and fighting and the sound of things breaking, but nothing like the zipping sound Elias once described to me. Alise and I leave it all behind.

We run to the river by the light of our joined hands and get our feet wet as we cross over. The light dims when we flip the world upside down together, but the sound doesn't. We laugh as we run to Elias's car, where he's left the keys in the ignition, never expecting to return. We throw his shoes out of the window and sing as we drive back to Alise's tiny flat above the grotty cafe. We yell as we strip each other naked and do the things each of us loves best. We wrap our lives with so much noise that the neighbours complain and we never, ever go back to the silent bridge.

Even if we wanted to, it's no longer there for us to go back to. In the early hours of the morning, shortly after we'd crossed the river, the capstone of the bridge crumbled into dust and brought the rest of the bridge down with it. It filled the water with stone and broken mortar, and it filled in something else besides. When they cleared the rubble and rebuilt the bridge with concrete and iron, there was nothing beneath it but the river.

It doesn't matter a bit to us. We never wanted a quiet life.

You Can't Go Back

Fighting centaurs isn't as easy as it looks, which is to say that instead of being just fiendishly difficult, it's actually virtually impossible. Most of those who try it end up getting trampled before they can even think about swinging whatever phallic implement they're wielding, and those who do manage to join combat are hampered not only by their relative lack of stature, but also by the horrendous crick in the neck occasioned by trying to keep their opponent in sight. It's not for the novice hero.

Fortunately, Odie is no novice. After ten years spent waging a pointless trade war at the very edges of civilisation, she's faced almost every enemy the known world has to offer. Fighting her way through the local cryptid population to get back to her fleet and off this godsforsaken wasteland is, if anything, a welcome break from all the bronze-armoured pillocks she's spent the past decade deshelling. At this moment, she is in her element.

Shoulder to shoulder with her army and crew, she lets loose three arrows in quick succession, each of which finds its home in a centaur's vital organ, then she hands off her bow and buries the butt of her spear in the ground with the point angled towards the charging enemy. The horse-human hybrid barrelling towards her notices the danger too late to slow his feet, which slide and scrabble in the dirt as he runs his own breast inexorably into the bronze tip, impaling himself with such force that his momentum flips his ungainly body up into the air and over the heads of Odie and her battalion. Halfway through the arc, his weight snaps the spear shaft and the whole thing collapses like a broken trebuchet, sending Odie's battle line into disarray.

She's not worried, though. None of the Ithacans are. They know their leader, and they know her strengths. They know what happens when she lets the anger take her. When she pulls her ornate bronze blade from its scabbard, it sings like the bards who will soon be hymning the victory she'll win this day.

She smiles. She stalks forward. She cuts.

She is bathed in wine-dark blood when she is done.

'Ten years,' Odie says.

She's standing on the deck next to her lieutenant, Yuri, as the crew rows the bireme away from the place they have called home for so long. There are twelve ships in all, following each other along the coast like ants on their way back to the nest.

'It's a while to be away from home,' Yuri says.

'Particularly when you have a family waiting for you.'

Odie turns to look at him. 'I didn't know you were married,' she says, tracing the cragged lines of her second's face with her eyes. He looks like exactly what he is: a weather-beaten soldier with little respect for personal hygiene and even less for good manners.

'I was talking about yourself,' he says. 'You've people waiting on you.'

Nell.

The name is so precious to Odie that she can no longer bring herself to whisper it, let alone say it out loud. She doesn't need to, though; her crew knows it well.

In those early days, the stories came easily. They sat together around the fires they made on foreign shores at night, talking about the loved ones they'd left behind, imagining their triumphant homecomings. Back then, they thought it would be a matter of months – maybe weeks if they were lucky – before they were turning for home in ships laden with shining riches and newly-minted heroes. Instead, they'd stayed away so long that the memories of home became painful, and even the weight of treasure in their holds couldn't overbalance the agonising lightness of all the friends they had left behind, buried in the sand between two rivers stained with their blood.

There will be families to inform on their return. That task is Odie's alone, and it hangs over her like a cloud. For once, she is grateful for the length of the journey home; perhaps by the time they finally reach Ithaca she will have found the right words to deliver the worst of news.

But Yuri is right; her own family will be waiting, and she is not yet dead, despite the best efforts of soldiers and seas.

'Are you worried?' he asks her.

Odie pushes away her memories and turns her attention back to her lieutenant. 'About what?'

'Well… it's been years. It would be natural to worry that she might not be waiting still.'

Odie laughs. 'You wouldn't have asked that if you knew her.'

'Maybe not,' Yuri says, but he looks unsure.

'She'll be waiting,' Odie says with all the assurance she doesn't feel. 'Even if every suitor on the continent is knocking at her door, she'll keep faith.'

And it feels true, every word. However long the journey takes, and whatever might occur during her absence, Odie knows that her wife will remain exactly as she remembers her: blameless, prudent, wise Penelope.

They waste years on the wind. At first they're tacking with the breeze, catching every helping hand the weather can offer to speed them on their way, but the moment Odie adjusts their course to fill the sails, the winds seem to switch and twist beyond her grasp like dragons of air sliding serpentine around the mast and away.

The crew might have dealt with these trials easily enough – after all, they have two banks of oars and they can slog the whole way home against the wind if they have to – but for the storm that zeroes in on their ships as though it has been sent against them by some vengeful god.

Four ships are lost under the waves with all hands. Two are wrecked beyond salvation, but the rest of the fleet manages to save at least a portion of their crew before they're swept away by the current. The remaining six ships are blown so far off course that they lose sight of the coastline they were using to guide their route and can't find it again.

They see no land. They see no ships except their own. Even the sun and stars seem to come out of alignment to cheat Odie's instruments, leaving her with no idea what course to plot.

In the end, low on water and half-starved, they follow the birds.

To a cluster of islands Odie doesn't recognise, spread out in an archipelago so large that it covers the horizon, and yet somehow appears on no map she has ever seen. People live there in sociable clusters, fishing in the shallows and rivers from hand-carved canoes decorated with patterns more ornate than even the finest carpenters back home can manage. They are welcoming and hospitable, despite the lack of common language, and they – along with the abundance of fruits, meats and sweet-tasting fresh water – make the tree-covered islands feel like paradise.

'We could stay,' Odie suggests to Yuri after three days of good eating, drinking and resting in the warm shade have weakened her resolve.

'Stay?' Yuri replies. He's been watching the ships every waking second since they paddled ashore and left them anchored in the bay, as if he's desperate to continue their journey. If Odie didn't know better, she'd think he had a reason to hurry home, but there's nothing left back in Ithaca for him except ashes and bones.

'I don't know where we are, or how to navigate from here,' she says. 'If the options are living out our days on these islands or risking it all on tides we can't trust, perhaps it's wiser to stay. Besides, after all they've been through, how can I ask the crew to carry on? Look at them. They're happy here.'

And, truly, they are happier than they have been since… well, ever. Odie can see them, spread out across the beaches and under the canopies of huts with food and drink in hand, battle-hardened men and women relaxing so hard that anyone would think they'd reached the end of their travails. Even Perry, who hasn't cracked a smile for years, is laughing with his crew mates as though they haven't lost a quarter of their number on the journey here, and more still in the war that they left behind.

It's a little eerie.

But still. They seem so happy.

'You want me to drag them away from this on the promise of… what?' Odie says. 'More storms, more lost lives?'

'You're not the only one with people waiting on you,' Yuri says. 'They have families too.'

'It's been thirteen years. Who knows what's waiting for us at home?'

'Do you doubt your wife?' Yuri says, with a challenge in his tone.

'Of course not.'

'So why do you think the others should doubt theirs?'

It's a fair question that she can't answer.

'A week, then,' she says.

'A day,' Yuri counters.

'Five days.'

'Two.'

'Four.'

'Three, and then I'll give them the choice,' Odie says. 'If they want to go home, we go. But if they want to stay…'

'Fine,' Yuri agrees reluctantly. 'Three days.'

With the clock running, Odie doesn't waste time. Perhaps she should be looking after her people. Perhaps she should be talking to the islanders, trying to establish some method of communication so she can work out where they are and how to get home from here. Instead, she finds a quiet corner of the beach sheltered under shady fronds and goes to work on a stash of food and drink her crew has saved for her. There's sweet liquid that cracks from the inside of a furry, hard-shelled seedpod, there's tender fish grilled over sandy campfires and, above all, there's a fruit that grows in clusters on the trees a little further inland. It's so heavy with nectar that the branches bow down under the weight of their burden, so sweet that the hummingbirds line up to prick it open and sup, and so fragrant that even with its delicate scent, it overpowers every flower on the islands. The fruit is the size of a fist, covered with a soft skin that peels back as though eager to reveal its secrets. The flesh beneath is the colour of gold, filled with juice, and if it contains any seeds at all, they're too small to be discerned. In sum, it is the perfect food. Odie has begun to believe that a person might survive on this fruit alone for the rest of their days and neither require nor miss any other form of sustenance.

They call it lotus, a name they whisper.

Later, Odie understands why.

After one fruit, she is merely hungry for more. After two, she feels as though the sunshine nectar is reaching out through her body and somehow healing her hurts. After three, she begins to remember things she has almost forgotten.

The night Nell first came to her bed in a dream of dark hair and golden eyes, a dream Odie couldn't believe was true until she woke the next morning to find the siren still asleep in her arms.

The day they were bound together in the orchard on her father's palace – now her palace, hers and Nell's – and the night that followed with soft lips and hard breaths.

The morning she left Nell crying in the garden and ran to the dock, too afraid of her own weakness to stay a moment longer with the woman she loved.

She couldn't go back.

There's a shadow over the palace and the darkest parts of Odie live inside it.

She can't go back.

After four fruits, Odie forgets that she has forgotten anything at all.

Three days later, Yuri finds her on the same beach under the same shady fronds, surrounded by discarded lotus skins and crabs that have sidled up the sand to pick them dry.

'It's time,' he says.

Odie can only moan and rub her eyes. For a second, a

moment, a minute, her mind is empty and she struggles to fill it.

'You were going to talk to the crew,' Yuri reminds her. 'About leaving. Did you forget?'

Nell is waiting.

She has not forgotten.

'I'll put it to them,' she promises.

It takes half a day just to gather herself up, then another half day to gather the crew in one place, and even then they're missing several of their number. Whether they've dispersed over the archipelago or disappeared into the sea, or whether they're just avoiding Odie, there's no sign of them. Odie sets out the options for the rest, but when – unbelievably – half of them elect to return home, Yuri doesn't offer her the same choices.

'Don't you want to go back?' he asks.

She should, she knows, but when she weighs the journey up against the joyful oblivion of the lotus fruit, she struggles to make the scales tip towards home.

'You're their leader,' he says. 'Their king. Would you abandon them? Would you abandon your wife?'

'Of course not,' she lies.

'Well, then.'

Yuri doesn't give Odie time to renege. Within the hour, they leave the lotus eaters behind and strike out for the ships, heading into unfamiliar waters. They have only enough sailors left to crew four biremes, so that is all they take.

There are more storms. There are bad winds. There are hostile peoples and forbidding shores. Still, the remnants of Odie's crew press on into the unknown, hoping that they will one day find a landmark that sparks a memory and sets them on a course for home.

Before that day comes, the monster finds them.

The location is unremarkable: just another green hill behind another sandy dune beside another seaweed-stinking bay. Odie and her nomad crew have seen hundreds of hills just as green and nondescript over the years as they've drifted around these seas. In the beginning, this one seems no different from any of the others. Then they see the sheep.

Meat.

The word is whispered at first, then shouted in excitement. It's been months since they last ate any meat that didn't come out of the sea. The sheep aren't even afraid of them, coming so close that the sailors might catch them simply by waiting with their arms outstretched, and there seems to be no one around to whom the flock belongs. The crew doesn't wait for Odie's permission, they just take. In those circumstances, she can do little but order them to build spits and share the meat fairly.

The carcasses are already bare when a roar splits the air and the earth begins to shake. The crew turn inland as one, looking for the source. As they watch, the shaking continues in a rhythmic pattern that, it soon becomes clear, is exactly what it seems to be: the footsteps of a giant. Its head crests the hill fully sixty seconds before the rest of it becomes visible, so they have time to appreciate every inch of its immense form. Its fists are the size of boats, its teeth the length of javelins; the single eye in the middle of its forehead is the size of a boulder, and its clothing so voluminous that Odie could collect all the sails in her fleet and still not have enough material to cover it.

When the monster spies Yuri, sitting in a place of honour at the largest fire, it is to him that it addresses its enquiry.

'What is your name, stranger?' it booms in their own language.

'Yu— Ooo!'

Odie subtly stamps on her lieutenant's foot before he can speak his name in full. No matter how many gods and tricksters they encounter, he can't seem to get it into his head that there is power in a name.

'*You*,' the monster muses. 'A strange name for a thief.'

'Who are you calling a thief?' Odie asks, bridling. Perhaps she should be scared, but she can't just sit by and allow the honour of her lieutenant to be called into question. Whatever else Yuri might be, she knows that he is an honest man.

'What else would you call a man who steals and butchers another man's sheep, then sits picking his teeth with their bones?' the monster asks.

It's another fair question that she can't answer.

'And what should the penalty for that man be, do you suggest?' the monster continues. 'It seems to me that the only proper recompense is for the man to be butchered himself, so that his bones might become toothpicks for the man whose sheep he stole.'

'Hang on—' Yuri says, quickly discarding the sheep bone and getting to his feet.

'Then what would be the penalty for the man who

butchers him?' Odie asks, talking right over Yuri. 'No. Come now, we'd end up going back and forth until everyone was butchered and eaten, and where would that get us?'

'It would get me a full stomach,' the monster rumbles.

'For a few seconds, perhaps,' Odie concedes, pulling her spear from the ground. 'Not much longer than that, I'd wager.'

'You mean to fight me?' the monster says, incredulous. '*Me*?' When it laughs, little pebbles rumble loose from the top of the hill and skitter down towards Odie's feet.

It's a bad idea. Odie knows this, and she's sure her crew does too. Really, they should try to placate the monster, or strike out for the ships, or run and hide in the brush, but where would be the glory in that? Besides which, the monster's scorn has provoked the part of her that can't back down. Her pride won't let her consider any other option, so instead of doing the clever thing she catches up her spear and hurls it at the beast, aiming for the heart.

It strikes true.

Then bounces off the monster's skin and drops harmlessly to the ground.

The monster smiles. 'The woman has doomed you, You,' it booms, then it crouches down and grabs for Yuri.

Yuri ducks, just in time, and the monster's hand knocks the spit and the tripod that supported it into the fire. The monster yells in frustration, then snatches up two of the crew in one gigantic fist and dashes their brains out on the rocky ground. With the other fist, it grabs two more of Odie's friends, and soon their broken bodies are lying at her feet.

The rage warms her soul like the sunshine warms her skin.

In this state, she doesn't need to think. There is an unbreakable connection between her body and her instincts that's been trained to perfection over years of combat, and she relies on it now. She doesn't consciously take the hot spit from the fire at her side, but it is now in her hands. She isn't aware that she's been tracking the monster's movements, but she can anticipate them well enough to know when he will bend down again for another swipe. She lets the anger take her. It lends strength to her limbs as she runs the burning stake into the creature's eye, blinding it in a gruesome burst of boiling liquid. Odie doesn't hear the monster's screams. She doesn't feel the disgust that overwhelms more than one member of her crew as they watch; she is safe in the hot embrace of her rage.

She returns to herself only when the monster stumbles away, howling as it clutches its face.

'POLLY?' a voice booms from over the hills.

'Help me!' the monster cries out.

Yuri looks at Odie and says, 'Now you've done it. It has friends.'

'What's wrong?' the voice shouts back.

'Someone has stolen and eaten my sheep, and blinded my eye!'

'Who?'

'You!' the monster shouts out.

'I did not!' his friend shouts in reply.

'No, You did!'

'I did *not*!'

'Not very bright, these monsters, are they?' Odie says to Yuri.

'No.'

'And nor are we if we hang around,' she adds. 'Let's go.'

The crew quickly gather up their things and clamber into their dinghies while the monster stumbles around blindly, calling for his friend to come to his aid. By the time they reach the biremes, the monsters are fighting one another on the shore. The newcomer throws a rock at the retreating ships, smashing one of them to smithereens. The remaining three biremes row on, dodging more rocks, leaving any survivors to swim to shore alone, if they dare.

'Your father would be proud,' Yuri says to Odie, but his tone doesn't match the compliment she finds in his words. She's saved as many as she could, and she's maintained her honour. Her father *would* be proud, even if Yuri is not.

Odie's second never had the stomach for this job. She should have replaced him long ago, but she finds his disdain reassuring. It reminds her that she is made to be a hero, and he is not.

She will not flinch from what needs to be done.

She will not back down.

The years run like water through Odie's fingers. They aren't any easier than those that came before, but they seem less substantial, like spectres of time passing. It's hard to grasp onto them because, like the hours, the travellers never stop moving.

Until they see the island through the pouring rain.

'The crew's tired,' Yuri cautions Odie. 'They need to rest. This could be the place.'

'*This* place?'

'It looks magical.'

And, from a distance, it does. That's Odie's objection: no island should look so rich and welcoming. Even from miles out, she can see that the vegetation is lush, the rivers are plentiful, and there's even a little stream of smoke issuing from the chimney of a cosy-looking home in the hills. Everything about the island feels too… nice.

When they drop anchor and row ashore, Odie's fears are not assuaged. There's a woman waiting on the beach to greet them, draped in fine fabrics with a doe at her side. The creature is even wagging its stumpy tail.

'Welcome,' she says as Odie and Yuri drag their boat up the sand with the first load of sailors.

'Hello,' Yuri says politely.

'And what is your name, stranger?' the woman asks.

'Yu—'

'—should know better than to ask that of a stranger,' Odie interrupts, shooting a glare at Yuri. Will he never learn?

The woman switches her attention to Odie as she narrows her eyes with sudden interest. 'It appears that I have misread the situation. Captain?' she says to Odie.

Odie tips her head to acknowledge the title.

'Then perhaps you and your crew would like to follow me? You must be tired from your journey, and I can offer you food, drink and shelter.'

Odie hesitates, because there's something about the woman that's unsettling her, but their would-be host insists.

'Please,' she says, 'allow me to extend my hospitality.'

Her people are hungry and soaked through. The night will be cold. The woman is beautiful. How can she refuse?

And oh, the woman is beautiful. The day after their arrival, Odie lays her down on the grass in the orchard and unwraps the gilded scarf from around her hair. When the locks spill out into Odie's hands, they run in slick streams the colour of old blood. They remind Odie of something she thought she'd lost a long time ago and half the world away, and she grasps the strands in her fists as though by holding onto them she can hold onto the things she has forgotten. The woman's lips taste like perfumed sunshine.

Odie doesn't intend to stay so long.

A night, she thought, perhaps a week, a month at the outside, but the years carry on running while Odie takes the woman to the orchard and lays her on the grass. One kiss becomes ten, becomes a hundred, becomes a thousand, until there are so many that they can no longer be counted at all.

'I can't go back,' Odie whispers into the woman's blood-red hair, inhaling the fragrant scent of her skin.

'You won't.'

Nell.

'I have to.'

'You don't.'

But Odie knows she will, sooner or later. She can feel

the guilt eating her from the inside out; besides which, the crew are becoming restless. Yuri has told her more than once that they want to leave. At first, they welcomed the break. After six months had passed, a few began to pine for their homes. Now, they're starting to grumble amongst themselves, and Odie knows enough about her people to know that it won't be long before their grumbling turns into misguided action.

That day comes sooner than she predicts.

'They're taking the boats,' Yuri says, running into the orchard to disturb her.

'How many?'

'About half the crew, I'd guess, but they're taking everything. They mean to strand us here.'

She rouses herself unwillingly from the woman's arms and, pulling her clothes on as she goes, follows Yuri as he runs to the beach. The crew must have been working on this plan for weeks, because the barnacle-covered biremes have been careened and she can smell the fresh pitch on the boats that they're dragging down into the water.

'What do you think you're doing?' Odie asks.

Most of the crew just carry on with their work, ignoring their captain as though instructed to do so, but Ellie – a fierce soldier and able sailor who captains one of the biremes – meets Odie on the tideline with her hand on her scabbard.

'Stay here if you want,' Ellie says, 'but we're going home. We've rested long enough.'

'You can swim if you want,' Odie counters, 'but you're not taking my fleet.'

'Your fleet? Your fleet is two ships.'

'*Two*? We arrived with three.'

'And you neglected one so poorly that the timbers rotted right through. We were lucky to be able to save the two we did, and if we stay here much longer, we're all going to rot with them. You've lost yourself, Captain,' Ellie says, pouring scorn into the title, 'but we're not going to sink into oblivion with you. I'm taking them home.'

Odie draws the blade from her belt and says, 'No, you're not.'

Ellie tries to draw her own sword, but she can't rely on her instincts the way Odie does. No one has her reflexes, her speed, the inner core of anger that keeps her sharp. Ellie hasn't even pulled her own weapon half out of its scabbard when the tip of Odie's blade lodges in Ellie's eye socket, with unerring accuracy. Perhaps Odie doesn't mean to push the sword all the way in. Perhaps she means only to menace Ellie a little. Whatever her intentions, the result is the same: Ellie lies dead on the sand and Odie has to put her foot on the woman's head to get enough leverage to extract her blade.

The crew are no longer moving.

'Boats back up the beach,' Odie says quietly, demanding their attention as she wipes her sword clean on the leg of her trousers.

Still, no one moves.

'Back up the beach!' she yells. 'Everyone!'

Bereft of their rebel leader, they jump to the task. Not one of them meets Odie's eye as they return the boats to the top of the sand, beyond the tideline, and flip them over into a neatly-stored rank. The two seaworthy biremes remain at anchor, the eyes painted on their prows watching Odie as she follows the crew back up the dunes and into the heart of the island.

Her heart is waiting for her there.

For now.

The months begin to run like blood, slowing and congealing in the sun.

The crew are resigned to their fates on this island, so resigned that there is no longer any talk of returning to families or friends. Instead, they are focused on building new lives here. But in the meantime, Odie's thoughts have finally begun to turn to home.

It isn't that Odie doesn't like the woman of the island. She thinks she might love her, maybe, and she certainly would were it not for the memory of Nell, who casts a shadow she can't escape. The problem is that Odie has begun to notice all the ways in which the woman is not quite as vivid as Nell is in her memory: her hair is a little less bright, her skin a little less clear, the colour of her eyes a little less brilliant and enthralling. Aside from that, she doesn't make Odie laugh or thrill the way she remembers laughing and thrilling with Nell. And so, although she is conscious that the deficit may be in her memory rather than in reality, Odie cannot help but long for the more complete version of a love that she half-remembers, and pine.

She has taken the pining far enough that she has a plan.

There is a herb that grows on the island, a herb that imparts safety from poison to those who consume it. Odie eats that herb, then picks another plant that she recognises and crushes its leaves into the bottle of wine she shares with her lover before bed. While the woman sleeps, drugged into unconsciousness by the plant, Odie – immune to its effects – creeps around the house and searches for what she knows must be hidden somewhere in the woman's rooms. There have been other sailors who've reached this island. Odie knows this because the woman has hinted as much, and because Odie has found their bones and broken ships in a cave by the shore. That is proof enough that they came, and that they never left this place.

Odie does not mean to meet the same end.

After hours of searching by the light of her oil lamp, Odie finally discovers the thing for which she is searching, tucked at the bottom of a wooden chest beneath folded coverlets and clothing from ages long since past. It's a map, and there are places on it Odie recognises. Using those waypoints, she can navigate a path to Ithaca. After the storms last winter, she has only one bireme left, but with a chart to guide their way, it should be enough.

Finally, they are going home.

Odie begins to make her way quietly back to the bedroom through the kitchen, her path lit only by her lamp and the embers of the fire, and is startled to find the woman by the hearth. Odie's lover shouldn't be awake, not with the amount of sedative she's consumed, but here she is, sitting in her chair with a bowl of dark liquid on her lap. Patterns and colours play across the surface beneath her fingertips.

'You're going to fail,' she says. Odie would swear that she's smiling, just a little.

'Don't prophesy dire fates for me, witch,' Odie says. 'You know nothing of me or my journey.'

'I know you, king of Ithaca,' the witch says, reaching out to grasp Odie's hand in her own. 'You don't need to tell me your name for me to see that you will never find your home.' As she speaks, she looks into the still, black pool. It paints a dark reflection of her face, distorted with barely-restrained glee. 'There's nothing for you in your kingdom anymore.'

'There is less for me here,' Odie replies, shaking the woman's hand away.

'Is that the truth you know in your heart, or simply a lie you choose to believe? I am here. She is there, but she is not waiting for you.'

The blow that follows is an instinct that surges out of Odie's heart.

Faithful Nell would never betray her. The witch is a spinner of deception. Her lips are spitting lies.

Odie's palm stings and the air sings. The bowl has been knocked from the woman's hands and now it rolls in circles on the floor, spilling water onto the flagstones.

The witch clutches her cheek in her hand for a second, then reveals it again so Odie can see the mark she has left. There is blood on the skin, scratches from the rings Odie wears on her fingers.

'Your anger will not change the fact that you have lost her,' the woman says, settling her shoulders back as she regains her imperious composure. 'You can't go back.'

'I will go back,' Odie insists through the red-hot shame-rage. 'I am going back. Right now.'

'With what crew, exactly? They know what you are now. They'll never follow you.'

'They will. They always have.' Odie turns to walk away.

'You can't go.' The witch is grasping at her hand again, pulling her back, reaching for her arms, her shoulders, her neck as though she means to overwhelm Odie here in this foggy little room in this dank little house on this grim little island and bury her within its bones. She'll imprison Odie in her arms just as surely as the lotus fruit imprisoned the crew in their own heads and hearts.

'No,' Odie says, and the rage fills her.

She can't describe exactly what happens next, because she doesn't truly live it. Those moments are inhabited by another creature, one made of fire and fury. It isn't Odie. She's set apart from it. This isn't her. It *can't* be her.

There's a knock on the door and Odie can hear Yuri calling for her on the other side. There was noise in this room a moment ago, but now everything is silent. That's when the horror sets in.

'We're leaving,' she says, wiping her hands on her trousers as she leaves the room and closes the door firmly behind her. With that action, she erases everything she's left behind inside.

'Is everything all right?' Yuri asks, glancing at Odie's hands, at the door.

'Of course.' She smiles, and her smile is so genuine that you might think she really, truly believes the words she's delivered with it. Perhaps she does.

'You want to leave?' Yuri asks, uncertain.

'Didn't you say it was time for us to go?'

'Months ago, yes, but—'

'Well, you were right, so we're going. Gather the crew.'

'Captain, I don't think—'

'They get in the boats or they answer to me,' Odie says, tapping at the hilt of her sword with one bloody hand. 'Understand?'

They have to make two journeys in the small boats to get the whole crew safely to the last bireme. Not one of them tries to stay behind.

From that point on, the journey home is a dream. There are pleasant beaches, abundant springs, kind winds and bounties of fruit and meat large enough to fill their hold several times over. It seems that everywhere they put to shore has been designed purely for the purpose of accommodating them. Soon enough, Yuri spots a familiar rock formation, and they are drawing into the harbour at Ithaca within a year. It all passes so smoothly that Odie can barely remember a thing about it.

Her homecoming, at least, is memorable.

The crew carries her aloft off the ship and into the city, shouting their praise for their captain and king, the woman who led them safely through wars, harsh seas and monstrous encounters to deliver them home to their families. As they parade her through the streets, she can hear the whispers already as the crew passes stories to the people lining their route as they go. By the time she reaches the palace, she's surrounded by snatches of her adventures, imparted in reverent tones.

Felled a one-eyed giant as large as a mountain…

*crewed the ship single-handed through a hurricane...
outsmarted a witch... freed them all from her
enchantment... blood on her hands...*

Or maybe the tones aren't so reverent after all. As the
remains of her army lift her up the steps towards the
grand palace gate, she starts to hear the censure beneath
the praise.

*Blinded the poor creature... nearly got them all
killed... sure she was a witch? Just because she spoke
unfavourable words... and so few came home...
murderer... only one eye... never saw her again...*

Everything is slipping.

'Put me down,' Odie says quietly to her crew.

They can't have heard, because they carry her
onward.

'I said put me down!' she snaps.

A hush falls over the crowd, and Odie begins to feel
uneasy. She remembers leaving this place in a
triumphant parade much like the one that has heralded
her return home, but is that memory even real? Weren't
there whispers in the undercurrent back then too?
There's a memory itching at the back of her ear and
turning her stomach over in its grip, a memory as
elusive as it is visceral, and it's drawing a dark cloud
over the palace like a shroud. It happened here,
whatever it is she's not remembering. She has a feeling
that it's something so important she should never have
forgotten it.

Nell.

She just needs to see Nell, and then everything will
be fine.

Unfortunately, when Odie throws open the palace

doors and strides inside, it's not Nell that she sees. Odie's sister is the image of her, so similar that they might have been twins, in form at least. In substance, they are nothing at all alike. Odie has her father's determination and strength, destined for greatness from childhood, but Seia is weak in body and will. Not even willing to accompany Odie to the war, let alone fight in it, Seia earned the contempt of Odie and her father. She bends like a river weed, allowing herself to be drawn along with the current, never standing against anyone or for anything. She is everything that Odie despises.

Seia's posture changes when she sees Odie. In a moment, she is all jutting lips and hands on hips, standing between Odie and the door that will take her into the inner sanctum of the palace, to Nell. Coming from her pliant sister, the opposition is unexpected.

'You dare to stand in my way?' Odie says.

'Someone has to.' Seia practically spits the words.

'I'm going to see Nell.'

'No, you're not.'

'I'll fight my way through you if I have to.'

'Because that's your answer to everything, isn't it?' Seia says, braver than Odie has ever seen her, and clearly resolved on her course. 'Nell doesn't want to see you.'

'I don't believe that,' Odie says, but she's starting to get that slipping feeling again, as though she's the only one who doesn't realise that the world has turned upside down.

'We didn't think you'd ever come back,' says Seia. 'Not after what you did. Gods, how could you dare to show your face here?'

'What are you talking about?' Odie says slowly, as the first tendrils of horror wrap their way around her chest.

'Did you forget?' Seia says mockingly. 'Because she didn't. I haven't. It doesn't matter how hard you try to convince the world that you're a hero. We know what you really are.'

'And what's that?'

Seia doesn't reply. Instead, she reaches for her belt and unsheathes a short dagger that Odie hadn't even realised she was wearing. The hilt is bejewelled and the blade is sharp, honed to an edge so fine it could cut silk. Odie knows this because she's the one who honed it, her favourite knife, the one she hasn't seen since—

Here is the thing that Odie has forgotten.

When it comes, it comes in a deluge, as though a dam has broken somewhere in her head and let the memory come flooding in. She remembers the rage. She remembers that first time, two long decades ago now, when the heat poured over her skin with an urgent need to be spent.

Her emotions were always hot with Nell. What had it been? One smile at someone else, just a fraction too warm. One night Nell returned to bed, just a fraction too late. One question asked and answered with an explanation that was just a fraction too weak. Odie had let the anger take her then, and it had burned too fiercely for Nell to quench it with her words.

Blood on her hands. Rings curled in her fists. Ugly words shouted as the gilded scarf bites into her lover's skin. One eye staring up at her, while the other… goes.

As the memory floods in, Odie is already backing

away from the palace, her feet carrying her without thought out of the side gate, through the blighted orchard, along the bloodstained path that she took that night as she fled. She runs to the dock and jumps into the fishing boat that's moored there, the same one she sailed in as a child, the one her father built with his own hands. Seeing the wood he hewed, it's difficult not to remember the other things he worked into shape with his arms, his fists, his blades. Everything he built, he built to last, and Odie was his greatest creation.

The witch was right.

You can't go back.

Odie grasps the oars and rows with all her might, breaking through the surf to the calmer seas beyond. There is one route, and one route only, that she can use to return home, and it tastes like sugar and sunshine.

She thinks she can remember the way.

Thank you so much for reading this book. I really hope you enjoyed it. If you'd like to read more from me, then I have suggestions!

***

Join my Readers' Club and receive a FREE short story!

www.josiejaffrey.com/subscribe

***

If you enjoyed this collection, why not read *Ring the Bell*? You can get the chapbook from my online store at www.josiejaffrey.com

Scale the mountain. Ring the bell. Buy your freedom. Or trade the prize to change the world.

***

Please leave a review!

If you enjoyed this collection, I'd be so grateful if you would please review it. Book reviews can make a huge difference to the success of a novel, particularly those of self-published authors like me. If you have time to leave a review, even if it's just a sentence or two, then I'd really appreciate it.

***

Get in touch!

I love hearing from readers! If you'd like to contact me, you can do that through my website at www.josiejaffrey.com

Acknowledgements

Huge thanks first and foremost to Adie Hart, my wonderful writer friend and fellow editor at Indie Bites. Most of these stories were written for that publication initially, with Adie's encouragement and editing. Without her support, I wouldn't have written *Broken Wings, Invidious Bitches, Good and Beautiful, Lead Me Not into Temptation, The Mermaid House, The Mirror Weir, How the Other Half Lives, A Quiet Life* and *You Can't Go Back*. It's wonderful to be able to collect them all here, with her help again! But Adie has read and given me feedback on almost every story in this collection over the past many years, and I am so grateful for her input.

Thanks also to Hayley Macfarlane, who published *The Biting Cold* and *The Forest at the End of the World* in the *Once Upon a Season* anthologies from Macfarlane Lantern Publishing.

Another chunk of these stories started out as pieces I wrote for my old Patreon supporters, so a huge thank you to everyone who supported me over there while I was writing *Peyton's End, Last Christmas* and *SnapShot*.

Thanks to the amazing Silverse Squad for everything they do to help promote my books and short stories.

And thanks always to Max, who has read and given feedback on a lot of these stories as they've been coming out, and has a particular soft spot for *Invidious Bitches*.
This one's for you, Ace. It's about time, right?

CONTENT WARNINGS

General warning for violence, death, swearing, sexual content

Broken Wings
Amputation (medical and self-inflicted)
Magical animal death

Invidious Bitches
Magical racism/bigotry, ageism

The Biting Cold
Loss of limbs due to frostbite
Hunting animals for food

Good and Beautiful
Implied rape
Implied and on-page sexual assault
Miscarriage due to violence

Lead Me Not Into Temptation
Suicide
Post-partum psychosis

The Mirror Weir
Suicide

Last Christmas
Parental/spousal abuse
Gun violence

The Forest at the End of the World

Starvation, thirst
Child endangerment

A Quiet Life
Misogyny
Forced marriage

You Can't Go Back
Domestic violence and abuse
Magical drug taking

www.ingramcontent.com/pod-product-compliance
Lightning Source LLC
Chambersburg PA
CBHW011550190726
48287CB00010B/2830